GW01337135

Also by the Author

The Erin O'Reilly Mysteries

Black Velvet
Irish Car Bomb
White Russian
Double Scotch
Manhattan
Black Magic
Death By Chocolate
Massacre
Flashback
First Love
High Stakes
Aquarium
The Devil You Know
Hair of the Dog

Punch Drunk
Bossa Nova
Blackout
Angel Face
Italian Stallion
White Lightning
Kamikaze
Jackhammer
Frostbite
Brain Damage
Celtic Twilight
Headshot
Vino Blanco (coming soon)

Tequila Sunrise: A James Corcoran Story

Fathers
A Modern Christmas Story

The Clarion Chronicles
Ember of Dreams

Headshot

The Erin O'Reilly Mysteries
Book Twenty-Six

Steven Henry

Clickworks Press • Baltimore, MD

Copyright © 2024 Steven Henry
Cover design © 2024 Ingrid Henry
Cover photo © 2024 under license from Shutterstock.com (Credit: Josiah_S/Shutterstock)
Additional cover photo © 2024 under license from Shutterstock.com (Credit: boommaval/Shutterstock)
NYPD shield photo used under license from Shutterstock.com (Credit: Stephen Mulcahey/Shutterstock)
Author photo © 2017 Shelley Paulson Photography
Spine image used under license from Shutterstock.com (Credit: Vlad Ageshin/Shutterstock)
All rights reserved

First publication: Clickworks Press, 2024
Release: CWP-EOR26-INT-P.IS-1.0

Sign up for updates, deals, and exclusive sneak peeks at clickworkspress.com/join.

Ebook ISBN: 979-8-88900-026-6
Paperback ISBN: 979-8-88900-027-3
Hardcover ISBN: 979-8-88900-028-0

This is a work of fiction. Names, characters, places, organizations, and events are either the products of the author's imagination or used in a fictitious manner. Any resemblance to actual persons, living or dead, is purely coincidental.

For Pam Jacobel, who probably saved my life.

We've got a bonus story for you!

We're so grateful for the love and support you've shown for Erin and Rolf. As a special thank you, we want to give you a free bonus story starring Dr. Sarah Levine.

Keep reading after Headshot to enjoy

Zombie
A Dr. Sarah Levine Story

Dying can be contagious.

Headshot

Mix 1 oz. vanilla vodka, 1 oz. raspberry vodka, 1 oz. Absolut vodka, and 6 oz. orange juice in a highball glass and serve.

Chapter 1

"Are you lost, ma'am?"

Vic Neshenko had on his public-relations face. He wasn't smiling—Vic's smile tended to unsettle civilians—but he wasn't scowling either. If you ignored his twice-broken nose, the scars on his knuckles, and his overdeveloped musculature, you might even think he looked concerned and helpful.

Erin O'Reilly wasn't fooled. She folded her arms and glared at him. At the other end of the leash that dangled from her right hand, Rolf copied her stare. The Shepherd's tail waved slowly back and forth, like a mountain lion deciding on the perfect moment to pounce.

"I think I'm exactly where I'm supposed to be," she said.

"I don't think so, ma'am," Vic said. "You see, this is the Major Crimes office. Even if you need to report a major crime, you have to talk to the sergeant at the front desk. You must have passed him in the lobby. I'd show you down myself, but I'm a detective with the NYPD and I really do have a lot of work to do. It's your tax dollars paying my salary, ma'am, and I'd hate to see them wasted."

"Ha ha," she said. "You're a riot, Vic. I missed you too."

He cocked his head. "You know, from just the right angle you look a little like some lady I used to work with," he said.

"Except the resemblance isn't really that strong. You're a lot tanner, you look like you've been getting enough sleep, and maybe you've been eating healthy. Nobody'd mistake you for a detective."

"I haven't been gone that long," she said.

"You kidding?" he retorted. "It's been three friggin' months! Three months you left us here, holding our dicks!"

"I thought if you did that more than four hours you were supposed to consult your physician," Erin said.

Then Vic did smile. It didn't scare Erin; under his thuggish exterior was one of the best friends she'd ever known. "You look good," he said, opening his arms. "Get over here."

She crossed the office and gave him a hug. It was surprisingly tight and even a little emotional.

"I missed you, you big lug," she said. "You look the same as you did."

But it wasn't true. Vic looked tired. He had dark rings under his eyes. Despite some questionable personal habits, he'd almost always showed up for work clean-shaven, but now he had about three days' stubble on his chin. But there was something else about him, something hard to define. Erin stepped back to arm's length and studied his face, seeing that elusive something lurking at the back of his eyes.

"What?" he said, the smile slipping off his face. "I feel like you're about to bust me for shoplifting or something. I swear, Detective, I didn't do nothin'."

"You look... happy," she said.

"Well, yeah," he said. "What'd you expect?"

"I missed something," she said.

"You missed a lot," Vic retorted. "Three months! You take off in December for Hawaii or some godforsaken place, you get a lot of sun, you probably get laid a lot, which I don't wanna hear about, or even think about, you come back with the deepest tan you've ever had in your pasty Irish life, and you think everything's just the way you left it? C'mon, Erin, do the friggin' math! Who don't you see in this office?"

"Lieutenant Webb," she said at once.

"Besides him," Vic said impatiently. "He's at the monthly CompStat meeting."

Then Erin got it. "I feel like an idiot," she said. "Zofia! The baby! She must've had it. When? Did everything go okay?"

Vic's smile came back, warmer and more genuine than she remembered it. "Yeah," he said. His hand went into his hip pocket and came out with his phone. He thumbed the screen and brought up a photo of NYPD Officer Zofia Piekarski lying in a hospital bed with a newborn baby in her arms. The baby looked confused, which Erin supposed was a natural reaction to being born. Piekarski looked tired, sweaty, and radiant.

"Mina Angelica Piekarski, born March 13," Vic said proudly. "It's short for Wilhelmina, but we're not ever calling her that. Mina means 'resolute protection,' did you know that? Great name for the kid of a couple cops."

"I didn't," Erin said. She grabbed Vic's hand and pulled him into a hug. "And you're absolutely right. Congratulations, Dad!"

He grimaced. "I'm not used to that yet," he said. "Anyways, Zofia's on maternity leave. She gets bored hanging around our place with just the kid, so she sometimes brings Mina into the office to see me. You'll get the chance to meet her pretty soon. I got two weeks off myself, but poor Webb was getting snowed under trying to manage the office all on his own. I think he actually missed us, if you can believe it. Not that he'd ever admit it."

"Of course not," Erin agreed. "I'm sorry I haven't been in touch. You should've called!"

"And interrupt your vacation?" he replied. "You needed to get away from it all. Besides, I haven't had time to talk much, or think about anything. It's been pretty crazy, what with Mina and our lousy half-squad trying to close cases."

"Catch any interesting ones?"

"Nothing worth talking about. Just assholes killing other assholes. SSDD."

"Same shit, different day," she agreed.

"Something's different about you, too," Vic said, and it was his turn to study her. "I'm not talking about the tan. Did you change your hair?"

"It's a little longer, I guess," she said. "I need to get it cut. If I grow it out too long, it gives the perps too much of a handhold."

His eyes traveled down her. Then he saw her left hand. He blinked.

"Holy shit," he said.

"What, this?" Erin nonchalantly held up her hand. On the ring finger, a big emerald glittered.

"You dumped that gangster, found Mr. Right, and got married in Vegas!" he exclaimed. "Wow, that ring looks almost genuine."

Erin punched him in the shoulder, putting her weight into the swing. It had basically no effect, and felt like hitting a heavy training bag filled with cement. She winced. "I did not dump 'that gangster,'" she retorted. "He proposed on a beach in Maui at sunset. It was beautiful and romantic and I said yes, you damn knucklehead. And it's a real emerald, thank you very much. One more crack like that and I won't invite you to the wedding!"

"You sure about that?" he asked.

Erin shook her head. "No, I was kidding about the wedding invite. Of course you're invited, and if you try to beg off I'll cuff you and drag you there."

"No, I mean the other thing. Carlyle. You sure this is what you want?" His eyes were serious.

"I've never been more sure of anything," she said. "And he's not a gangster, Vic. Not anymore. All that's behind him. He's just a bar owner now."

"Didn't his bar burn down?"

"The renovation's done," she said, brightening. "We got a good line on some really solid contractors. Corky gave us the recommendations and they've really come through. Most of it's finished, and we can get along without the rest for a while. The Barley Corner is reopening! And the upstairs apartment's fine. We were able to move right in when we got back Sunday evening."

"Congratulations," he said. "I guess."

"For the bar repairs or for getting a fiancé?"

"Both," he muttered. "But remember what I said about him a while ago?"

"That if he broke my heart you'd break his arms?"

"It's still true."

She grinned. "I don't think he's forgotten."

"How about the mutt?" Vic asked, turning his attention to Rolf. "Last time I saw him, he had on a cast and one of those stupid cones. He was pretty well out of commission."

Rolf appeared mildly offended at the suggestion he would let something as insignificant as a broken paw even slow him down, let alone take him out of action.

"All better," Erin said.

"Thank God for that," Vic said. "We can use him. With Zofia on half-time on account of the whole mom thing, we're still shorthanded, even with you back in the rotation. What I figure is, as soon as the Lieutenant gets back—"

He was interrupted by his phone. Erin noted he'd changed his ringtone to the theme music from "The Terminator."

"Speak of the devil," he said, glancing at the screen and setting the phone to speaker. "Neshenko here, sir. Guess what?

You don't have to worry about leaving me in charge anymore. I'm under adult supervision now. Some hotshot Detective Second Grade just turned up, walking in like she owns the place."

"Hello, sir," Erin said.

"O'Reilly," Lieutenant Webb said. "Glad you're back. And great timing. I'm stuck in this purgatorial meeting for another... God help me, three hours. Maybe longer. I just stepped out for a minute, and I need to get back in, so I'll keep this short. I need you to get to McQuillan's Bar in Hell's Kitchen."

"Sounds like my kind of place," Erin said. "A good Irish bar?"

"I don't know about that," Webb said. "You'll be investigating the scene along with a rep from IAB."

"Internal Affairs?" Vic demanded. "What do we want with those weasels?"

"That's for you and O'Reilly to sort out," Webb said. "You'll understand when you get there."

"Give me something more than that, sir," Erin said. "Why IAB? Is a cop a suspect?"

"No," Webb said. "He's a victim. I've been told there's an NYPD officer dead in the restroom, shot by his own gun."

"We're on our way, sir," Erin said into the phone. She hung up.

"Vacation's over," Vic said.

Chapter 2

"It's nine-twenty," Vic said. He was in the passenger seat of Erin's Charger, sharing a strip of beef jerky with Rolf through the hatch between the seats.

"That's right," Erin said. She was only half listening. After a quarter year away, Manhattan traffic was something she had to get used to again. Most of her attention was focused on the road.

"On a Monday morning," he went on.

"So?"

"So don't you think it's a little weird, a guy eats his gun in a bar restroom on a Monday morning?"

"Or a Sunday night," she replied.

"They would've found him if he'd done it before closing," Vic said. "Or somebody would've heard the shot."

"Did you turn into a detective while I was gone?"

Vic grinned. "Somebody had to pick up your slack. Were you in Hawaii that whole time?"

"Yeah. Carlyle rented a beach house. It was really nice."

"I'll just bet it was. Sheesh, three months! They give me two lousy weeks! I didn't know you had that much vacation time banked."

"I didn't. Some of it was medical leave."

"Right. For you and the dog both. How's your head?"

"Fine."

He snorted. "I asked for that. We both know that's what you'd say even if it fell off and you were carrying it around like Ichabod Crane."

"The horseman was headless," she said. "Not Ichabod."

"You sure? Oh, right, Johnny Depp doesn't get his head chopped off in that movie. He's about the only one who doesn't. You ever notice we don't get many decapitations?"

"I'm sorry, *what?*" Vic had her attention now.

"Decapitations. Guys with their heads cut off. Doesn't happen often."

"Are you saying you want more of them?"

"No! I'm just saying, most murders are done with guns or knives these days. You can't cut off a head with a gun. I guess you could do it with a knife, but you'd have to work at it. I mean, even a really sharp knife, you'd have to saw away for something like ten minutes."

"We're here," Erin said. "Thank God. You can stop talking now."

She steered into the parking lot next to McQuillan's. She'd never been to this particular Irish bar, and didn't know what it looked like, but the pair of NYPD blue-and-whites blinking their flashers out front were a dead giveaway. A Patrol cop stood on the sidewalk by the front door, arms crossed, shooing curious bystanders away.

As Erin unloaded Rolf from the Charger's rear compartment, a motorcycle pulled in behind them and parked alongside. The biker was female, to judge from her height and build, and clad in black leather with silver trim. Her face was hidden by a black helmet with a reflective visor. The biker dismounted and started toward the bar behind the detectives.

"Whoa there," the Patrolman said, stepping in front of the door. "Bar's closed."

Erin held up her shield. Vic was wearing his on a chain around his neck. "Major Crimes," she said.

"And IAB," the biker said over Erin's shoulder.

Erin spun around in time to see the woman pull off her helmet, revealing a shock of spiky hair, dyed electric blue at the roots and crimson toward the tips. The biker's face was a familiar one.

"Kira!" Erin exclaimed. "You're the one Keane sent?"

"I'm the lucky girl," Kira Jones said, tucking the helmet under her arm and smiling. She'd been with Major Crimes before transferring to Internal Affairs. She and Erin had maintained a slightly distant but genuine friendship.

"All the stray cats are showing up today," Vic said. "Decided to get out of the office and pretend to be real police?"

"If you can pretend, so can I," Kira shot back.

"Nice wheels," he said, giving the motorcycle an appreciative once-over. It had a custom paint job of purple and white lightning bolts. "Kawasaki?"

"Ninja 400," Kira said. "I just got it last month."

"And there I thought you transferred out of Major Crimes because you were a fraidy-cat," Vic said. "Those things will kill you faster than a bullet."

"I wear a helmet," Kira said. "And this isn't just leather. I've got armor inserts in the pants and sleeves. Something's going to kill me someday, but it's not going to be this bike."

"I always kinda wanted a Harley," Vic said. "Zofia says they're not safe."

"Zofia's right," Erin said. "Who's in command on this case?"

"Major Crimes," Kira said. "I'm here primarily as an observer. Unless it turns out our guy was murdered by another cop, IAB ought to keep mostly clear of this one. Lieutenant

Keane didn't even think we should bother, but I volunteered. I used to work up here in the Kitchen, you know."

"I thought it sounded like a suicide," Vic said. "Beats the hell out of me why we're even involved."

"Stomach flu," Kira said.

"Huh?" Vic said.

"Half the Homicide squad went down with it," Kira explained. "They're really shorthanded and the brass don't want detectives puking all over crime scenes."

"That actually makes sense," Erin said.

"Lucky you got back when you did," Vic said.

"I know you were on leave," Kira said. "Have any fun?"

"A little," Erin said. "If you're ready, let's see what we've got here."

They found a Patrol Sergeant inside, taking a statement from a fat, balding man at the bar. The detectives ignored the two men for the moment and made their way to the restrooms. McQuillan's was an old joint, dark and a little dilapidated. It had thus far resisted Hell's Kitchen's gentrification efforts. Erin was certain the wiring wasn't up to code.

A pair of uniformed officers stood guard outside the men's room. The detectives flashed their gold shields again and one of the uniforms opened the door for them.

Erin blinked at the smell of cleaning fluid and fresh blood. The bathroom was small, equipped with only a single sink and one stall. The tile was yellow with age. A cheap fluorescent bulb over the mirror made an annoying buzzing, flickering fitfully.

Vic wordlessly pointed to the floor under the stall. A startlingly large, dark pool of blood had oozed out into the main part of the room.

Rolf lowered his head and snuffled at the pool, nostrils flaring. Erin saw a pair of feet, clad in dark blue trousers and black shoes, resting on the ground in front of the toilet. Next to the right foot lay the black, boxy shape of a Glock 18 pistol identical to the one on Erin's own belt. She sidestepped, carefully avoiding the blood, and pulled on a pair of disposable gloves. The stall door was ajar. She nudged it open. Vic and Kira stood behind her. All three had a pretty good idea what to expect. None of them wanted to see it. But that was the Job. Nightmarish images were all in a day's work.

It wasn't as bad as Erin had feared. The entry wound wasn't even visible. She guessed the muzzle had been in the dead man's mouth. The exit wound would be terrible, to judge by the spatter on the back wall and the sheer quantity of blood on the floor, but she couldn't see it from where she was standing.

The dead man's left hand lay in his lap, clutching an open copy of the *New York Times*.

"Oh, shit," Kira said in a weak, watery voice.

"Come on," Vic said. "We've seen plenty worse ones than this. Jesus, don't you have any stomach for this kind of work? On Patrol, I used to find bodies that'd been marinating in bathtubs for a week, sometimes! This guy's practically good as new! At least he doesn't have his pants down. Now that'd be disturbing."

"No," Kira said, and something in the way she said it made Erin turn toward the other woman. Kira's eyes were huge in her head and they were filling with tears.

"Kira?" Erin said. "Do you know this guy?"

Kira nodded. "It's Bill. Bill Ward. We were on the same squad together, in the Gang Task Force. Oh my God."

"Shit," Vic said. "I'm sorry. Look, what I just said there, I didn't know."

Kira waved a hand, silencing him. "Forget it. I'm fine. I wasn't expecting... you know. A face I knew. I just need a second."

"Take your time," Erin said. "We're waiting on the ME

anyway."

"Yeah," Vic said. "Doc Levine gets real pissy if we touch anything before she gets here. So do the CSU guys. This is just like being at a strip club. We can look, but we better keep our hands off the goods."

"Yeah," Erin said, giving Vic a look. "Exactly like a strip club. Congratulations. You were a sensitive, caring guy for almost ten seconds. I think that's a new personal record."

"It's the dad thing," he said. "It's making me soft."

* * *

CSU were the next to arrive. The crime scene techs shooed everyone else out of the bathroom and started photographing everything in sight. While the technicians collected evidence, Vic went to see about the bartender's statement. Erin and Kira moved to a corner of the bar.

"How long did you work with Bill?" Erin asked.

"I was on the Task Force for two years," Kira said. "Bill was there the whole time."

"How well did you know him?"

"The crew was pretty tight. We spent a lot of time working, of course, but we hung out off duty, too. I hadn't really kept in touch with him." Kira leaned on the bar and put her head in her hands. "I should've called him. Maybe, whatever he was dealing with, I could've helped."

Erin laid a hand on her shoulder. "Hey. This isn't on you. We don't even know it's a suicide yet."

"Keane said it was," Kira said.

"How would he know?" Erin retorted. "That's what we're here to figure out."

"Dispatch sent him the call. The stall was locked from the inside."

"So what? Somebody could've shot him, locked the stall, and crawled out under it. This isn't exactly a sealed bank vault. Do you think Ward shot himself?"

"I don't know," Kira said miserably. "If you'd asked me yesterday, I would've said hell no. I mean, it's common. Almost two hundred cops kill themselves every year in this country. But not a guy like Bill."

"You've studied this?" Erin asked.

"Of course I have," Kira said. "IAB has to investigate every time an officer takes a nine-millimeter retirement. This isn't the first one I've been to."

"Then why don't you think Bill was the type?"

"He's got family. Friends. Geez, he's got a *kid!* Three—no, he'd be four now I guess. Where does the time go? Oh shit, who's going to do the family notification?"

"You or me," Erin said grimly. "It's either that or Vic."

"One of us," Kira agreed without hesitation.

"Were he and his wife doing okay?"

"As far as I know. He talked about her all the time. Trisha, that's her name. Short for Patricia, I assume. He carried a picture of her in his wallet, along with a whole bunch of shots of his kid. Good-looking woman, great smile. She looked really happy. Bill smiled a lot too."

"Sometimes the guys who put up the best front are the unhappiest on the inside," Erin replied. "Remember Robin Williams?"

"Jesus, yeah." Kira shook her head. "I still can't believe that. Maybe something happened to Bill in the last couple of years. Like I said, we kind of lost touch. I still think it's more likely he was killed. I don't know what to hope for."

"Our job isn't hope," Erin said. "We're supposed to find out the truth."

"Yeah," Kira said. She cleared her throat and wiped her eyes.

"You look good, Erin."

"Thanks. It was a good vacation, and I needed it."

"I'll say. You really got put through the wringer last year. Everything going all right with you and your guy?"

Erin glanced down at her own left hand. Kira caught the gesture. Her eyes widened.

"Oh my God! You got a ring? Let's see it!"

Erin dutifully extended her hand. "See that clasped-hand shape?" she said. "It's called a Claddagh. It's a really old Irish symbol of love."

"It's beautiful," Kira said. "Is that a real emerald? God, it's huge!"

"I don't think I'll wear it all the time on duty," Erin said. "I probably shouldn't have brought it at all. Too many things can happen to your hands on the Job. But I was getting used to wearing it in Hawaii. We don't have to make a big deal out of it."

"Like hell we don't! What're you doing after your shift?"

Erin shrugged. "Going back to the Corner, I guess. I'm barely unpacked. We still need to settle in, and I want to see how everything's going with the reopening."

"No, no, no," Kira said. "We're going out on the town and we are going to celebrate! I'm going to get smashed and hit on the prettiest boy or girl in the place, and you're going to have a good time. I know this great spot about six blocks from the Eightball, you'll love it. C'mon, Erin. I'm feeling really bummed about Bill. The least you can do is help distract me."

Erin smiled. "Okay, fine, if you twist my arm. Who else is coming?"

"We'll ask around," Kira said. "Vic's invited, of course, but only if he promises to behave."

"He may have to go home and help with the baby," Erin said. "But we can offer."

"First round's on me," Kira said.

"That might convince him," Erin said.

The smile trickled away from Kira's lips. "Here's the ME," she said. "I guess we'll know what happened to Bill soon enough."

When Erin saw how pale Sarah Levine looked next to her own sun-bronzed skin, she wondered if Levine was sick with the same flu that had laid the Homicide squad low. Then she figured it was probably just the normal New York winter pallor, exacerbated by staying in basements all the time and working lots of nights. Erin thought it unlikely Levine was a vampire, but the possibility couldn't be completely ruled out.

"Where's the dead guy?" Levine asked.

Erin pointed a thumb toward the men's room. Without another word, Levine went in. The door swung shut behind the Medical Examiner.

Vic wandered over to join the two women. "Doc's doing her magic?" he inquired. "Romancing the dead?"

Kira grimaced. "Necromancy?" she guessed.

"Yeah, that's the one," Vic said, snapping his fingers.

"Did the barkeep have anything useful?" Erin asked.

"Not really," Vic said. "He came in at eight. Nothing out of the ordinary. Around eight-thirty, he had to use the john. When he saw the blood, he freaked a little and kicked open the stall door. He said he thought maybe somebody was hurt and needed help. But he swears the stall was locked and nobody else was inside."

"What about the exterior doors?" Erin asked.

"He unlocked them when he got here," Vic said. "He claims the place was deserted except for him and the guy in the bathroom."

"This seems weird," Erin said. "If you're going to shoot yourself, why do it in a seedy bathroom in a closed bar?"

"Privacy?" Vic guessed.

"Nobody was going to walk in on him," Kira said. "If he wasn't sure he wanted to go through with it, he might've wanted some time to think it over or work up to it. And there wouldn't have been any chance of anyone else getting hurt. Bill never would've put an innocent at risk."

"But he could've had plenty of privacy at home," Vic said.

"Yeah," Kira said. "As long as he didn't care if his wife or their kid found his body."

"Jesus Christ," Vic said, staring at her. "He was a dad? How old?"

"Four," Kira said.

Vic abruptly turned on his heel and stomped out of the bar.

"Geez," Kira said. "What'd I say?"

"I told you he had a kid," Erin said. "A newborn."

"Oh shit," Kira said. "That's right. It slipped my mind. Is he okay?"

"I have no idea," Erin said. "He's not used to having all these feelings. I think it's making him uncomfortable. Life was easier when he could just be a thug with a shield."

"Should I go after him?" Kira asked. "Apologize?"

"I'll go," Erin said. "You stay here and keep an eye on things. I'll bring him back as soon as I can."

Chapter 3

Erin and Rolf found Vic standing at the corner, leaning against the brickwork. He was staring at a cluster of cigarette butts in the gutter.

"Hey," Erin said quietly.

"Times like this, I understand why the Lieutenant smokes," Vic said. "I sure could use a drink, too."

"Kira and I are going out on the town tonight," she said. "You're welcome to join us."

He didn't give any indication of having heard her.

"What the hell?" he muttered. "The dumb bastard's got a little kid and he goes and blows his own brains out? What's his son gonna think when he's old enough to understand? I bet twenty bucks the brat thinks it's his own fault. That's the sort of thing that'll screw a kid up for life."

"Vic?" she said, touching his arm. "You're not going to mess up like that."

He gave her the bleakest look she'd ever seen from him. "If it's not that, it'll be some damn thing," he said.

"Of course you're going to make mistakes!" she retorted. "Show me a perfect dad. And Mina's going to have issues, because every kid does. But you and Zofia will take pretty damn good care of her. She'll grow up knowing her mom and dad love her and I'll bet *you* twenty bucks she turns out pretty much okay."

"That's if her mom and dad are around," he said hollowly.

"What sort of bullshit is that?" Erin snapped.

"We're both cops," he said. "It's a dangerous job. Suppose the next time I kick down a door, I catch a bullet right in the face? Or Zofia gets stabbed by some junkie? There's a hundred things that can happen. I didn't used to get scared, Erin. You know, I thought Kira was a damn coward when she transferred to IAB. But now? Maybe she's the smart one."

Erin didn't have a good answer to that, so she decided to ask a question instead. "Vic, you don't talk about your dad a lot. What's his deal?"

Vic shrugged. "He died."

"Oh. I'm sorry."

"Eight years back," he went on. "Heart attack. He was young for it, I guess. Fifty-two. I guess I should be glad he didn't kick off until I was grown up."

"Was he a good father?"

"I dunno. He was okay."

She looked him in the eye. "You're going to be better," she said. "And you're not going to get killed. You're the second-toughest guy I know."

A spark came back into his eyes. "Only number two?" he said. "Who's the toughest?"

"You don't want to know."

"Of course I do. You don't get to say something like that and then not tell me who the competition is. So c'mon, Erin. Who've I gotta beat up to take the top slot?"

"Ian Thompson."

Vic rolled his eyes. "You're just saying that because he's this big war hero with a bunch of medals who's killed a couple hundred dudes."

Erin smiled. "That about covers it," she said. "But you're a close second, if that makes you feel any better."

He considered this. "Yeah," he said. "It does."

"And if you want, we can take turns," she said. "Kicking down doors, I mean. I can go first sometimes."

Vic had recovered. "Hell no," he said. "You think I'm letting you steal half my fun? I dunno what I was thinking. We all gotta die of something, sure, but the bullet with my name on it hasn't even been made."

"That's more like it," she said. "Look, if you need to stay out here for a bit, that's fine. There isn't a lot for us to be doing right now anyway."

"Nah," he said. "Let's go back in. Maybe we missed something exciting."

* * *

Kira was talking to the bartender when they entered. She waved them over.

"Mr. McQuillan, tell them what you just told me," she said. "Erin, this is Angus McQuillan. He owns this place."

Erin was hoping for a thick Irish brogue. She was disappointed. McQuillan had obviously been born and raised right there in Hell's Kitchen. His accent was pure, blue-collar New York.

"Your friend here was just showing me a picture of the guy in the bathroom," he said. "I know him. I mean, we wasn't friends or nothing, but he's been hanging around. He'd come in once, maybe twice a week. Always ordered the same thing. A bottle of Schlitz and a shot of Johnny Walker Red."

"Did you know he was a cop?" Erin asked.

McQuillan shook his head. "No way. He never showed no badge or nothing. And he sure as shit wasn't wearing no uniform. He just looked like an ordinary-type guy."

"Did he drink alone?" Erin asked.

"He'd come in alone," McQuillan said. "And he'd sit in the corner, that booth right there. He'd set the shot down on the table and start nursing his beer. Then another guy would come in and sit across from him. They'd talk a little and then your guy would drink his shot and he'd leave. The other guy would hang around a bit, maybe buy a drink, and then he'd go, too."

"This other guy," Erin said. "What did he look like?"

"That's the thing," McQuillan said. "It wasn't always the same guy."

"Come again?" Vic said.

"Sometimes it was one guy, sometimes another," McQuillan said. "There must've been three or four different mooks. I don't remember their faces good enough to describe, but I'd know them if I saw them. But none of them looked like guys you'd want to mess with."

"How so?" Erin asked.

"They was tough guys," McQuillan said. "You know, scars and tattoos and stuff."

"Weapons?" Vic asked.

McQuillan shrugged. "Nothing I saw. Hey, if I'd seen guns or knives hanging off them, I would've called you folks. I don't want no trouble in my place."

"What *were* they carrying?" Erin asked. "In their hands, I mean."

The bartender rubbed his chin. "Now you mention it, your guy was always carrying this briefcase. He'd set it down under the table while he had his drinks."

"And the guys he met?" Vic asked. He'd figured out where Erin was going with this. "Did they happen to be carrying real similar briefcases?"

"Yeah," McQuillan said. "And I thought that was a little weird, on account of them not looking like the kind of guys who use briefcases. These wasn't lawyers or guys in suits, know what I mean?"

"I do," Erin said. "Do you remember anything else about these other gentlemen? Did you hear what they were talking about?"

He shook his head. "It gets kinda noisy in here," he said. "And I'm behind the bar, and they was way down the other end of the room. They looked like tough guys, like I said. They had beards and leather jackets, like bikers wear."

"When did our victim come in?" Kira asked. "What time of night? What day of the week?"

"Nothing regular," McQuillan said. "I can't remember, sorry."

"Was he in here last night?" Erin asked.

"Yeah," McQuillan said. "He was."

"Mr. McQuillan," Kira said. "I notice you have a security camera over the bar. Is it turned on?"

"Yeah," he said. "But it only shows the bar and register."

"We need to take a look at that," Erin said.

"Sure, sure," McQuillan said. "I don't believe it. A guy gets killed in my own bar. I never thought I'd see it. And a cop, too! I'm not gonna get in trouble for that, am I?"

"Should you?" Vic asked, giving him a hard stare.

"I didn't kill him!" the bartender protested.

Vic held the stare a few seconds longer, letting McQuillan get good and uncomfortable. Erin suppressed her laughter. Sometimes Vic drew a little too much mean pleasure from his work.

"We'll find out what happened," Vic finally said. "Thanks for your cooperation."

"Let's check on Levine," Kira suggested as they walked away from the bar.

"Good idea," Erin said. "Sheesh, Vic, did you consider *not* making our witness piss himself?"

"Witness, hell," Vic said. "The guy has keys to the bar. He knows our boy was carrying something, probably something valuable. How do we know he didn't ice him? Did you notice what wasn't in that bathroom?"

"A briefcase," Erin said. "I'd like to know where that went."

"And what was in it," Kira added.

"He was definitely making a handoff," Erin said. "Drugs for cash would be my guess."

"Or vice versa," Vic said. "Maybe he had a habit."

"Levine will know if he was shooting heroin," Erin said. She knocked on the bathroom door.

"This room is currently occupied," Levine said through the door.

Vic snickered. "Whaddaya know," he said. "Doc's got a sense of humor. I thought it'd been surgically removed."

Levine opened the door. "A sense of humor is not something which can be surgically removed," she said. "The closest approximation would be a frontal lobotomy, which I hypothesize would have no discernible effect on you, Detective."

There was a brief, stunned pause.

"Did she just make a joke?" Kira finally asked.

Levine blinked. "I read an article last week in one of my journals which touted the benefits of witty banter within organizations whose purview includes the handling of stressful, life-and-death situations," she said. "So-called gallows or dark humor, including sharp or idiosyncratic statements and apparent insults, are valuable to the maintenance of unit morale. Did I do it wrong, or apply the theory improperly?"

"No," Erin said. "That was good, at least until you explained it."

"You appeared perplexed," Levine said. "I thought perhaps you were insufficiently perceptive to reap the full benefit of the humorous statement."

"She's getting better at this," Vic said. "I think she's a natural."

"What do you have on our victim so far?" Erin asked.

"Body temperature places time of death at approximately two o'clock in the morning ," Levine said. "Preliminary cause of death is a single gunshot wound to the soft palate. The wound was administered by a handgun bullet, probably nine-millimeter, at contact range. Powder tattooing inside the mouth indicates the muzzle of the weapon was inside the teeth when the shot was fired. The bullet exited the cranial cavity through the upper rear portion of the skull. Death was instantaneous."

"Any other injuries?" Erin asked.

"I found no defensive wounds on the hands or fingers," Levine said. "Nor are other injuries in evidence on the exposed portions of the victim's body. I will have a full answer on this once I have conducted my postmortem examination."

"What about gunshot residue?" Vic asked.

"That is a question for the Crime Scene Unit," Levine said. "Fortunately, they are also present and usefully employed."

"Hey, buddy!" Vic called over Levine's shoulder at one of the CSU techs. "What've you got for GSR?"

"Powder residue on the right hand," the man called back. "There's a Glock nine-mil on the floor and a single shell casing against the side wall, also nine-millimeter. Best guess, one shot fired."

"Any sign of anyone else in the room?" Erin asked.

"It's a restroom," the tech replied. "There've been dozens of guys in here. But I can't see any evidence of a second party at time of death, nor any indications of more than one shot being fired. We're going to dig the slug out of the wall, but that'll take a little time. Once we get it back to the lab, we ought to be able to match it to the weapon, most likely the Glock."

"I just ran the pistol serial number through the system," the CSU supervisor added. "It's registered to Officer William Ward, NYPD, as his off-duty piece."

"Our initial conclusion is death by self-inflicted gunshot wound," Levine said.

Erin thought the ME seemed a little depressed by this revelation. "Anything weird about the scene?" she asked. "Anything that doesn't fit?"

"No," Levine said. "It's extremely straightforward. Unless additional evidence presents during the autopsy, I will be reporting this as suicide."

"Did anyone find a briefcase?" Vic asked.

"No," the CSU supervisor said. "The victim is holding a copy of the *Times* in his left hand. Nothing else. But we've only checked the restroom. Should we expand our search area?"

"Definitely," Erin said. "Dust for prints, try to find out where Ward was sitting last night. Then go over that booth with as fine a comb as you've got. See if you can get an ID on whoever else was sitting there. And keep your eyes open for a briefcase."

"Will do, Detective," the CSU man said.

"I still have work to do," Levine said. She immediately turned her back and returned to her examination of the late William Ward.

"I, for one, am thrilled at our Medical Examiner's enhanced social skills," Vic said with a straight face. "If she continues to improve, I predict she may be mistaken for human by the end of the year."

"Excuse me," the bartender said, sidling his way into the conversation.

"Yeah?" Vic said.

"I dug up the security tape," he said. "I have a player in my office, if you want to take a look."

"That'd be great," Erin said. "Thank you."

* * *

McQuillan's "office" was a corner of the back room, surrounded by cases of beer. His desk was an old door laid across two stacks of beer crates, upon which perched an ancient, boxy computer monitor and an equally ancient television screen with a built-in VCR.

"Wow," Vic said. "It's like being in a museum. Do they even make these things anymore?"

"Funai Electric is still making them," Kira said. "But they're the only company that does, and they're planning to discontinue production in a few months."

"How could you possibly know that?" Erin asked.

"I've got a better question," Vic said. "*Why* would you possibly know that?"

Kira shrugged. "You know me and my head for trivia."

"That reminds me," Vic said. "Have you finished memorizing the Patrol Guide?"

"Not yet," Kira said. "I'm getting there."

McQuillan pointed to the TV screen. "Here we are," he said. "Have a look."

The detectives crowded around the bartender and watched the grainy, black-and-white footage. The timestamp indicated it was 10:33PM.

"There's Bill," Kira said, pointing. A blurry form walked across the screen to the bar. It was carrying a briefcase in its left hand.

"You sure?" Vic asked. "I couldn't pick out my own brother with this shitty resolution. How come security cameras are always crap?"

"People like them to be cheap," Erin said.

"The main point of cameras is deterrence," Kira said. "Half the time, they might as well not have film in them. Sometimes they don't. You should be grateful we've got anything at all."

"There he is buying his drinks," McQuillan said. "Beer and a shot, just like every time."

"Now he's walking to his booth," Erin said.

"Dammit, he's out of frame," Vic said. "How come your camera doesn't cover the rest of the room?"

"The bar's where I have the expensive liquor," McQuillan said. "And the cash register. The camera's for if anybody tries to rip me off and I can't get to the Louisville Slugger under the counter."

"You'd really take a baseball bat to an armed robber?" Vic was skeptical but slightly impressed.

"Well, not if he pulled a gun on me," McQuillan said. "I ain't stupid. I love my bar, and I like money, but ain't neither worth dying over. Anyway, you can see everybody who walks in."

They watched for a few moments. Then McQuillan stabbed a finger at the VCR, freezing the image.

"There's the guy!" he said. "That was his drinking buddy last night."

All four of them examined the indistinct shape.

"I think it's a person," Vic finally said. "But not beyond a reasonable doubt."

"It's a man," Kira said. "Look at the shape of the shoulders and hips. And he's definitely carrying a briefcase."

"He's wearing a hat," Erin said, disappointed.

"Oh, is that what that is?" Vic said. "I thought it was a big-ass wig, or maybe an afro. Does he have a beard? Or is that a design on his shirt?"

"It's a white guy," Kira said. "Or Hispanic or Asian, I guess. Not black at any rate."

"Great," Vic said. "We can put out a BOLO for a white guy, probably."

"Let's hope CSU can lift a print from their table," Erin said. "Mr. McQuillan, can you point out the right table to our evidence guys?"

"Sure thing," he said.

"And we'll need this tape."

"I figured. Is the City gonna pay me back for it?"

"You can submit a claim," Erin said.

"Nah, forget about it," McQuillan said in the finest New York style. "I'm doing my civic duty. Glad to help."

"You're an inspiration," Vic said.

"Is this guy jerking me around?" McQuillan asked.

"It's hard to tell with Vic," Erin said. "I always assume he is, when it's me."

Chapter 4

"No witnesses," Erin said.

"Not unless McQuillan's lying," Vic said. "You know how those Irish bar owners can be."

"Carlyle's never told me a single lie," Erin retorted.

"Really?" Kira asked.

"Really," Erin said. "He's an expert at misleading truths, though."

They were on the sidewalk outside McQuillan's, waiting on CSU and Levine. A couple of bored-looking uniformed officers were guarding the perimeter and wishing they were somewhere else.

"I don't know what the point of all this is," Vic said. "If the doc says Ward offed himself, then that's what he did. She's never wrong."

"I don't believe it," Kira said.

"You'd better," Vic shot back. "If Levine told me a guy was dragged into a grave by a friggin' zombie, I'd start stocking up for the undead apocalypse."

"It's never zombies, Vic," Erin said.

"I said *if*," he said. "My point is, the lady knows her shit. Suicide is suicide. It sucks, I get it, but what does it matter what shady shit this guy was up to? If nobody shoved the gun in his mouth, it's not our problem."

"Bill wasn't shady," Kira insisted. "He was a stand-up guy. We had all kinds of opportunities on the Gang Task Force. Money, drugs, girls, any one of us could've had any of it. He was clean."

"People can surprise you," Vic said. "I used to think Erin here was squeaky clean, but guess what? She blew that girl up outside the JFK Hilton last year."

"I did not!" Erin snapped. "And we shouldn't be talking about that."

"Why not?" he retorted. "The whole underworld knows about it by now, and they know the girl didn't really die, so what difference does it make?"

"I already knew about the bomb incident," Kira said. "I'm IAB, remember? The only really bad thing about that was that Erin didn't clear it with us before she did it."

"Oh," Vic said. "I thought the bad thing was setting off a car bomb in front of a busy hotel when I was standing twenty feet away. Silly me."

"I was half that distance," Erin said. "You were lucky."

"That's me," Vic said. "I got the luck of the Russians."

"Is that like the luck of the Irish?"

"It's the opposite," he said. "It's all bad luck."

"You believe me, don't you?" Kira asked Erin. "About Bill?"

"I believe there's more going on here than a simple suicide," she replied. "But if the ME rules it that way, we don't have a case. We need PC to investigate any peripheral crimes. It's not against the law to drink with bad guys in a dive bar."

"Good thing," Vic said. "Or you'd be in jail yourself."

"How long until Levine finalizes her report?" Kira asked.

"She likes to work late," Erin said. "She'll have the autopsy done by tomorrow morning at the latest."

"Then we have today and tonight to figure this out," Kira said.

"I love unpaid overtime," Vic muttered.

"Nobody's forcing you," Kira said.

"It's fine," he said. "It'll beat changing diapers. But where do you want to start?"

"The wife," Erin said. "The database ought to have her contact info, since Ward was one of us."

"You really think she knows what her husband was up to?" Vic asked.

"Does Zofia know the crap you do?" Erin shot back.

"I hope not," he said. "But she probably does. She's a lot smarter than any woman that hot's got any business being."

"Wow," Erin said. "That was efficient. Two sexist statements in the same sentence."

* * *

According to the NYPD database, Clarissa Ward worked at an insurance company less than a mile from McQuillan's. Her job description was "Enrollment Specialist," which might mean just about anything. Erin, Vic, and Rolf rode in the Charger. Kira trailed them on her Kawasaki.

They had to buzz in at the front door, then wait at the desk for a security guard to take them through another keycard-secured inner door. After that, they climbed into an elevator to ride to the eighth floor.

"These guys have more security than we do at the Eightball," Vic commented.

"This is health insurance," Kira said. "They have PHI to protect."

"PH what?" Vic asked.

"Personal Health Information," Kira explained. "Social security numbers, medical records, all kinds of private data."

"So?" Vic replied. "We have guns and drugs and violent criminals. You'd think we'd have a few more locked doors between us and the outside."

"Well, we do have our own guns," Erin said. "Along with Tasers, pepper spray, nightsticks, Rolf..."

Rolf opened his mouth in a smug grin and let his tongue hang out.

The guard led them to a cubicle with the name CLARISSA WARD pinned to the divider. A curly-haired, bespectacled blonde sat at a computer, talking into a headset about some insurance subject or other. The detectives waited for her to finish.

"Ms. Ward?" Erin asked as soon as the woman ended the call.

"Yes?" Clarissa spun her office chair around to face the cubicle entrance.

"Ma'am, my name's Erin O'Reilly," Erin said, holding up her gold shield. "NYPD Major Crimes. Is there a place we can talk privately?"

Clarissa had a round-cheeked, pleasant face. Erin watched all the fears of a police spouse come crowding into that face at once.

"Yes... yes, of course," Clarissa said. "There's a conference room this way. Just a moment."

She pushed a button on her phone, locked her computer, and stood up. She led the three cops and one dog into a generic corporate meeting room and indicated a wood-veneer table. They sat down, Rolf settling under the table at Erin's direction.

"We'd like to talk with you about your husband," Erin said. "When's the last time you spoke with him?"

"Yesterday evening," Clarissa said. "After supper. It's his bowling night. He stays out late with his friends."

"Did he come home last night?" Erin asked.

"Of course he did," Clarissa said. "That is... he always does. I didn't see him this morning. I had to take Eddie to daycare on my way to work. Ever since Bill was on night shifts, we... we sleep in separate rooms. He has those heavy blackout curtains so he can sleep during the day. You know how that is."

"Yeah, we do," Erin said. "Just to be clear, he told you he was going bowling last night, and then left your place?"

Clarissa nodded.

"When was this?" Erin asked.

"About seven-thirty, I suppose," Clarissa said. "Ms. O'Reilly, you're scaring me. Where's Bill? Is he all right?"

Erin took a deep breath and got ready to shatter the other woman's world.

"I'm sorry, ma'am," she said. "Officer Ward was found at a Hell's Kitchen bar this morning. I'm afraid he's been shot."

Clarissa blinked. "Shot?" she repeated blankly. "Is... is he at the hospital? Is he all right?"

There was no easy way to say it, so Erin just said the words. "He was killed," she said, then repeated, "I'm sorry."

Clarissa's expression froze. She shook her head, slowly at first, then more emphatically. "No," she whispered. "No, no, no. It's not true. It's a mistake."

"Ma'am," Kira said gently. "I worked with Bill for a couple of years on the Task Force. I recognized him. I'm sorry, but there's no doubt."

The wail started deep down in Clarissa's stomach. It began as a low moan and got louder and higher pitched as it worked its way up and out of her, cresting in a sob that tore pieces out of Erin's heart. Kira leaped out of her chair and wrapped her arms around the howling woman, holding her in what was half embrace, half restraint.

The door flew open and a man in a business shirt and tie rushed in. "What in God's name is going on?" he demanded. "What is that gosh-awful racket? We're trying to run a business here!"

"Sir," Vic said, putting himself between the man and Clarissa. "Step out of this room and close the door."

"I don't know who you think you are," the guy blustered. "But you're disrupting our office environment and I demand—"

"NYPD," Vic growled. "You want to talk disturbance? This lady needs not to be disturbed, so I'm telling you to get out right now."

The businessman was a full head shorter than Vic and, while their weight was probably similar, on Vic it was muscle. The guy swallowed and retreated. Vic closed the door firmly behind him.

Kira continued holding Clarissa. "It's okay," she lied, pressing the woman's head against her shoulder. "Shh, it's okay."

After a few minutes, Clarissa subsided into hiccuping sobs. Erin found a box of tissues in the corner and slid them down the table. The detectives waited for the new widow to get a little more control of herself.

"What... what happened?" Clarissa finally managed to ask.

"We're still trying to determine that," Erin said. "Can you think of anyone who might have wanted to hurt him?"

"Bill's a cop," Clarissa sniffled. "Of course people want to hurt him. But he doesn't... he didn't... oh God. He didn't have *enemies*. Not as far as I know."

"Are you familiar with McQuillan's Bar?" Erin asked. "Do you know why he might have gone there?"

Clarissa shook her head. "No," she said. "I've never heard of it. Bill doesn't go to bars. He is... he was an alcoholic. A recovering alcoholic. He stopped drinking a couple months after we got married."

Kira nodded. "That's true," she said. "Bill never went to the bar with the rest of the squad after work. And he never took a drink. I forgot all about that!"

Erin exchanged glances with Vic. What was a recovering alcoholic doing knocking back shots in a bar? Clearly, Bill Ward had been living a life of which his wife was completely unaware.

They asked a few more questions, but it became increasingly evident they'd learn nothing from Clarissa. The poor woman was beside herself, and insisted she'd had no idea what Ward had been doing. At last, Erin handed her a card with her own phone number and the number of the NYPD's grief-counseling hotline. By sad necessity, the Department had plenty of resources in place for a woman like Clarissa.

* * *

"Another dead end," Vic said as they walked out of Clarissa's building. "If that lady knows why her husband died, she's not telling. Did you believe her?"

"Yeah," Erin said. "If she's playing dumb, she ought to quit that corporate job and move to Hollywood."

"I don't think Bill was having marital problems," Kira said. "Or if he was, his wife didn't think they were serious. You saw her in there. She was crushed, and it didn't look like remorse to me."

"We've got two options," Erin said. "Either Ward had a problem his wife didn't know about, one that pushed him to shoot himself, or there's a killer out there who's clever enough to spoof the best Medical Examiner I know."

"I really don't like that second option," Vic said.

"Me neither," Erin said. "But we have to consider it. Remember the Janitor case?"

"I have a vague recollection of hanging by my fingernails over a stage show," Vic said.

"That guy was able to make murders look like accidents," she said. "So it's not unprecedented. But it strikes me as unlikely."

"When you remove the impossible," Kira said in tones of recitation, "whatever remains, however improbable, must be the truth. Sherlock Holmes said that."

"Sherlock Holmes was a stuck-up British asshole," Vic said. "He would've made a lousy street cop. Him with his damn violin and his silly hat."

Kira sighed. "I don't want to think Bill did it to himself," she said. "But what if he did? I didn't think he was drinking anymore, and it looks like I was wrong about that. Look, guys, I appreciate you helping me with this, but if it really was a suicide, you're wasting your time. That makes it a straight-up IAB case, open-and-shut, and definitely not Major Crimes' jurisdiction."

"Forget about it," Erin said. "Like you said, we have until Levine files an official cause of death. Right now I don't have any other cases going."

"That's because you just got back from vacation," Vic said. "We've got a few open ones."

"Anything we can do on them right now?"

"No," he admitted. "We're waiting for lab results and to hear back from a couple other departments."

"Then we don't have anything better to do," Erin said. "Besides, something's bothering me about the timeline."

"What?" Vic asked.

"According to McQuillan's security tape, Ward goes into the bar around ten-thirty," she said. "McQuillan seemed to think these meetings of his never lasted that long."

Vic nodded. "So what's he doing dying in the bathroom four hours later?"

"McQuillan didn't say Bill hung around," Kira said. "The bar closed at one-thirty. I checked the sign."

"Of course you did," Vic said. "What are the hours of operation at Ms. Ward's company?"

"Eight to four-thirty, Monday through Friday," Kira rattled off. "What does that have to do with anything?"

"Not a damn thing," Vic said, grinning. "I was just checking to see if you'd looked. You can't help yourself, can you?"

"I like to know things," Kira said. "You never know when a detail's going to be important."

"Ward left the bar," Erin said. "Then he snuck back in hours later, just in time to die."

"We don't know that," Kira said. "He might've been at the bar for a while before death. We have no idea what he was doing over that period."

"And we don't know how he got back into the bar," Erin said. "Or why."

"And what he was doing with the *Times*," Vic added. "Who the hell does a crossword puzzle right before offing himself? Maybe he couldn't figure out number seven across. Then he was overcome with despair and frustration, so he shut himself up in the john and ate his gun."

"That's the dumbest thing I've ever heard," Erin said.

"I doubt that," Kira said.

"Okay, it's the dumbest thing I've heard today."

"All right, hotshot Detective Second Grade O'Reilly," Vic said. "What's your theory?"

"I don't have one yet," Erin said. "But I think it'll have something to do with the missing briefcase. I have the feeling if we can find it, we may be able to figure out what was going on."

"Good plan," Vic said. "All we need to do is search the West Side of Manhattan for a plain, ordinary briefcase. And after that, you can help me with a little problem. I seem to have lost a needle. I can't remember which haystack I put it in."

"Your optimism is a credit to the Force," Erin said.

Chapter 5

"I know where to find a needle," Erin announced suddenly.

"Oh?" Vic said. "Where's that?"

"A sewing kit."

He rolled his eyes. "Look, the needle thing was a metaphor."

"I know," she said. "So is this."

"Listen up, Kira," Vic said. "Erin's about to give us the benefit of her wisdom."

"The Gang Task Force is a pretty tight-knit group, isn't it?" she asked Kira.

"Yeah," Kira said. "I miss them. They're like you guys in Major Crimes."

"Or like SNEU," Vic said. "Zofia never stops talking about those damn cowboys."

"IAB isn't the same," Kira said.

"Cops don't like to bring their work home," Erin went on. "Ward probably tried to hide his problems from his wife."

"But he might've talked to his squad," Kira said, nodding. "That makes sense. But they won't want to spill to outsiders."

"Good thing we've got an insider, then," Vic said, giving her a meaningful look.

Kira scowled at him. "When they gave me a gold shield, I left the Task Force behind. They may not want to talk to me anymore, especially now that I'm IAB."

"You were one of them once upon a time," Erin said. "That has to count for something."

"You didn't piss any of them off, did you?" Vic asked. "Unhappy love affair, that sort of thing?"

"I don't sleep with my coworkers, Vic," Kira said.

Vic started to say something, thought better of it, and shut his mouth. Erin knew he'd slept with not one, but two of his female colleagues, one of whom was the mother of his newborn daughter.

"What Area of Service does the Task Force operate out of?" Erin asked.

"This one," Kira said. "The One-Oh-Four."

"That's convenient," Vic said. "Think we should drop in and say hi?"

"Are they likely to be at the station?" Erin asked.

Kira shrugged. "Depends on whether it's a paperwork day," she said. "If they're not, somebody ought to know where they are. Do you really think this is our best lead?"

"You wanted to work Internal Affairs," Vic reminded her. "That means investigating other cops, unless I'm mistaken."

"Yeah, but not my friends," Kira said unhappily. "They're going to hate me."

* * *

Kira directed them to the Gang Task Force's office. It was tucked away in the basement of the Precinct 104 station, in a concrete-floored room. The ceiling was a tangle of steam pipes. Beat-up desks, secondhand office furniture, and rusty file cabinets huddled in the corner.

"Nice place," Vic said. "Reminds me of my first apartment."

A man's head popped up. He had bloodshot eyes, a three-day growth of stubble, and a wild, unkempt shock of hair dyed a lurid shade of orange. He glared at Vic.

"What do you want?" he demanded. "We turned the music down, just like Cap said! We're trying to work here!"

"Hey, Scarecrow," Kira said. "How's it going?"

The man's face lit up. "Kira!" he exclaimed. "Hey, guys! Jones is back!"

Two more heads came into view. They belonged to a fat-faced, balding man and a black-haired younger guy who looked like an extra from "Grease," complete with black leather jacket, white T-shirt, and slicked-back hair.

Rather than come around the desk, Scarecrow planted a hand on it and vaulted straight over, narrowly missing his computer monitor. Erin understood the nickname. He was long and lanky, moving with a loose-jointed motion. He was almost skeletally thin and vibrated with nervous energy.

Kira held out a hand. Scarecrow ignored it, flung his arms around her, and gave her a hug. He was stronger than he looked. He swept her off the ground and spun her around before letting her stagger away. His two companions approached more slowly, but they were all smiles.

"Just a guess, but I don't think they hate you," Vic said in a stage whisper.

"Who're your buddies?" Scarecrow asked, turning his attention to the detectives.

"Erin O'Reilly and Vic Neshenko," Kira said. "Major Crimes. The K-9 is Rolf. He belongs to Erin."

"I belong to him," Erin corrected her.

"I got a dog at home," Scarecrow said. "Shih-Tzu. Not exactly NYPD material. I'm Stuart Kristofferson, Scarecrow on the street. This is Louis Loren Lamont."

"Extra-Large," the man in the leather jacket said. "Three Ls, you know?"

"And Sergeant Osborne," Scarecrow said, nodding to the bald guy. "Or just Oz."

"The Great and Powerful?" Erin asked.

Osborne chuckled. "That's me," he said. "We thought about calling Lamont the Cowardly Lion, and that would've made Ward the Tin Woodman."

"And I would've been Dorothy," Kira said. "But it was corny, so it didn't stick."

"What're you doing here?" Scarecrow asked, clapping her on the shoulder. "I see you're still hanging with Major Crimes."

"Not exactly," Kira said. "I'm with IAB now."

There was a short, awkward pause.

"C'mon, guys," she said, shifting her shoulders. "I don't have horns growing out of my head, or three eyes, or anything. I'm still the same old Kira."

"Okay," Scarecrow said, but he sounded more cautious now. "Jesus, I didn't think the music was that big a deal."

"We're not here about music," Erin said. "What're you talking about, anyway?"

"Lamont likes to crank up his tunes," Osborne explained.

"I didn't think it'd be a problem," Lamont said. "Seeing as how we're way down here in the dungeon. But the music must've resonated with the pipes or something."

"The Captain called down a few minutes ago," Scarecrow said. "He said his radiator was shaking. He thought it was going to explode."

"Is this all of you?" Erin asked.

"We're down one," Osborne said. "Officer Ward didn't come in today."

"That's why we're here," Erin said.

Every eye in the room was on her, even Rolf's.

"Officer Ward was found shot in the men's room at McQuillan's bar this morning," she said. "He's dead."

"Shit," Lamont said. The word fell flat and dead into the silence that followed Erin's declaration. Nobody else had anything to add for a few moments.

"Do you know who shot him?" Osborne finally asked.

"The ME thinks Ward did," Erin said.

"Suicide?" Osborne asked.

She nodded. "It's looking that way."

"But you're Major Crimes," he said. "And you're here. Of course IAB would look into this, but suicide isn't major enough for you hotshots. How come you're involved?"

"Because something else is going on," she said, looking directly at him. She'd dealt with squads of dirty cops in the past. In her experience, you didn't tend to get just one bad apple.

Ward's comrades didn't look shifty or guilty. Lamont blinked several times, backed up, and sat down on the edge of the nearest desk. He looked like he was about to throw up, break down in tears, or maybe both. Scarecrow just looked stunned. Osborne's eyes went very cold and hard.

"You think somebody was screwing with him?" he demanded.

"Maybe," Erin said. "Do you know anything?"

"I know we're going to do everything we can to help," he said. "You name it, Detective. What do you need?"

"Information," she said. "Did you notice anything unusual about Ward?"

"Yeah," Scarecrow said. "He wasn't coming to meetings anymore."

"Department meetings?" Vic asked.

"AA meetings," Scarecrow corrected him.

"How do you know?" Kira asked.

"Because I've been going with him," he said.

"Really?" Kira gave him a surprised smile. "Good for you! How long?"

"Just got my six-month pin," he said. "It's been hell. I've been compensating with tobacco and caffeine."

"That's not much better," Kira said.

"One addiction at a time," he said. "Anyway, Ward and I would go to meetings together sometimes. But the last couple months, he'd given it up. He said he didn't need them anymore, but I'm sure I smelled booze on him a couple times."

"And he was super edgy," Lamont added.

"That's true," Osborne said. "This job can make anyone paranoid, but he was really nervous."

"Yeah," Scarecrow said with a shaky, almost hysterical laugh. "I've been working with these guys, I thought they were just taggers, but it turns out they're peddling fentanyl and they're putting codes in their graffiti. I'm worried they'll find out I know and they'll pop me. They come out at night, so I'm hardly sleeping these days. I'm a mess, but Ward was even worse. I swear, that guy had a bag of cats in his head, know what I mean?"

"What was he scared of?" Kira asked.

"Drug dealers," Osborne said. "Ward was infiltrating a pretty hardcore biker gang that's been running Mexican brown up from Texas."

"Can you get us his files?" Erin asked eagerly.

"Sure," Osborne said. "But you told me he got shot in a bathroom?"

"That's right," Erin said.

"That's not these guys' MO," Osborne said. "They want to kill you, they take you out of the city, tie a chain around your ankles, and drag you down the highway behind their bikes. Leave nothing but a red smear on the asphalt."

"Jesus Christ," Vic said. "No wonder he was twitchy."

"He was meeting some tough guys at McQuillan's," Erin said. "Could that have been part of his case?"

"If it was, I didn't know about it," Osborne said. "And I should've. He was supposed to report all his contacts to me. Do you know who he was meeting, or what they were talking about?"

Erin shook her head. "We hoped you'd be able to tell us that."

It was Osborne's turn to give Erin a searching look. "Do you think Ward was on the take?" he asked.

She matched his stare. "We don't know," she said.

"He was exchanging briefcases with the guys he met," Kira said. "Do you know what he would've been swapping with them?"

"No," Osborne said. "But I'll see what I can find out."

"Discreetly," Erin blurted out.

The Sergeant blinked. "What do you mean?"

Erin didn't know what to say. She'd spoken on instinct, out of her old undercover habits. How to explain that she didn't know who to trust, even within the NYPD?

Kira came to her rescue. "If it was suicide, it's a sensitive thing," she said smoothly. "We don't want gossip getting around the One-Oh-Four. His family's going to have a hard enough time with this."

"Of course," Osborne said. "We'll keep it quiet."

* * *

It was about noon, so they stopped at a nearby deli for sandwiches. Vic ate quickly, then stepped away from the table to call Piekarski and check up on Mina, leaving Kira and Erin sitting opposite one another and Rolf at Erin's feet.

"I still can't wrap my head around Vic being a dad," Kira said.

"It's pretty weird," Erin agreed. "But when you think of all the strange people we run into, they had parents, too."

"Yeah." Kira swallowed hard. "I keep thinking about Bill. He must've really been struggling. Maybe, if I hadn't taken that transfer to Major Crimes…"

"No." Erin put a hand out, laying it on top of Kira's. "Don't go there. This isn't on you."

"It's on *somebody*," Kira said. "This didn't just happen."

"Not necessarily," Erin said. "He was having problems. He'd picked up drinking again. You said it yourself, Gang Task Force guys have lots of temptations."

"I knew he was in recovery," Kira said. "I sometimes think half the NYPD are alcoholics. At least Bill had the guts to admit it."

"Maybe he just slipped," Erin said. "You know the old joke about how it's so easy to quit smoking? Some people quit ten, fifteen times, it's so easy to do."

"I also know why a lot of us drink," Kira said. "The Job wears us down. We see all this heinous shit and we have two choices: either stop caring permanently, or find a way to cope day to day."

"If IAB sacked every cop with a drinking problem, we'd lose a third of the Force," Erin said.

"I was exaggerating," Kira said. "There was a study back in 2010 that found eleven percent of male cops and sixteen percent of female ones used alcohol in at-risk quantities."

"Of course you'd know that," Erin said. "I wonder why women have more of a problem than men."

"Either it's our sensitive and fragile nature…" Kira began.

Erin snorted.

"...or maybe it's because we're already under higher stress in this bullshit male-dominated job," Kira finished. "Take your pick: chauvinism or feminism, it ends up the same. It's really not all that bad, though, when you consider the level of alcoholism in the populace at large is about ten and a half percent."

"We should be better than the average Joe," Erin said. "But Carlyle once told me the world doesn't run on 'should.'"

"Ain't that the truth," Kira said. "Know what's ironic? This is exactly the sort of conversation we ought to be having over a couple of beers. Instead, what've we got? Reubens and diet sodas."

"What do you think?" Erin asked.

"About what?"

"Ward's death."

"I *think* he shot himself," Kira said. "I just don't *believe* it."

"That's a pretty fine distinction," Erin said.

"It's the difference between my head and my heart," Kira said. "You know how people always say, 'I never thought he'd do it?' That's how I feel about Bill. That man loved life. If you'd known him, you'd see what I mean. He loved playing jokes on people. He was always screwing around with the squad. He loved riddles and games."

Kira stopped talking and stared past Erin into space. Erin took the opportunity to finish her sandwich, chasing it down with a gulp of Diet Coke.

"Hey," she said after a few moments. "You okay?"

"Games," Kira said again, lost in thought. "That's it!"

"What is?" Erin asked.

"Bill really liked logic puzzles," Kira said. "He was a clever guy. Whenever we worked Sundays, he'd have the *Times* crossword with him and he'd do it over his breaks. In *pen*. He had the *Times* right there in the stall with him, remember?"

"Yeah," Erin said. "I thought that was weird."

"He did riddles and all that stuff. Did you ever try one of those Escape Rooms?"

"What, you mean the ones where they lock you in a room and you have an hour to get out?"

"Yeah."

Erin shook her head. "Too much like work."

"Well, Bill loved them," Kira said. "He always wanted to make one up himself."

"Hold on," Erin said. "Are you saying he used his own death to set up a puzzle?"

"Maybe," Kira said.

"That's insane," Erin said.

"Maybe," Kira repeated. "But think about it. Let's suppose, just for a moment, that Bill was in some sort of serious trouble. Maybe he found something out about someone important, or stumbled on some big, scary secret. And he couldn't tell anyone, because his family would be in danger. But he knew if he shot himself, IAB would have to investigate. And he knew I was in IAB."

Erin was shaking her head before Kira had finished. "You're talking about some sort of conspiracy," she said. "And this one cop figures it out, but he can't tell anyone directly, and so he decides to *kill himself* in a weird way, just hoping the case will get handed off to the one IAB officer in New York who knows him well enough to figure it out?"

"When you say it that way, it sounds pretty nuts," Kira admitted.

"It sounds like paranoid schizophrenia," Erin said.

"Well, maybe that's not what happened," Kira said. "Maybe it's what Bill *thinks* happened. You might have a point about the paranoia."

Erin put a hand over her face. "Good Lord," she muttered.

"Come on!" Kira insisted. "I'm not saying his head was screwed on straight. If he was stressed out, if he'd fallen off the wagon, he might have been jumping at shadows. Even if there isn't some big conspiracy, if he thought there was, it might explain what he did."

"This is some secret agent bullshit," Erin said. Then she gave Kira a wry smile. "But it's worth thinking about. If there's someone Ward was afraid of, it might explain this. I hope so, because right now it makes no damn sense at all."

Kira returned the smile gratefully. "Thanks," she said.

"But how can we tell?" Erin asked. "If it's all a big game?"

"We look for clues," Kira said. "If we find ones he deliberately planted, we'll know."

"And how can we tell which ones are deliberate?"

"I have no idea."

"This is a new one," Erin admitted. "You think our victim set up his own death to solve another crime? Sheesh, and I thought *I* was dedicated to my job."

"Maybe he was going to die anyway," Kira said. "He just chose the particular time and place."

"I can't wait to explain this to Vic," Erin said. "And Webb's going to be even more fun. He's going to think we're the ones who've been drinking. What're you planning on telling Keane?"

"As little as possible," Kira said.

* * *

"Bullshit," was Vic's verdict when he returned to the table and heard Kira's theory.

"I know it sounds far-fetched," Kira said.

"*Star Wars* is far-fetched," Vic said. "You want me to list everything wrong with what you just said?"

"No," Kira said. "But I don't think it matters what I want."

"He couldn't have known you'd catch the case," Vic said. "This is a big city with a lot of IAB punks. No offense."

"The One-Oh-Four doesn't have an active IAB unit," Kira said. "We pick up their slack. And no offense taken."

"But you're not the only dick Keane's got in his pocket," Vic said. "Okay, that came out wrong. But what if one of his other guys got the nod?"

"I'd still hear about it," Kira said. "Even if I didn't get the case, once I learned it was Bill, I'd dive into it.

"But Ward didn't know that'd be the case," Vic said.

"Why not?" Erin asked. "If he knew her as well as he thought?"

It was Vic's turn to roll his eyes. "Fine. Whatever. Our super-genius, who blew his own brains out in a bathroom, is a master of psychology. But if this is some fancy-pants escape room puzzle, where are the clues?"

"The clues are in the room," Kira said. "That's how these things work."

"This would be the restroom at McQuillan's?" Vic asked. "The same restroom CSU's gone over with a fine-toothed whatever?"

"That's the one," Kira said.

"Then CSU's gonna find the clues," he said.

"I don't think so," Kira said.

"Why not?" Erin asked.

"Because they're looking for evidence in a criminal investigation," Kira said. "They're not trying to solve a puzzle."

"How's that any different?" Vic demanded.

"I think we'll know when we see it," Kira said

"So we're going back to McQuillan's?" Vic asked.

"Looks like it," Erin said. "And we need to see that newspaper he was holding."

"For a squad that spends as much time in bars as we do, we really don't drink enough," Vic said.

"We drink all the time," Erin said.

"My point stands," Vic said.

Chapter 6

The Crime Scene Unit had mostly finished by the time the detectives got back to McQuillan's. They were packing up the evidence into their van, but the bathroom was still taped off and a very bored Patrolman was standing guard over it. Fully processing a scene could take a day or two.

Erin showed her gold shield to the head evidence tech, Detective Burrows. "I need to see the newspaper," she said.

"What for?" the CSU guy asked. "Newsprint doesn't carry prints."

"Just let us take a look," she said.

The *Times* had been carefully bagged, but the bag was clear. CSU had left it the way they'd found it, open to the crossword puzzle. It appeared to have been about half finished.

"That's Bill's handwriting," Kira said. "At least, I think so."

"Why'd he stop?" Vic wondered. "If I was gonna off myself, I'd finish the damn puzzle first. Otherwise it'd bug me all through the afterlife."

"You're right," Kira said. She scanned the puzzle, examining every bit of it.

"What're you looking for?" Erin asked.

"Clues," Kira said.

Vic rolled his eyes. "It's a crossword puzzle," he said. "It's full of clues."

"Look," Kira said, pointing to one of the answers.

"'Graffiti,'" Erin read aloud. "What's your point?"

"That's not the right answer," Kira said. "Number 129-across. The clue is 'Perfecto!' 'Graffiti' doesn't make any sense."

"What's the right answer, then?" Erin asked.

"What the hell difference does it make?" Vic demanded.

"The first letter is N," Kira said. "And 79-down should be 'Unfriended,' so that makes the sixth letter D. Then with the last letter being T, that should be... 'Nailed it.'"

"Okay," Vic said. "What is it?"

"That's the answer," Kira said.

"What is?"

"'Nailed it.'"

Vic looked confused for a moment. Then he smiled. "Gotcha. This was one of those Abbott and Costello 'Who's on First' moments. But why would he write the totally wrong answer?"

Erin was already turning toward McQuillan's. "Because he wants us to look at the graffiti in the restroom," she said.

The bathroom stank of blood, disinfectant, and chemicals. The meat wagon had carted William Ward's body off to the morgue, where Levine was doubtless up to her elbows in the poor bastard by now. A pool of dried blood remained to mark the spot. There was no chalk outline; that was a myth. In this age of digital photography, the evidence techs snapped a few dozen high-res photos of the body and called it good.

"We're looking for another clue?" Vic asked. He was avoiding the blood with a squeamishness Erin might have found amusing in other circumstances.

"That's right," Kira said. "That's how these things work."

Vic pointed to a ragged hole in the wall. "CSU must've dug the bullet out there," he said.

Erin nodded. She was looking at the restroom stall. It was typical of a tavern's men's room. The latch was broken. A roll of cheap toilet paper, lightly spattered with blood, hung from the metal wall. The wall itself was decorated with graffiti, most of it sexual.

"'Doreen Davis is a slut,'" Erin read aloud. "'Donnie Evans licks my balls.' Not exactly great literature. Here's a drawing of a body part I don't have. It's kind of weirdly proportioned. Vic, you're a guy. Why do guys have this urge to draw dick pics on everything?"

"It's sort of like wolves in the wild," he explained. "They piss on things to mark their territory."

"Thanks for clearing that up," Kira said. "You do know girls really aren't impressed by dick size, right?"

"Says you," Vic said.

"Vic?" Kira said.

"Yeah?"

"I'm a girl, in case you'd forgotten. I know a little more about being one than you do."

"We're wasting our time," Vic growled. "Nothing's here."

Erin ignored his griping. She was still scanning the graffiti. Some of it was kind of funny, even clever.

"Get a load of this one," she said. "I think it's a haiku: 'Gloria Danvers/Promised me forever, but/One night was too long.'"

"Cute," Vic said. "At least he put some effort into it. Probably more than he put into Gloria."

"This guy's an idiot, though," Erin continued. "'For a time you won't forget, try Chelsea, the Fat Witch, 759-01059.'"

"Some guys like bigger girls," Vic said. "That doesn't make him an idiot."

"That's not what Erin's talking about," Kira said. "That isn't even a real phone number. It's got an extra digit."

"Yeah," Erin said. "But I think Vic's right. This is a washout. Unless..."

"Unless what?" Kira asked after a moment.

"Shh," Vic said. "Erin gets like this when she's about to say something smart. Wait for it."

Instead of speaking to them, Erin rushed out of the bar. The CSU van was just pulling away from the curb. She leaped in front of the van and waved them down.

Burrows stuck his head out the passenger window. "What is it, O'Reilly?" he asked.

"Did you find anything in Ward's pockets?" she asked.

"Yes," Burrows said. "Wallet, keys, some loose change... let's see, that'd be a dollar eighty-five. Six quarters, three dimes, one nickel. And a black permanent marker."

Erin's heart leaped. The Fat Witch graffiti had been written in black marker and looked fresh.

"Thanks," she told him.

"He had a holster on his belt," Burrows went on. "Empty. One extra magazine for a Glock nine-millimeter semi-auto, seventeen bullets. The belt was leather, an imitation Burberry. Not a very good imitation. One pair Levi's slacks, thirty-six inch waist—"

"That'll do," Erin interrupted. "Thanks, Detective. I appreciate it."

"You need us to hang around?" he asked.

"I don't think so. But I may give you a call."

She went back in, ignoring the questioning looks leveled at her by Kira and Vic, and sniffed at the graffiti. The familiar acrid tang was just noticeable under the reek of blood and the faint whiff of gunpowder.

"That's one hell of a suicide note," Vic said, bending his head to peer into the stall alongside Erin. "Who's this Chelsea chick?"

"Not who," Erin said. "Where."

Kira, catching Erin's drift, already had her phone out and was scanning a map of New York. "There's a Chelsea Market between West 15th and West 16th," she reported. "Off 9th Avenue."

"And?" Erin prompted.

"In the market is a bakery," Kira said. "The Fat Witch Bakery, to be exact."

"What's the address?" Erin asked.

"75 9th Avenue."

"Seven Five Nine," Vic said, pointing to the first three digits of the number scrawled on the wall. "That can't be a coincidence."

"Why a bakery?" Kira wondered.

"We'll find out when we get there," Erin said. She took a quick snapshot of the message with her phone camera. "Let's go."

* * *

"Is this a shopping mall?" Vic wondered aloud.

"It's an indoor marketplace," Kira said. "Totally different."

"What's the difference?" Vic asked.

Kira didn't answer, probably because she didn't know. Chelsea Market was a sprawling brick building that stretched between 9th and 10th Avenue. It contained a grocery store, a florist, a few restaurants, a bookstore, and the bakery. The market was built very much like a strip mall; a central corridor lined with shops on either side. Skylights would have been nice, but this was Manhattan and real estate was expensive, so apartments were piled on top of the market.

The detectives stood in front of the Fat Witch Bakery. Rolf's nostrils were twitching at the aroma of fresh bread that wafted out into the corridor. So were Vic's.

"Who's hungry?" Vic asked.

"We just ate," Kira said.

"One sandwich," he said contemptuously.

"I hate men," Kira said. "They can eat anything they want."

"Speaking of which," Vic said. "See that place a couple doors down? Mayhem Beer and Sandwiches? Sounds like my kind of joint."

"Maybe later," Erin said. She led Rolf into the bakery.

"Welcome to the Fat Witch," said a pleasant-faced young woman. She was slender, pretty, and just about the furthest thing from a fat witch. Her hair was a dramatic side cut and was dyed magenta.

"Good afternoon, ma'am," Erin said.

"Ma'am?" the woman echoed, wrinkling her nose. The nose had a gold ring in its septum and a diamond stud on the left side. "My mom's a ma'am. I don't figure I'll be one for another ten, fifteen years. If ever."

"Sorry, Miss," Erin said. She held up her shield. "I'm Detective O'Reilly, NYPD Major Crimes. These are my colleagues, Detective Neshenko and—"

"Kira Jones," Kira interjected, smiling at the woman. "What's your name?"

"Dana," she replied. "Dana Featherwood. It's a weird name, I know, but it wasn't up to me."

"Would it be okay if we asked you some questions?" Erin asked.

Dana shrugged. "Sure. But we haven't had any major crimes here at the Fat Witch. I'm pretty sure I would've noticed. I mean, that's stuff like murders and kidnappings, right?"

"That's right," Kira said. "We're investigating the death of a police officer."

Dana blinked. "Wow," she said. "A cop was murdered? I hadn't heard anything about that. We don't even have shoplifters in here."

"We're still determining what happened," Erin said. "Do you know Officer William Ward?"

"I don't think so." Dana shook her head. She had three earrings in her left ear and two in her right. They jingled and clinked.

Kira produced her phone and showed the screen to her. "Here's a picture of him," she said.

Dana's face lit up. "Oh! Yeah, I've seen him!"

"Really?" Kira said excitedly. "When did you see him last?"

"Yesterday," Dana said. "This was so weird. You aren't going to believe it."

"I bet we will," Vic said. "Or they will, at any rate. I might not."

"He came in right before closing," Dana said. "He looked rough."

"Rough how?" Erin asked.

"Like he was drunk," Dana said. "All red-eyed. But he talked okay. He didn't slur or forget what he was saying. But he was acting strange."

"What did he do?" Kira asked. She was watching the other woman closely.

"He didn't tell me his name," Dana said. "Or if he did, I didn't remember it. But he showed me his badge and said he was on some sort of important job. A 'covert assignment,' that's what he called it. And he wasn't wearing his uniform, but he had a gun. He kept touching it."

"The gun?" Vic asked.

"Yeah," Dana said.

"What kind of gun?" Vic asked. "Pistol? Rifle? Revolver? Automatic?"

"A gun," Dana said. "Like, a handgun. Just like that one."

She pointed at Erin's Glock where it rested on her hip.

"Did he take it out of its holster?" Vic asked.

"No," Dana said. "He just kept holding it, like he wanted to remind himself it was there. It was almost like he was caressing it. You know, as if it was a pet. Like stroking a dog's head or something."

Kira shuddered. Erin didn't blame her.

"What did he do?" Kira asked.

"He wanted to know if it was okay to post something on our board," Dana said. She pointed to a cork bulletin board that hung on the far wall. It was festooned with posters for local music groups, ads for cleaning services, and one notice asking whether anyone had seen a lost dog.

"What did you say?" Kira asked.

"I said sure," Dana said. "But he didn't have a poster. He just took a piece of scratch paper out of his pocket and scribbled a note on it. He told me to leave it up for at least a week. He told me it was important."

"Where's the note?" Erin asked. Vic was already scanning the board.

"Lower left corner," Dana said.

"Here," Vic said, pointing. Erin and Kira hurried over. Rolf lost interest immediately. Humans were always concerned about paper with funny little marks on it. All he cared about was what had been wrapped in the paper—food wrappers were always fascinating—or who had been handling it.

"'If you see Susie Derkins, call the police,'" Kira read aloud. She scratched her head.

"Like I said," Dana said. "Weird."

"It's another puzzle," Erin said. "The handwriting's the same as on the bathroom stall."

"Definitely," Kira agreed. "And it's black Sharpie. This was Bill."

"This dude was nuts," was Vic's opinion. "Didn't he have anything better to do than lay out goddamn breadcrumbs for us? I feel like Hansel, and you two can share being friggin' Gretel."

"Well, we *are* in a bakery," Kira said. "We should be able to get some breadcrumbs."

"That name is familiar," Erin said.

"Of course it is," Kira said. "Didn't you read the funny papers when you were a kid? *Calvin and Hobbes*?"

"Oh, right!" Erin said, snapping her fingers. "Suzie was Calvin's girlfriend."

"She wasn't his girlfriend," Kira said. "Those two hated each other."

"Calvin was six," Vic said. "Little boys pester girls they like. So do bigger boys. Erin's right. He totally had a crush on her."

"I love *Calvin and Hobbes*," Dana said. "Especially the stuffed tiger."

"Me, too," Kira said.

"But it doesn't get us any closer to figuring out what the hell Ward was hiding," Erin said. "We don't have much to go on here."

"No numbers," Vic said. "No address. Just a name, and it's not even the name of a real person."

"We don't know that," Erin said. "Check the directory."

"Why me?" Vic asked.

"Because I outrank you and I said so," Erin said.

"But is Major Crimes even in charge of this case anymore?" he asked.

"If IAB is, then I'm ranking officer," Kira said. "In which case *I'm* telling you to. You're outranked either way."

He grinned and took out his phone, bringing up the online New York directory. "Fair enough. Derkins... let's see. Nope, no Susie or Susan or Susannah. Got a Sarah Derkowitz, but that's as close as we come."

Erin was still staring at the paper. "We're missing something," she said.

"What tipped you off?" Vic asked. "The part where we've got no idea what this message means?"

In answer, Erin pulled the pin out of the board and lifted the slip of paper close to her face. It was rectangular, a few inches long, and crumpled, like it had been riding around in a pocket. She squinted at it.

"Invisible ink, maybe?" Kira guessed. "When I was a kid, we used to screw around with lemon juice. You put it in the oven and it turns visible."

"We've got ovens," Dana said. "I mean, we're a bakery."

"Maybe," Erin said. She turned the paper over. "Nothing's written on the backside. Looks like it's a claim slip from a laundromat."

"Which one?" Kira asked.

"Jiffy Laundry, a block over on 14th," Erin said. "I don't know it. But..."

She trailed off into silence.

"What?" Vic demanded. "I wish you'd stop doing that. You're making me twitchy."

Erin held up the claim slip and pointed to the call number stamped on the corner of the slip. The digits read 01059.

"That's the fake phone number," Kira said. "The one on the stall."

"The message isn't the message," Erin said, knowing it sounded insane and not caring. She felt a strange excitement, the thrill of the hunt. "Our next stop is Jiffy Laundry."

"Thanks for your help, Dana," Kira said. "If you think of anything else, here's one of my cards. You can give me a call any time, day or night."

"Do you really think Miss Featherstone, or whatever her name is, knows anything?" Vic asked as they hustled through the market.

"Of course she doesn't," Kira said. "She's completely peripheral."

"Then why'd you bother giving her your card?"

Erin snorted. "And you call yourself a detective," she said.

"Huh? What'd I miss?" Vic was indignant.

"Vic," Kira said patiently. "I thought she was hot. And she definitely gave me vibes like she was interested. I gave her my number."

That shut Vic up for almost ten seconds. Then he said, "Boy, do I feel like an asshole."

"I hope she calls you," Erin said to Kira. "A good-looking girl who knows how to bake is someone to go after. Just ask my dad."

"Yuck," Kira said. "It was going so well, but then you had to go and ruin it. Do *not* bring your parents into my love life."

Chapter 7

Jiffy Laundry was a little mom-and-pop place sandwiched between a pair of vacant storefronts. The one directly to the west advertised space to lease. The one on the other side was boarded up. Someone had painted the slogan FEAR IS NOT AN OPTION on that display window.

"Nice, upstanding neighborhood," Vic said.

"Remember, anything can be a clue," Kira said.

"This isn't police work," Vic said. "It's a whacked-out scavenger hunt. We're not gonna have to steal some poor schmuck's license plates, are we?"

"We're just picking up some dry cleaning," Erin said. She pushed open the laundromat's door.

A little bell tinkled as the door brushed it. The smells of detergent, fabric softener, and lint filled Erin's nostrils. Rolf shook his head and snorted.

This wasn't a self-service laundry. Instead of ranks of washers and dryers, Erin found herself in a narrow room furnished with an old counter and an ancient cash register. An Asian woman who looked older than the register was sitting behind the counter, reading a magazine.

"Good afternoon," Erin said. She held up her shield. "I'm Detective O'Reilly, NYPD Major Crimes. I'd like to ask—"

"Pick up or drop off?" the woman interrupted in heavily-accented English.

"Um, pick up," Erin said. She placed the claim slip on the counter.

The woman scooped up the slip of paper, glanced at it, said "One minute," and disappeared through a door into a back room.

"Five bucks says she comes back with something weird," Vic said.

"Define weird," Erin said.

"Not normal street clothes," he said. "I'm talking really bizarre, like a rubber gimp suit, or Freddy Krueger's sweater, or pants with no crotch in them."

"I don't think rubber needs to be dry-cleaned," Kira said.

"*That's* your problem with what he just said?" Erin demanded.

The old woman returned, carrying a plastic garment bag. "Here you are," she said. "Twenty-two fifty."

"Hold on," Vic said. "Wasn't this already paid for?"

"Twenty-two fifty," the woman repeated stonily.

"Good thing I'm not the ranking officer," Vic said, grinning at Erin. "Or I might be expected to pay for this."

"You've got a new baby," Erin said. "Kids are expensive. I'll get this one."

"You can expense it to the Department," Kira suggested.

"Do you really think we're going to file paperwork on this?" Erin shot back, fishing out her wallet.

The bag was bulky, obviously containing multiple articles of clothing, but it was opaque. Saying a quick thank-you to the laundry lady, she handed the bag to Vic. She was about to suggest they wait until they were somewhere more secure before looking inside, when Vic tore open the bag.

"Dress blues," he said, disappointed. "That's not as weird as I expected."

"Ward's dress uniform," Erin said, baffled. The uniform was pristine; the laundry had done a good job. A little baggie was looped around the coat hanger; it appeared to contain a number of metal accoutrements.

Kira reached out and tore the baggie loose, spilling its contents into her palm. She pointed to the nametag, which read WARD.

"At least we know we're on the right track," Erin said. "What else do we have?"

"Cufflinks," Kira reported. "Nothing fancy. They're set with some sort of black stone, maybe jet or onyx. My gemstones identification is sketchy."

"I thought you knew everything," Vic said.

"His decorations," Kira went on, pretending she hadn't heard. "Community Service Commendation, Meritorious Police Duty medal, Firearms Proficiency Bar."

"I've got one of those," Vic said, to nobody's surprise. The Firearms Proficiency award was given to officers who were certified as expert shooters. "That's a little ironic, don't you think?"

"Why?" Erin asked.

"Because it looks like he shot himself," Vic said. "Point-blank. That doesn't exactly take a marksman."

"Anything else?" Erin asked Kira.

"A key," Kira said. She held it up. "Looks like it goes in a storage locker. Or maybe a safe-deposit box."

"Which one?" Vic asked.

"How am I supposed to know that?" Kira retorted.

"There'll be a locker number on the key," Vic said, his tone as pedantic as if he was explaining it to a four-year-old.

"Yes, Vic," Kira said, matching his tone. "I know that. But if you look here, you'll see the locker number has been filed off."

Vic rolled his eyes. "Jesus friggin' Christ," he said. "If this guy wasn't already dead, I'd smack him. How many hoops we gotta jump through?"

"There has to be a number somewhere," Erin said.

"There's his shield," Kira said doubtfully. "Number six-six-three-two. Do you think that could be it?"

"We don't even know where the goddamn locker is!" Vic snapped. "Do you have any idea how many storage lockers there are in this city? How many bus stations? Train stations? Self-storage units?"

"One thing at a time," Erin said quietly. She was trying to think. "Why a laundromat, do you suppose? And a bakery? It has to mean something."

"I have a guess," Kira said. "The laundromat is a joke. Don't you get it?"

"Yeah, it's hilarious," Vic said. "Oh wait, no. I don't. Because jokes are supposed to be funny. Do you hear me laughing?"

"Bill was laundering information," Kira said triumphantly. "He was making sure nobody could get to what he was hiding by accident. They'd have to follow the clues. *All* the clues."

"Okay," Erin said. "Meaning what, exactly?"

"The uniform is obviously his," Kira said. "Anybody could get at it and go through his pockets. There'd be no point filing the numbers off the key if the same numbers were in the bag. They have to be somewhere else."

"So we gotta go where?" Vic asked. "Staten Island? Newark, maybe?"

"You have a really negative attitude, you know that?" Kira said.

"I know," Vic said. "I've been practicing it for years. I think I'm getting good at it. Zofia thinks so, too."

"The bakery's a wasted step," Erin said. "If he was trying to throw people off his trail, that is. Like you said, this uniform's pretty conspicuous, and it's obviously his. There must be a reason he sent us there first."

"Maybe the number's back at the bakery," Vic said.

"Lemon juice," Kira said.

"Huh?" Vic said.

Kira spun and lunged toward the counter, startling the old woman badly. The laundress dropped her magazine and said something indignant in a language Erin thought was Chinese.

"Give me that claim slip!" Kira exclaimed. "The one we just gave you!"

Utterly bewildered, the old woman opened a drawer under the counter and extracted the slip. Kira snatched it out of her hand and held it up to the light.

"Damn," she said after a moment. "I can't tell. We need an oven."

"We're going back to the bakery, aren't we," Erin said.

"Of course we are," Vic said. He was smiling now. "That hot chick with the pink hair is there, right?"

"Shut up," Kira said. "That's got nothing to do with this. Do you know an oven anywhere closer?"

"You're interested in Dana's oven," Vic said, still grinning.

"Thanks for reminding me," Kira said.

"About Dana?"

"No, about what an asshole you are sometimes."

"Don't mention it."

"Something's bothering me," Erin said.

"Yeah?" Vic said. "What's that?"

"I'm starting to think Ward was smarter than we are."

He snorted. "The man put a nine-millimeter round through his own brain. How smart could he be?"

"I'm thinking maybe we're finding that out," Erin said.

"That's not what's bugging me," Kira said quietly.

"Well, as long as we're airing our grievances, by all means, share your concerns," Vic said with mock politeness.

"Bill went to a lot of trouble to hide whatever this is," Kira said. "I'm wondering whether we really want to figure it out."

* * *

"Hello again," Dana said when the detectives trooped into the Fat Witch. "Is there something else I can do for you?"

"Yeah," Vic said. "We want to stick something in your—ouch!"

Erin was five-foot six, a decent height for an American woman, but a size that left her at a disadvantage compared to the average thug. Some women compensated for height difference with high-heeled shoes, but since Erin's job often required her to stand or run for prolonged periods, she had to make do with comfy shoes with a modest two inches under the heels. It was hard to run down a perp when every step risked a twisted ankle.

Kira was only five-four, but she'd transferred into a cushy desk job. Her biker's boots looked hardcore, but they also had impressively tall heels. While these were frowned on by the NYPD for street wear, Kira had just demonstrated they were not entirely without practical use. With expert precision, she'd planted her right heel on the top of Vic's more pragmatic but less spiky footwear. As she'd leaned into the motion, she'd been able to put almost her entire body weight behind a contact point less than two square inches in area. Vic was going to have one hell of a bruise.

"We were hoping we could take you up on that offer of the use of one of your ovens," Kira said smoothly. "Oh, sorry, Vic. Did I step on your foot? I'm so clumsy sometimes."

"For the invisible ink you were talking about?" Dana said, her eyes lighting up. "Sure! Come on back. We just pulled some cinnamon rolls out of Number Three, so it should still be nice and hot."

They followed the bakery girl behind the counter, Vic trailing the others, limping slightly and muttering curses under his breath.

"What's this all about, anyway?" Dana asked.

"The NYPD can't comment regarding ongoing investigations," Vic said, glaring at Kira.

"Don't mind him," Kira said. "He's always like that. But he's really a nice guy underneath."

"Deep, *deep* underneath," Erin added.

Dana came to an industrial-sized oven and hauled it open. She pulled on an oven mitt and held out her hand. Erin passed the claim slip to her and Dana placed it carefully on the rails.

"Do I need to close the door?" Dana asked.

"No," Kira said. "Just give it a couple minutes. The lemon juice should show up in brown."

"Assuming there is any," Vic said.

They waited. Erin stroked Rolf's ears. Vic examined a tray of cinnamon rolls and licked his lips thoughtfully. Kira chatted with Dana, quickly discovering the other woman shared an interest in motorbikes.

"I ride a Kawasaki Ninja 400," Kira said.

"Nice," Dana said. "I'm between bikes. I used to ride a Harley Iron 883, but some idiot in a Humvee sideswiped me last month and totaled it. I'd like to see that Ninja sometime."

"I'd be glad to show you," Kira said.

"Things are definitely heating up in here," Vic muttered in Erin's ear.

"No kidding," Erin said. She grabbed a spare mitt and leaped at the oven, snatching up the piece of paper, which had started to turn brown and curl up at the edges. She drew back from the heat and laid the paper down on a cooling rack.

The others crowded excitedly around her. "Well?" Vic said.

Erin had to squint to make out the writing. It was barely legible, and the oven had been a little too hot, so the paper had turned almost the same color as the ink. "Sky Ring, I think," she said. "Then the number twelve."

"Sky Ring?" Vic echoed. "Never heard of it."

Kira put the name into the web browser on her phone. "Nothing," she said after a moment.

"Maybe it's a, whaddaya call it, a metaphor," Vic said.

"For what?" Erin asked.

"Beats me."

"Are you sure that's what it says?" Kira asked.

"Pretty sure," Erin said. "The first word is definitely 'Sky,' and that's an R."

"That last letter isn't a 'g,'" Vic said.

"I think it's a 'k,'" Dana suggested. She'd managed to work her way between Kira and Erin and was peering at the note with interest.

"Sky Rink?" Erin said doubtfully.

"The Sky Rink!" Kira exclaimed. "That's it!"

"I swear that's supposed to mean something," Vic said. "But it beats the hell out of me."

"It's a skating rink," Kira explained. "On Chelsea Piers, just a couple blocks from here."

"An ice rink would have equipment lockers," Erin said, nodding. "And this must mean what we want is in locker number twelve. Let's go."

She was almost out of the bakery when she realized Kira wasn't behind her. She paused and saw the Internal Affairs detective saying something to Dana. Then Kira jogged after them.

"Sorry," she said. "Dana... Miss Featherwood wanted to know how this whole thing came out. I told her I couldn't give her all the details, but I'd be happy to share what I could. Over dinner sometime."

"You got a date!" Vic exclaimed. "Get some, girl! You know what they say about chicks who dye their hair?"

Kira put a hand up and ran it along her own blue-and-red-tinted scalp. "What do they say?" she asked in a deceptively soft and pleasant voice. Her other hand curled into a fist.

"Vic?" Erin said.

"What?"

"If you don't want Mina to be an only child, you'd better stop talking right now, while you still have functioning balls."

"I just got a great idea," he said without missing a beat. "Let's stop wasting time and go skating."

Chapter 8

The Sky Rink stood on the bank of the Hudson River in the middle of Chelsea Piers. The Piers were a sprawling complex of indoor sporting facilities, including not only the skating rink but a driving range, a swimming pool, and a bowling alley.

"Did you ever come here?" Kira asked as they assembled outside, staring at the big blue and gray building. "As a kid, I mean?"

"I grew up in Queens," Erin reminded her. "In case you've forgotten, it's a blue-collar kind of place. We do have pools and bowling alleys down there. Why go all the way to the West Side?"

"Brighton Beach for me," Vic said. "If we ever got bored, we'd just have a pick-up fistfight with some of the punks a couple blocks over."

"My dad brought me here a few times," Kira said. "I was a pretty good skater."

"Triple axels and shit?" Vic asked.

"Hockey," she replied.

"That's more like it," he said.

"So you know where the lockers are?" Erin asked.

"Yeah," Kira said. "Follow me."

She led them into a maze of concrete-block corridors lined with decorative blue tile. They passed the entrance to the skating rink and paused a moment to admire it. The indoor rink was a huge space, the ceiling supported by massive steel crossbeams. It was midafternoon on a weekday, so the ice was only sparsely populated by skaters.

"Gotta love good insulation," Vic said, zipping up his jacket. "It feels like friggin' January in here."

"What'd you expect?" Erin retorted. "It's an ice rink, Vic. They don't want it to melt."

"The lockers are this way," Kira said, directing them down a cross-hallway. They found themselves in a curiously-shaped little room, walls lined with wood-frame lockers, their contents screened by metal mesh. Each locker was secured by a combination lock. Three big, bearded men stood next to one of the lockers. The guy in the middle was doing something to the lock. It popped open with a squeal of protesting metal.

"We interrupting something?" Vic asked.

The three guys froze. The one in the middle was holding a crowbar. The men looked at the detectives for a long, awkward moment.

"Forgot the combo, huh?" Vic said. "No sweat, happens all the time. Now, if you were breaking into a locker that wasn't yours, then we'd have a problem, because that's against the law and we're with the NYPD."

"Ah, shit," the guy on the right said. "Listen, buddy, we don't want no trouble. And no offense, but you don't look like no cops I ever seen."

"That one's a biker bitch," the one on the left said, jutting his chin Kira's direction. "I bet they're with the Devils."

Erin pulled back the flap of her jacket, revealing her gold shield and holstered pistol. "Wrong," she said. "We're NYPD all right. Back off and keep your hands—"

The man in the middle rushed her, swinging his crowbar. His buddies went for Vic and Kira at the same time.

"*Fass!*" Erin shouted, backpedaling as the crowbar whistled down. She didn't even try to draw her Glock. A handgun was a great thing to have in a fight, but it took about a second to pull the pistol and bring it in line. That was a second she didn't have. The whole point of a gun was that it allowed you to hit the other guy from a distance, and these punks were already way too close.

The forked end of the crowbar slashed air less than an inch from her eyeball. Erin lost her footing and went down on her ass. The floor was rubberized, so it didn't hurt as much as it might have, but the impact still jarred up her spine. The thug whipped the crowbar around and up, getting ready for another swing.

Rolf leaped over Erin and plowed into the man, teeth snapping shut on his forearm. The guy gave a startled cry that cut off with a whoosh of involuntary air as he smashed against a locker, Rolf's ninety pounds of canine ferocity driving the breath from his body. The crowbar clattered across a row of benches and into a corner.

Erin planted a hand and made a sideways half-roll up onto one knee, reaching for her Glock. Rolf had her opponent under control. Vic and the second thug were in close contact, raining blows on one another. On Erin's right, the third goon had Kira by the throat. Even as Erin cleared her pistol and brought it up, the guy picked Kira up by the neck and banged her head against a locker door.

Erin sighted down the barrel of the Glock, lining up the sight with the man's ear. The first day back from vacation, she thought, and here she was about to shoot a guy. "Drop her!" she shouted.

The man paid no attention, pulling Kira's dangling body back to slam her again. Erin's finger slid inside the trigger guard and began to tighten.

Kira's hand came up. She was holding something bright yellow. Erin, on the verge of firing, recognized an X-26 Taser. Kira shoved the business end of the weapon directly into the thug's nose and triggered it up his nostrils.

The effect was immediate and spectacular. The man's head snapped back as if he'd been smacked with a baseball bat. His jaw went rigid and his knees buckled.

His fingers turned rubbery and he sank to the ground making a weird sound that wasn't quite a moan and wasn't quite a scream, but something in between. He pawed ineffectually at his face, his eyes rolled back so far only the whites were visible. Kira kept the trigger pressed down, the Taser giving off its vicious rapid *click-click-click* as it delivered its voltage into the man's face.

Erin turned her attention back to Vic just in time to see him administer a short right hook to his opponent's kidney. The man grunted and countered with a hook of his own. His fist looked weird, misshapen somehow. Erin caught the glint of reflected light on some sort of blade. Even as she registered this, it flashed across Vic's cheek, drawing a line of fresh, bright blood.

Erin decided to shoot this asshole. Nobody knifed her partner. But Vic was standing too close and both men were moving too fast. If she fired, she might hit Vic either by missing her target or through overpenetration. She took aim again and waited for her opening.

Vic knew he'd been cut, but it just made him mad. He didn't waste time flinching or clapping a hand to his face. Blood was beginning to stream down his cheek. He growled and caught the man's next swing with a hand around the guy's wrist. Then he grabbed the man's weapon, pulled, and twisted it all the way around. There was a faint but distinct crackling, like a guy cracking his knuckles, and a pop like a champagne cork. The man gave a surprisingly high-pitched, almost girlish scream.

Vic jerked on the thing over the man's hand, yanking it loose, which drew another scream. Vic stared at the weapon in disgusted surprise.

"An ice skate?" he shouted. "You cut me with a friggin' *ice skate*? I oughta cut your balls off with this, you stupid son of a bitch! What's the matter with you?"

The thug, clutching his arm, paid no attention.

To Erin's right, the clicking of the Taser finally stopped. Kira was leaning against the wall next to her assailant, rubbing the back of her own head. The man was curled into a tight ball, whimpering. Rolf had his guy down, too. The K-9 stood with the goon's arm in his mouth, just like a happy suburban dog fetching a stick. His tail was wagging.

"You're all under arrest," Erin said. "For assaulting police officers. I'm guessing you already know your rights, but we have to remind you."

"They're not the top of the class anyway," Vic said. He tossed the bloody ice skate aside. "Fat-head lard-ass idiots."

"You're bleeding," Erin said.

Vic gave her a look. "You think I don't know that? I got cut with a goddamn ice skate. That's the sort of thing a guy notices. Let's get the cuffs on these bastards so I can get a Band-Aid or something."

"I think you might need stitches," Erin said. "That's a lot of blood."

"Shit, I hurt myself worse than this shaving," Vic snorted. "You assholes have the right to remain silent, so keep your mouths shut. If you say anything, we'll use it at trial and you'll be sorry. You've got the right to an attorney, if any of those bottom-feeding lowlifes are willing to talk to you. Oh, and we'll give you a couple phone calls if we're in a good mood. You understand?"

The three men gave distracted sounds of assent. All three were pretty uncomfortable. Erin guessed two had broken arms. The third probably didn't have any permanent damage, but he'd taken a triple Taser jolt up his nose. That was a full fifteen seconds of electric pain straight to the sinuses. He'd suffer no long-term effects, but his memory of what had happened might be a little spotty. The detectives cuffed the men without further resistance. Vic called Dispatch to send a couple Patrol units to pick them up.

"Erin," Kira said quietly as Vic lined the men up on a bench to wait for the cavalry.

"What?"

In answer, Kira pointed to the locker the men had jimmied open. A metal plate above it was engraved with the number 12.

"That's not a coincidence," Kira murmured.

"No," Erin said. "It isn't. I wonder how they knew."

"That's a good question," Vic said. He turned to the man who'd cut him with the skate. "Hey, Tonya Harding. Why were you breaking into that locker?"

"You broke my friggin' arm!" the man spat. "Screw you! I don't have to tell you shit!"

"You want me to break the other one, too?" Vic replied.

"We can't break their arms once we've got them in cuffs," Kira said wearily. "And they don't have to say anything, just like it says in the rights you just read them. Sheesh, Vic, guys like you are the *reason* we have the Miranda warning!"

"Vic, take these guys outside and wait for the Patrol boys," Erin said.

"And let you ladies have all the fun in the locker room?" Vic replied. "Shit, that came out wrong. I meant—"

"I know what you meant," Erin interrupted. "And that wasn't a suggestion. I'm ranking officer, so that makes it an order. Once you get them sent to lockup, you're going to the hospital to get your face stitched up. That's another order."

"Give a good cop a little power and she turns into a real bitch," Vic muttered.

"I'll give you a pass on that," Erin said. "On account of your injury. Now get going. Unless you're scared you can't handle these guys on your own, that is."

"You kidding?" he said. "They've got four good arms between them. I could take them with one of my own tied behind my back. Come on, assholes."

He grabbed two of the men by the upper arms and yanked them to their feet, giving the third a hard nudge with the toe of his boot. The three goons reluctantly went with him, Vic keeping behind them so he could watch them.

"We really should have another officer with him," Kira said as the locker room door swung shut behind Vic and his prisoners. "They might jump him."

"He's hoping they'll try," Erin said. "Three injured mopes, already in cuffs? Don't worry about Vic, he'll be fine. We'd be scraping those bastards off the street with a spatula. Now we need to work fast."

"What do you mean?" Kira asked.

"Once the uniforms get here, this becomes an official crime scene," Erin explained. "They'll tape off this whole room, and especially the locker. If we want to see what's in there first, we'd better look now."

"Right." Kira unzipped a pocket of her leather jacket and removed a roll of disposable gloves. She handed a pair to Erin and pulled on two for herself. "Let's have a look."

They peered into the locker. It contained a hockey jersey, a helmet, a skate matching the one that had cut Vic, a set of hockey pads, and a black briefcase.

"Bingo," Erin said, grabbing the briefcase. "It's not even locked."

She laid the case on the bench and popped the clasps. She swung the lid open.

"What is it?" Kira asked, craning her neck. "Cash? Drugs?"

"What the hell is this?" Erin asked nobody in particular. She was staring at bundles of banknotes, but they weren't what she'd expected. For one thing, they were the wrong color.

"Monopoly money?" Kira said, bewildered.

Erin took one of the bundles out of the briefcase and ruffled it. She saw the familiar colors of the funny money she'd played with as a kid.

"Is this some kind of sick joke?" she wondered. "Jesus Christ, Kira, Ward's dead! Don't tell me he shot himself over this!"

"There must be something else in the case," Kira said.

Erin dumped the bills out onto the floor. "Nothing," she said. "Maybe he left a message on one of them, but it'll take hours to go through them all."

"There's a message somewhere," Kira said. She was studying the locker and absentmindedly rubbing the back of her head. "The briefcase is the booby prize. It's the thing a thief would take without bothering to look inside. But what if that's the point?"

"You think the real clue is something else?"

"Why not? He used the backside of a note, invisible ink, fake graffiti. Bill liked misdirection."

"Okay," Erin said. "What else do we have here? That asshole used one of the skates on Vic. Here's the other. I don't see anything on them."

Kira rapped the helmet with her knuckles. "Standard hockey equipment," she said. "I don't see anything written on it. The brand name's Bauer, if that means anything. It's a good brand, pretty standard."

Erin took hold of the jersey. "It's a Rangers jersey," she said. "Number 10. The name Calvin on the back."

"I don't know anybody on the Rangers roster with that name," Kira said. "Do you follow hockey?"

"No," Erin said. Then she smiled suddenly. "But I know Susie Derkins and her boyfriend."

Kira slapped her own forehead and winced. "*Calvin and Hobbes*," she said. "Ow."

"Are you okay?" Erin asked, suddenly concerned. "How hard did you hit your head?"

"I'm fine," Kira said.

"You ought to get yourself checked out," Erin said. "A knock on the head is no joke. I should know. I got shot in the head before Christmas."

"I know," Kira said. "I always thought you had a thick skull."

"Just barely thick enough," Erin said.

"Seriously, I'm fine," Kira said. "It's just a bruise."

"Good job with that Taser," Erin said. "But did you have to cram it up his nose?"

Kira smiled wryly. "He was trying to strangle me. It seemed like a proportional response."

"Calvin Ten," Erin said. "What does that mean?"

"It means the number ten is important," Kira said. "And this jersey is the clue, whatever it is." She flipped up the tag at the back. "Look! A name's written on it. Looks like it's in black Sharpie."

"Just like the graffiti on the bathroom stall," Erin said. "I know how Vic feels. I think maybe I'm going a little crazy chasing after this guy. What's the name?"

"Chase," Kira said, grinning.

"I wonder who that is," Erin said.

"Not who," Kira said. "What."

"Chase Manhattan?" Erin guessed. "The bank?"

"We have a safe-deposit key," Kira said.

"I thought that was to open this locker," Erin said.

"This locker?" Kira repeated. "The one with a combination lock?"

"Oh," Erin said, feeling silly. "Right. But what's the combination?"

In answer, Kira quickly spun the dial to the numbers 1, 5, and 9 in rapid succession. The lock clicked open.

"The numbers on the bathroom stall," Erin said. "Okay, so the key belongs to a safe deposit box, probably box number ten, at the nearest Chase Manhattan branch. And I'm guessing whatever's in there is a lot more valuable than a few thousand bucks in Monopoly money. But what's the point of all this?"

"I don't know," Kira said.

"Ward could've just mailed you the key!" Erin burst out. "He didn't have to do all this crap! The man was about to die, and what'd he do with his last hours? He spent them setting up this stupid time-wasting game!"

"If you're asking me what was going through his head, I don't know," Kira said. "I'm open to suggestions."

"He's leading us around," Erin said quietly. "Maybe the locations are important. McQuillan's is where he met his underworld contacts. The laundry might be a hint about money laundering, especially when we combine it with the funny money here. But why the ice rink? And the bakery? And who the hell were those mopes breaking into the locker?"

"We should be able to answer that last question, at least," Kira said. "I'll bet you five thousand Monopoly dollars all three are in the system."

"I'd take some of that action," Erin said. "Except it's unethical to steal money from a crime scene, even play money, so I'm not about to do it, especially in front of an IAB detective. Someone needs to look into those thugs and interrogate them. Someone else needs to get to the bank."

"The bank can wait," Kira said. "I feel like we ought to stick together. The whole point of safe deposit boxes is that they're safe, right?"

"I know," Erin said. "But we're on a clock here, and not just because of Levine's autopsy. We're following a trail, but we've got competition and they know things we don't. For all we know, that box has more than one key, and they've got the other. You have your bike. Vic and I will take the Charger. I'll go to the station with him and the prisoners. Then I'll get him some medical care. You take the key and go to Chase Bank. But be careful."

"Copy that," Kira said. "I'll let you know what I find. Good luck with the perps."

"Don't worry about us," Erin said. "And Kira?"

The other woman was already on her way to the door. She paused and half turned. "Yeah?"

"It's good having you back on the team."

Kira smiled. "I missed you guys too," she said. Then she was gone.

Chapter 9

"You really should go to the hospital," Erin said.

"For what?" Vic retorted. "If I went to the doc every time I got a scratch like this, I'd max out my insurance. I'm not letting you have all the fun sweating these losers."

"We can wait until you get stitches."

"Forget about it. This is a good look for the guy playing bad cop."

They were standing outside the Precinct 10 interrogation rooms. The perps were split up, each waiting his turn. Rolf was having a nap in one of the observation rooms.

"We know who they are," Erin said. "We need to know what they were looking for." The detectives had run the thugs' fingerprints and compared them with mugshots. To nobody's surprise, all three had lengthy criminal records.

"And why they thought it was worth mixing it up with us," Vic said.

"They probably thought they could take us," Erin said.

"You and Kira, maybe," Vic said.

"That guy who hit you with the skate is pretty big," Erin said. "He might've figured he had a chance of taking you out."

"How'd that work out for him?" Vic said. "Now he's cuffed in a chair with his wrist busted, which probably hurts like a son of a bitch."

"You ready?"

"Always."

They went into the first room. The best play when interrogating multiple suspects was to start with the weakest link in the chain. If you could break or flip one man against his buddies, you were better than halfway home. Erin had picked the guy Kira had Tased in the nose. He didn't look as beat up as his pals, each of whom now sported a bandage on his arm, but the fear in this man's eyes when he saw Erin and Vic was gratifying.

"Darryl Kortland," Erin said. "My name's Erin O'Reilly. We have some things to talk about." She laid a manila folder on the table in front of him. It was mostly for the sake of appearances; she'd read his file on the computer and only printed off his record so she'd have something to slap down for emotional emphasis.

"I wasn't doing nothing," Kortland muttered sullenly. "That bitch zapped me in the face! That's police brutality!"

"No," Vic growled, leaning on the table and glaring at him. "It isn't. You want to see what that really looks like?"

"We know about your arrangement with Bill Ward," Erin lied. "You're in a lot of trouble, Darryl. All three of you are. But this is your lucky day."

"If you think so, lady, luck don't mean the same thing to you it does to me," Kortland said. He sniffled loudly, then wished he hadn't. He tried to rub his nose. His hands were cuffed to a ring in the tabletop, so he had to bend his head forward to reach.

Erin gave him a tissue.

"Thanks," he said in muffled tones, blowing his nose. The tissue came away bloody. "Look what she did to me!"

"You were choking Jones out when she did it, asshole," Vic reminded him. "You think she should've given you a hug?"

"Didn't know you was cops," Kortland said.

"You think that makes it okay?" Vic snapped. "You think you can just go around choking girls and nobody gives a shit? And we identified ourselves, numbnuts!"

"Don't look like cops," Kortland insisted.

"O'Reilly showed you her friggin' shield!" Vic was yelling at him now. His wide, angry eyes, coupled with the bloody gash on his cheek, were genuinely frightening. Even Erin, who knew and trusted him, and knew he wouldn't actually hurt the man, had to fight down the urge to take a step back. Kortland, who was nearly as tall as Vic and considerably heavier, shrank down in his chair.

"Sorry," he said in a whisper that was almost a whimper.

"We're wasting time with this limp-dick loser," Vic said, turning his back on the man. "He's worthless. I say we toss him in a cell and go shake one of his buddies."

"Darryl," Erin said in a much gentler tone. "Take it easy, buddy. My partner gets pissed when people go after his pals. He thinks you're an idiot who doesn't know a thing, especially not how to save yourself. He wants to throw you in Riker's right now. But I think you're smarter than that. I think you want to help yourself, while you've still got the chance."

The good cop/bad cop routine was cliché because it worked. Scare the perp, then give him a reason to hope. Carrot and stick. It had worked dozens of times for Erin in her career, and she was betting on it working this time. Kortland hadn't lawyered up yet, for one thing, which meant he hadn't decided whether to talk or not. For another, he knew enough to know assaulting a cop could lead to serious jail time.

"What do you want?" he asked.

"You're a member of the Roadkillers," she said, naming his biker gang. If she hadn't known this from his police file, the tattoo on his bicep and the insignia on his jacket would have told her. Their logo was a cigar-chomping, bearded biker dragging caricature of a Hispanic man behind his bike. The Roadkillers combined habitual lawbreaking with white supremacy and racially-motivated violence.

"What about it?" Kortland said.

"Your gang competes with Mexican drug cartels," she said. "Coke, heroin, and fentanyl."

"I don't know nothing about that," was his predictable reply.

"You had guys meeting Bill Ward at McQuillan's," she went on, ignoring his denial. "You were doing swaps with him in the back of the bar."

"That wasn't me," Kortland said.

"But it was your guys," Erin said. "It's okay, I'm not asking you for names."

Kortland looked relieved she wasn't pressing him for IDs. Biker gangs weren't kind to snitches.

"I just need to know what your people gave Bill last night," she said. "What were you looking for in that briefcase in the locker?"

"That wasn't mine," Kortland said. "It was already in there."

"We know," Erin said.

"How come you're asking what was in it?" he asked, suddenly confused. "I mean, you got it. You can just look inside."

"I know what was in it," she said. "What was *supposed* to be in it?"

"What do you mean?" asked a very bewildered biker.

"She means it was full of this," Vic said, pulling an evidence bag out of his pocket and shoving it in Kortland's face. It was full of yellow hundred-dollar bills; the sort you got two of for passing GO.

"Huh?" Kortland said. "What's that?"

"Play money," Erin said. "I'm willing to bet that's not what your guy gave him last night."

"That son of a bitch," Kortland said. "He screwed us!"

It was Erin's turn to be confused. "How's that?"

"That ain't what's supposed to be in there!" he protested.

"It was supposed to be real money?" she asked.

"Yeah!" he blurted. Then he froze. "I mean, it don't matter. Even if we'd taken that out of the locker, which we didn't, it wouldn't be worth nothing. So it's not, like, a serious crime or nothing."

"Not like trying to strangle a member of the NYPD," Vic agreed, staring darkly at him.

"If your guys gave Ward a briefcase full of cash, why would you try to take it back again the next day?" Erin asked.

"I told you," Kortland said. "We wasn't at McQuillan's!"

Erin and Vic shared a surprised glance. "Then who was?" she asked.

"That was those sons of bitches," Kortland said.

"We've got a lot of SOBs in New York," Erin said. "Which ones do you mean?"

"Those goddamn taco vender wetback greaseballs," Kortland said with sudden venom. "Los Cuchillos Locos."

"The Crazy Knives," Vic translated. Every New York cop worth his salary picked up a little Spanish on the Job.

"The Mexican gang?" Erin guessed. She'd never heard of them, but wasn't about to admit it.

"That's them," Kortland said. "But we knew about Ward, see? He said he was on our team, but he was playing both sides, you know?"

"You and the Cuchillos were both giving him money?" Erin asked.

"Cheating no-good pig," Kortland said. "You cops are all the same. Yeah, I heard of you. Who hasn't? Junkyard O'Reilly, Cars Carlyle's attack dog. Took his money, then turned around and screwed him and everyone else. So don't go talking like you're better than the rest of us. We're all playing the same game. Everyone's in it, all the way to the top."

"Oh yeah," Vic said, rolling his eyes. "The old 'everyone's doing it' defense. That'll play real well at your trial."

"Look, Ward wasn't using that money," Kortland said. "He's dead now, right?"

"What do you know about that?" Erin challenged.

"Nothing! Word on the street is all. We didn't have nothing to do with him getting popped! We just heard, like, a couple hours ago. Donny said he'd been following him, and he knew he'd been into the skate rink and came out without the case. He said Ward wouldn't be needing it, so we might as well grab it."

"Why was Donny following Ward?" Erin asked.

"On account of we'd heard he was talking to those goddamn Mexicans. We needed to know what he was doing with them, whether he was gonna screw us or not."

"This is Donovan Burns we're talking about?" That was the name of the perp in Room 2, the one who'd taken the ice skate to Vic's face.

Kortland started to nod, then remembered he wasn't supposed to snitch on his buddies and stopped.

"So you're saying Ward's briefcase wasn't yours?" Erin asked.

"Wasn't you listening?" Kortland shot back. "It came from Los Cuchillos!"

"Why would they be giving him money?"

"Same reason—" Kortland bit off the remainder of his sentence.

"The same reason your people were," Erin said quietly. "Protection money? Or drug money?"

"Look, lady," he said. "You don't wanna go any further down this hole, you get me? You think it stopped with Billy? He didn't have that kind of pull. What was he? Glorified beat cop, that's all. There's big people, powerful people who want the Roadkillers to keep doing our thing. This is a business, just like bankers or truck drivers or whatever. We're providing a service, and it's a service this city wants. You take a ride down this road, you're gonna find out your own bosses don't wanna see where it ends. What's your problem, anyway? Why are you digging into this? You want in on the action?"

"You believe this friggin' guy?" Vic exclaimed. His disbelief wasn't an act. It wasn't every day a cop got offered a bribe in an interrogation room.

Erin shushed him with an impatient wave of her hand. She could say anything she wanted in this room in order to get the information she needed, as long as she steered clear of straight-up entrapment. And she hadn't asked Kortland for money. The offer had come from him, unsolicited.

"I'm not out to get the Roadkillers," she said. "We weren't even looking for you and your buddies. You picked the fight with us, remember? We were just following Ward's trail. I'm not with the Narcotics squad, I'm not DEA. You weren't my problem until you wrapped your hands around an officer's neck. So give me something I can use, and maybe we can forget about you."

"What do you want?" Kortland asked for the second time.

"What did you think was in the briefcase?"

"Cash."

"How much?"

"How do I know that, lady? I told you, it wasn't mine. But Donny figured fifty, maybe sixty large. Coulda been more."

"Ward gave another case to their guy in exchange," she said. "Any idea what was in it?"

"I dunno," Kortland said, but his eyes slid away from her and Erin was sure he was lying.

"Darryl," she said gently. "I can't help you if you won't help me. We're talking about your competition here. Whatever they were doing, it won't come back on you. Come on, I know you know this. What was in the other case?"

"I dunno, not exactly," he said. "Coulda been a couple things. But probably Mexican brown."

"Heroin? Ward was dealing drugs?"

"Yeah."

"Bullshit," Vic growled, bringing his hand down on the steel tabletop with a bang. Erin and Kortland both jumped. "The Cuchillos are bringing that shit in! Why would they be buying it from a goddamn cop? They've got their own suppliers!"

"That's what it was," Kortland insisted.

"Where's he getting the shit?" Vic demanded. He leaned way over the table, getting right in Kortland's face.

"Ask your own people!" Kortland shouted. "Where do you think? You guys got plenty of it lying around!"

Vic pulled back as if Kortland had swung a fist at him. "What the hell are you talking about?"

"He's talking about evidence lockers and seizures," Erin said softly. "Drugs our people took off the streets, getting funneled right back out there."

"I don't believe this crap," Vic said. "What a load of shit. He's lying."

"Screw you, man!" Kortland said. "Why are you asking me if you're not gonna believe me?"

"Is that what the Roadkillers were doing?" Erin asked. "Paying Ward for drugs and protection?"

Kortland said nothing. He was happy to throw the Crazy Knives to the NYPD, but he wasn't about to betray his own gang.

"She asked you a question, dipshit," Vic said.

"I want my lawyer," Kortland said abruptly. "I ain't saying another thing to you."

That was the cue Erin had been expecting, but hoping not to hear. She nodded reluctantly and stood up.

"If you want your lawyer, that's what you'll get," she said. "Sorry you weren't willing to play ball with us."

The biker shrugged and blew his nose again. A bubble of blood soaked into his tissue.

* * *

Vic held onto his self-control just long enough for them to step into the observation room, where Rolf eagerly pranced over to Erin's side. Then the big Russian exploded.

"This friggin' guy!" he said again in classic Brooklyn fashion. "We're interrogating *him!* He's the one who's under arrest, and what's he do? Tries to make us think we're the bad guys! I oughta go back in there and twist his goddamn ears off!"

"Easy, Vic," Erin said, dropping a hand instinctively to Rolf's ears and rubbing them. The Shepherd leaned against her leg and panted happily.

"No, I'm not gonna take it easy! He said the whole NYPD was nothing but crooks!"

"Don't take it personally."

"I'll take it however I want to! He tried to kill a cop, for Christ's sake! And no, I don't give a shit that it was an IAB cop!

Where does he think we are, friggin' Moscow? He offered us a bribe!"

"He thought I was dirty," Erin explained.

"That's because he's an idiot! The last punks who gave you payoffs all got thrown in jail. Some of them tried to kill us. See this scar? That's from that asshole who blew up that hospital room!"

"Vic!"

He paused. "What?" he asked in quieter but no less surly tones.

"You're a damn professional. Act like one!"

"Whatever you say, Mom," he growled.

"What Kortland's talking about isn't exactly unprecedented," Erin said. "Back in the Seventies, the NYPD's Narcotics squad was dealing out of their own evidence room."

"So you think Ward was dirty? Kira's gonna love that. She'll kick your ass for suggesting it."

"I don't know," Erin said thoughtfully. "I think it's worth looking into. He was giving those gangbangers something. It might've been drugs. If it was, either he'd gone rogue or he had permission."

"If it was official, his CO in the Gang Task Force would've known about it," Vic pointed out. "Sergeant what's-his-name. You know, the Great and Powerful Oz?"

"Osborne," Erin said.

"Yeah, him. And he didn't say a thing about it. But did Ward even have access to the evidence locker?"

"He might've been selling street seizures that never made it into Evidence," Erin said.

Vic shook his head. "Not like this. If he was dealing—and I'm not saying he was—he must've had a reliable source. He was doing it on a regular basis."

"Which means we might be looking at something a lot worse than one dirty cop," Erin sighed.

"You thinking conspiracy?" Vic asked.

Erin nodded. "I'm starting to think it's a good thing we've got an IAB cop on this case."

"No wonder Ward was paranoid," he said. "I can't wait to hear what Kira found in that deposit box."

Chapter 10

The other two Roadkillers were no help at all. Donovan Burns said "Lawyer" before Erin had even finished introducing herself, and the third biker, Earl Hollis, just spat a continuous stream of profanities until the detectives gave up and left.

"It'd be nice to have some corroboration," Erin said once they were back in the observation room with Rolf.

"Yeah," Vic said. "Especially if we're gonna accuse half the NYPD of being on the take."

"You're exaggerating," she said. "I don't think it's *that* bad."

"Can we drag the PC downtown while we're at it?"

"Wow," Erin said. "You really don't want to collect your pension, do you?"

Her phone buzzed, indicating an incoming text message. Erin glanced at it. Then she frowned and looked more closely.

"What?" Vic asked.

"It's Kira," she said.

"What's it say?"

"'We've got a problem.'"

"I know," he said. "But what's the text?"

"I was quoting it," Erin said, showing him the screen.

He rolled his eyes. "That's not helpful."

Another message came in. Erin read it aloud. "'Meet at coffee shop next door.' I assume she means next door to the bank."

"She could've clarified," Vic said. "By sending an actual address. Sheesh, this paranoia sinks into you. Let's go."

"We're going," Erin said. "But not to the same place. You're going to the hospital."

"Dammit, we've been over this."

"Yes, and we agreed you were going to get your face looked at after the interrogations."

"I don't remember agreeing to that."

Erin shrugged. "Then it's a good thing I'm in command here, so I can order you to do it whether you agree to it or not."

Vic pouted.

"I'll let you know what we've found out," she promised. "Now go. Zofia won't want to kiss a bloody, scarred-up cheek."

"You clearly have no idea what Zofia finds attractive," Vic said. "Besides, you've got the only car."

"Take a cab," she said. "And expense it to the Department."

He scowled and muttered darkly, but he went. Erin knew him well enough to recognize the pain hiding behind his eyes. He'd never admit it, but he was hurting.

"I thought I wanted to make Lieutenant someday," she told Rolf as she loaded him into the Charger. "But is this the kind of crap guys like Webb have to put up with? It's like having a toddler who won't brush his teeth."

Rolf had no opinion on the subject, but that didn't bother him. He was tired of being alone in the observation room. His compartment in the Charger was much better. It was familiar, it smelled like him, it let him stick close to Erin, and best of all, it meant going to work. That meant chasing bad guys. His tongue uncurled and he smiled.

The K-9's excitement lasted the few minutes it took Erin to drive from the Ten to Chase Bank. Sure enough, she spotted Kira's bike parked outside a coffee house next door. When Erin took Rolf inside, the dog remained optimistic, but when she sat down opposite Kira in a booth toward the back, he settled under the table with a sigh. It looked like another boring human conversation.

"What did you find?" Erin asked. "You wouldn't be acting so mysterious if you hadn't gotten the box open."

"Oh, the box opened, all right," Kira said. "Box 10. In Precinct Ten. You think that's a coincidence?"

"And…?" Erin said, trying to curb her impatience and almost succeeding.

In answer, Kira reached under the table and brought out a thick packet. She laid it on the tabletop.

"Is that what it looks like?" Erin asked.

"It's cash," Kira confirmed. "Fifty thousand dollars, in hundreds. Unmarked, non-sequential, used currency. And that's not all."

"Go on," Erin said.

Kira produced a thumb drive. "I don't know what's on this," she said. "But it's encrypted."

"How do you know?"

"Because it was wrapped in this," Kira said, unfolding a piece of paper. On it was written:

If you have the answer, you get more answers. The name you're looking for is the key that locks him away. Burn this after reading. Sorry for the games. I had to prove it was you. The really funny thing is, I don't know if I can trust you after all. Maybe you've been drawn into orbit, just like all the rest. Gravity's a hell of a thing. I wish I could've told my wife, but it would've only put her in danger. This is the only way she gets away.

Quis custodiet ipsos custodes, qui custodes custodiunt?

"He didn't even mention my name," Kira said quietly. "Or any names. The paranoid bastard."

"That last bit is Latin," Erin said. "It reminds me of that famous saying, 'who watches the watchmen?'"

"This one's a little more complicated," Kira said. "I think it means something like 'who watches the watchmen who watch the watchmen?' My grammar probably sucks, but that's the gist of it."

"He's talking about dirty cops," Erin said. "Internal Affairs are the ones who watch the watchmen. If you take it a step further..."

"He's asking who keeps Internal Affairs accountable," Kira said. "That means he thinks someone in IAB is compromised. That's why he didn't come straight to us with his problem."

"His problem is he was taking money from two different gangs," Erin said. She quickly repeated what she and Vic had learned from Kortland.

"And you believe that jerk?" Kira asked.

"The evidence backs him up," Erin said. "On some of it, at any rate. I don't know who to believe. We need to get into that drive."

"And we need a password for that," Kira said. "Look, it's getting toward the end of the day. Let me take it home and work on it overnight. Maybe I'll figure something out."

"Are you sure?" Erin asked. "Shouldn't we log it as evidence?"

"Evidence of what?" Kira replied. "Levine's going to rule Bill's death a suicide no matter what."

"You don't know that."

"Yes I do."

"How?"

"Because Levine's good at what she does," Kira said bitterly. "And it really does look like Bill shot himself. You saw the note. He knew what he was going to do. He did it to protect his wife, and he covered his tracks so nobody could possibly trace the information to him. That's why we've been chasing our tails all day."

"Are you going to burn the letter?" Erin asked.

"I should," Kira said. "But what if there's a clue in it somewhere? We'd better keep it a little while. And I'm not logging a damn thing into Evidence. Not even the cash. Not until we know who we can trust. I'm not talking to a single other cop about this, and neither should you."

"Except Vic?" Erin asked.

"Well, yeah, Vic's okay. He already knows most of it anyway."

"What about Lieutenant Webb?"

"I'm not telling my CO," Kira said. "You've had me looking at him, remember? That's a conversation we need to have, and soon. It's your call with Webb, but I wouldn't if I were you."

Erin rubbed her temples. "Jesus Christ," she muttered. "I thought I was done with this cloak-and-dagger shit."

"I guess it wasn't done with you," Kira said. "I'm sorry you got pulled into this."

Erin smiled ruefully. "I'm used to it," she said. "Anything I can do for you tonight?"

Kira shook her head. "I'm good," she said. "But I think maybe we'd better take a rain check on that celebratory drink. Too much to do. Say, did you and Carlyle set a date yet? For the wedding?"

"We're working on it," Erin said. "But don't worry, you're invited."

"I'll look forward to it," Kira said. "Say hi for me, and tell him I'm glad he turned out to be one of the good guys."

"Copy that," Erin said. "We'll do drinks later this week, once this whole thing blows over. What were you saying about Keane?"

Kira shook her head. "Later," she said. "I don't think it's got anything to do with Bill."

"How bad is it?"

"I'm not sure yet. I need to look a little closer. We'll have plenty of time for that can of worms once we've finished this one off."

"Okay. Take care of yourself."

"You're the one who keeps catching bullets, Erin. See you tomorrow."

* * *

Three months of construction and renovation had left the Barley Corner cleaner and newer. Even the smell was unfamiliar. The old Corner's odors had lingered all the way from Prohibition. Cigar smoke, bootleg moonshine, spilled beer, and spilled blood had impregnated the floorboards of the place. Now, as Erin and Rolf stepped through the brand-new front door, they smelled fresh varnish and sawdust underlying the more savory scents of good liquor and hot food. Rolf's nose twitched appreciatively.

All the woodwork was new. The fire that had gutted the basement had also wrecked the main floor. The floorboards had needed to be replaced, as had the bar, the tables and chairs, and the excellent selection of liquor bottles behind the bar. Even the dartboard and TV screens were new. The cost had been eye-watering, though insurance had paid the majority of it.

The pub had reopened at noon, without much fanfare. A large part of its prior clientele hadn't been able to attend, due to prior commitments requiring them to remain in their cells at

Riker's Island. But now, as the dinner hour approached, the place was hopping with new faces. The patrons were more diverse than before, by ethnicity, age, and sex. Erin saw whole families occupying booths. Couples on dates had gravitated toward the more secluded corners of the room.

Carlyle was sitting on a barstool, back to the bar, arms resting on top of it, surveying his domain as if he'd never left. He was dressed in his customary charcoal gray suit, a dark red necktie and pocket square providing a little color to his ensemble. A thin smile played across his face as he watched his customers.

A redheaded waitress bobbed into Erin's view. "Welcome to the Barley Corner!" she chirped. "Oh, hey, Erin. Good to see you again!"

"Hi, Caitlin," Erin said. "Busy night?" Caitlin Tierney was one of Carlyle's most reliable employees. She'd never been part of the Irish Mob, nor had Danny Sullivan, the evening-shift bartender. They'd lived through the Corner's gangster days as dedicated civilians.

"You know it," Caitlin said. "I thought maybe people wouldn't turn up, but Danny swore we'd be packing 'em in, and he knew what he was talking about. He says we're notorious now, and that's the next best thing to famous. We're a destination! We've got *tourists* in here, and I'm not just talking about guys from Jersey. I served a family from North Dakota. They said they read about us in *Time* magazine! Can you believe that?"

"I read the article," Erin said dryly. Her mother had sent copies to all their relatives.

"We had reporters here for the opening!" Caitlin chattered on, following Erin across the room. "There was this really nice lady from Channel Six News who wanted to interview me. She said I was pretty enough for Prime Time."

"That's great," Erin said, trying to think how to politely disengage from Caitlin. It wasn't that she disliked the young woman—Caitlin was hard not to like—but she was hungry, thirsty, and tired, and what she wanted was a good meal and some time with her fiancé.

Carlyle saw her coming and, ever the gentleman, stood up to welcome her. His smile widened.

"Evening, darling," he said. "What do you think?"

"It's... nice," she said. "I wasn't expecting it to be so crowded."

"Nor I," he said. "It's gratifying, though I've no notion if it'll last. At the moment there's value in the novelty of taking a drink at the infamous reformed gangster's bar. Caitlin, darling, I fear we're keeping you from your duties."

Caitlin went a little pink and hurried away, pretending she hadn't been listening in.

"Everything's running smoothly, thus far," Carlyle went on. "Marian did a bit of complaining about the kitchen layout, though I daresay she's happy enough with the new appliances. All the work was done on time and under budget, and that's a blessing bordering on a miracle."

"I don't suppose Corky had anything to do with that?" Erin asked.

"I'll not deny it's been useful knowing a lad with so many contacts in the construction unions," Carlyle said with a quiet laugh. "I rang him earlier. He's mending quite nicely from his late misfortunes."

"By which you mean, the multiple bullet wounds and the explosion in his hospital room?"

"Aye, those. He tells me he's getting the very best of care from his live-in nurse."

"I'll just bet he is," Erin said. Corky's caretaker was his lover, a Brooklyn schoolteacher turned witness. Teresa

Tommasino was operating under the very noses of New York's Mafia families, living in Corky's apartment with the assistance of a fake ID that claimed she was a Mexican nurse. Erin was still having trouble believing Teresa and Corky were getting away with it, but James Corcoran had made a career out of getting away with things. The very audacity of his schemes was what made them mostly successful.

"I've also touched base with Ian Thompson," Carlyle continued. "He sends his apologies for not welcoming us home in person. Apparently they're keeping him rather busy at the firefighters' academy. He'll be graduating presently, barring mischance."

"That's great! Who've we got running security now?" Erin asked.

"Ken Mason," Carlyle said, nodding toward the far wall. A lean, taciturn man with a military haircut stood there, arms crossed, giving the room a steady, hard stare.

"Mason's all right," Erin said grudgingly. "But Ian's a hard act to follow."

"He's a good lad," Carlyle said. "But enough about my business concerns. I'm anxious to hear about your first day back on the job."

"Excuse me?" a female voice asked.

Erin and Carlyle turned to see a girl, no more than twelve, standing in front of them. She wore a Yankees sweatshirt, jeans with torn knees, and a hesitant smile.

"Good evening, lass," Carlyle said with a smile.

The girl's attention was fixed on Erin. "Are you Erin O'Reilly?" she asked.

Erin's own smile was cautious. "That's right. What can I do for you, kiddo?"

"Can I have your autograph?"

Erin blinked. "My what?"

"Your autograph," the girl repeated. "I read all about you in the paper. In my English class, we have to write an essay about our hero. I was hoping... I mean, I'm writing about you. Because I think you're the best cop, and I want to be a police officer when I get out of school. Because of you."

Erin realized her mouth was hanging a little open and closed it. "Sure," she managed to say. "I'd be glad to. But I'm not a superhero or anything. I'm just a girl from Queens. Where are you from?"

"Brooklyn," the girl said.

Erin picked up a napkin off the bar. They had the Barley Corner's logo on them, which might lend extra authenticity to the signature. Carlyle had already pulled a pen from his coat's inside pocket and was holding it out to her.

"What's your name, kiddo?" Erin asked.

"Emily," the girl said. "Emily Matthews."

"Well, Emily," Erin said, scribbling out a quick note on the napkin and signing it, "being a cop isn't easy, but if you really want it, go for it. And if you do get your shield, and I'm still on the Force, look me up."

Emily took the note, eyes shining, and hurried back to the table where her family was waiting. Erin watched her go and shook her head.

"Is fame all you hoped?" Carlyle asked.

"That was really weird. But it's been a weird day." Erin turned her attention to the bartender. "Danny! Can I get a pint of Guinness, a shot of Glen D, and a bowl of Marian's Irish stew?"

"Sure thing," Danny said with a grin.

After making sure no more autograph-seekers were within earshot, Erin quickly explained the situation. Carlyle listened, rubbing his chin.

"It sounds to me like this lad got himself into trouble he didn't know how to get clear of," he said when she'd finished. "Suicide's a rather strong remedy, however. Why do you think he did it?"

"Like you said, he couldn't find a way out," Erin said. "I think he started trying to infiltrate a gang, but they got to him before he could get to them. It's a slippery slope. He probably took a little money for some favor that didn't seem like much, then they asked for a little more and offered a little more. You know how it goes."

"I do, aye," Carlyle said. "By the time he realized he was in too deep, the water was over his head, and there's only so long a lad can thrash about before he's pulled under. Was he the target of an investigation?"

"Not as far as I know," Erin said. "And if Ward had attracted IAB's attention, Kira would've known about it."

"Then the pressure wasn't coming from inside the Department," Carlyle said. "Do you suppose one of the gangs wanted him to cross a line he wasn't prepared to step over?"

"Maybe."

"He could still have taken the high road," Carlyle mused. "Turned everything in to your lads and resigned his job. Surely that's preferable to death, and more honorable as well. From what you say of him, he was rather a brilliant lad. I can't imagine he couldn't have figured a way forward, a simpler one than setting all those riddles for you."

"Like I said, it's weird," Erin said. She took a long pull at her Guinness. "I hope Kira gets that drive open. Maybe it'll have something we can use."

"Hope isn't a plan, darling," he said gently.

"I know," she said. "But it's a damn sight better than the alternative."

Chapter 11

Carlyle's upstairs apartment hadn't been seriously damaged by the fire, so it had been easy for Erin to move back in. She couldn't even smell the smoke anymore. The bed caressed her skin—Carlyle had invested in very expensive silk sheets, with a thread count she could only guess at—and she had every creature comfort she could hope for.

None of this explained why she was lying on her back at one in the morning, staring at a ceiling half-hidden by darkness, unable to sleep. Rolf was fast asleep; she could hear the adorable little yipping sounds he made while he was dreaming. He was curled up near the foot of the bed, paws and nose twitching.

Carlyle was downstairs. He didn't need to stay up so late anymore, now that the Barley Corner's business was a hundred percent legitimate. Gangsters weren't coming around for shady late-night meetings these days. But the Corner didn't close its doors until two o'clock, and he wanted to make sure everything ran smoothly. Erin supposed it was habit, too. She'd had trouble adjusting when she'd gone off the night shift herself. It was something to do with circadian rhythms. Your body got used to living by night, and three months' vacation hadn't quite broken him of his nocturnal habits.

Erin turned over, working her pillow into what she hoped was a more comfortable shape. It didn't do any good. She couldn't turn her brain off. Images of William Ward kept running through her head.

What was wrong with her? It wasn't like she'd never seen violent death before. Hell, she'd *caused* violent death more than once. She'd seen bodies disassembled in just about every traumatic way imaginable: bullets, explosives, fire, blades, blunt force, even a circular saw in one particularly nightmarish incident. Had she been off the street too long?

She sat up and turned on the bedside lamp. There was no point lying around in the dark. The best thing to do was either to get up and figure out what was bothering her, or take a stiff drink. Maybe both.

Erin had never been diagnosed, but she was pretty sure she was an alcoholic. That was no surprise; as Kira had said, a lot of the NYPD couldn't stay off the sauce. When she'd realized she was drinking too much as a coping mechanism, she'd tried to scale it back. The safest thing seemed to be never to drink alone.

She decided to go downstairs for a shot of whiskey. But first, she picked up her phone. Kira had said she'd be working on the case overnight. If she was still awake, maybe she'd have some thoughts to share. Erin fired off a text message.

"*You up?*"

She gave it a few moments. There was no response. The phone indicated Kira hadn't even seen the message.

"I guess she's asleep," Erin muttered. Rolf's right ear flicked upright. He raised his head and blinked sleepily at her. Then his jaws cracked open and he yawned hugely, his tongue unrolling like a party streamer.

"Sorry, kiddo," she said. "Go back to sleep."

Rolf stood up and stretched, yawning again. If Erin was up, so was he. The K-9 was no stranger to late hours.

Erin pulled on her old NYPD sweatshirt and a pair of jeans. She nearly left her gun and shield behind, but picked them up out of habit and hung them on her belt. Rolf bounded off the bed. By the time she was dressed he was standing at the top of the stairs, tail wagging, leash dangling from his mouth, one paw raised. Any time was walk time as far as he was concerned. Bad guys needed to be bitten during all shifts. You had to be ready.

The bar was more sparsely populated now. A group of young men were playing darts in the corner, two couples were lingering over their drinks in booths, and a few serious drinkers had their bellies against the bar. Ken Mason appeared not to have moved an inch since she'd left. Carlyle, too, was right where she'd left him. But he had a visitor on the stool next to his.

"Ian!" Erin exclaimed, feeling her mouth crack into a broad grin.

"Ma'am," Ian Thompson said reflexively, coming to his feet a half-second ahead of Carlyle. Then he smiled slightly and held out his hand. "Sorry, Erin. Old habits. Good to see you."

Erin ignored the hand and threw her arms around him, pulling the startled former Marine in for a hug. After an awkward moment, he returned it.

"What're you doing here?" she asked, coming back to arm's length and looking him over. He was as lean and fit as ever, but his face was different. Ian had always had one hell of a poker face, completely unreadable. Now he looked more open, more hopeful; younger.

"Couldn't sleep," he said. "Too much on my mind."

"Join the club," she said, sliding onto the stool on the opposite side of him from Carlyle. "Danny! Glen D, please, when you get the chance."

"Coming at you," Danny said, pouring a shot of Scotch and sending it deftly her way.

"Shouldn't you be resting?" she asked Ian. "I hear firefighting academy's tough going."

"Not compared to Parris Island," he said. "FDNY's got nothing on the Corps. I can hack it."

"The lad's near the top of his class," Carlyle said with undisguised pride. "I'm not surprised, mind, but it's grand."

"Class rank isn't that important," Ian said. "Just have to stay out of the bottom ten percent. They're the ones who wash out."

"I don't think there's any chance of that," Erin said, sipping her whiskey and giving an appreciative shiver as it burned its way down her throat. "I hope you won't be hung over, though."

"Not much chance of that either," Ian said, looking at the glass in front of him. "Don't know anyone who gets drunk on ginger ale."

"Ian came to welcome me home," Carlyle said.

"Would've liked to see both of you," Ian said. "Couldn't get away before dark. Lot to do. No excuse."

"Well, I'm here now," Erin said, still grinning. "How's Cassie?"

"She's good."

Erin waited, but apparently that was all Ian was prepared to volunteer on the subject of his girlfriend.

"They're planning to wed once the lad graduates and receives his posting," Carlyle said.

"Need a stable situation," Ian explained. "Cassie's had enough surprises."

"Good for you!" Erin said, reaching out and giving his shoulder a squeeze. "Congratulations! She's a lucky woman."

"What brings you down in these wee hours?" Carlyle asked. "Not that it's not grand to see you, darling."

"I couldn't sleep either," Erin said. "I'm thinking about our case. What's on your mind, Ian?"

"The war," he said.

"I should've guessed," she said. "Can Cassie help with that?"

"Sometimes," he said. "But she's not always around. Not staying over with her."

"You're not?" Erin was surprised.

"It's Ben," he explained. "Kid needs stability, has to understand what's going on. Cass and I talked it over, figured I'd better not move in until we make it official. That way everyone knows who's who."

"Your self-control is a proper inspiration," Carlyle said. "Anything we can do to help, Erin?"

"Mostly I needed this," she said, finishing her drink. She took out her phone and checked it. Kira still hadn't answered. "Dammit, I thought she'd be awake."

"Who?" Carlyle asked.

"Kira Jones," Erin said. "She's trying to break into the thumb drive we found. It's probably going to solve the whole thing. If she'd cracked it, I hoped she could give me some peace of mind."

"Perhaps she's letting you sleep," Carlyle said.

"Yeah, probably," Erin said.

"Worried about her?" Ian asked.

"No," she said. Then, "Damn it, I am *now*. Thanks for that."

"Sorry," Ian said. "No—"

"Don't," she said, forestalling him with an upraised finger. "Just don't."

"I'm sure the lass is perfectly all right," Carlyle said. "We've no reason to think otherwise."

"None," Erin agreed, but the word sounded hollow as it left her mouth. "Except for two violent drug-dealing gangs and some crooked cops who might've driven another officer to shoot himself. Shit. Now I'm going to worry until I hear from her. Screw it. I'm calling."

She dialed Kira's number and held the phone to her ear. It rang once, twice, three times, four. Then the voicemail picked up and a recorded voice informed her that she could leave a brief message after the tone.

"Kira," Erin said, speaking with the habitual caution she'd developed in her undercover days. "I'm just calling for an update on our case. Drop me a line when you get this, whenever you do. Thanks."

Carlyle and Ian were both watching her closely as she hung up and returned the phone to her hip pocket.

"Trouble?" Ian asked quietly.

"I don't know," Erin said. "I hope not."

"Where is she?"

"At home, I think."

"Where's home?"

"The Village, last I knew," Erin said. "I'd have to look up the address. I've never been to her place."

"Ten minutes from here," Ian said at once. "Give or take." He knew Manhattan's urban terrain as well as he'd ever known Afghanistan or Iraq.

"Surely you needn't go haring off on a whim," Carlyle said.

"No, Ian's right," Erin said. "I can take a half hour to drive up there, make sure she's fine, and get back, or I can stay up twice as long worrying."

She hopped off the stool and started for the door. "I'll be back before closing time," she said.

"I'll come with," Ian said, falling in step just behind her.

"You don't have to do that," she said. "You should go home to bed."

"Told you, can't sleep," he said. "Nighttime patrol should be just the thing. Never had any problem sacking out when I got back from Patrol in the 'Stan or the Sandbox."

"Have it your way," she said. "But we're taking my car."

* * *

"Do you think you're going to like it?" Erin asked as she steered toward Greenwich Village.

"Like what?" Ian asked. He was in the shotgun seat, scanning the Manhattan streets for threats. His eyes were quick and alert, picking up every detail of the cars and pedestrians they passed. He couldn't help it. Hypervigilance wasn't something you could turn off.

"Being a firefighter."

"Affirmative."

"You don't think it'll make... you know, some of the stuff you're dealing with worse?"

He considered this for a few moments.

"Don't think so," he finally said. "Might even make it better. Cass is behind me a hundred percent. Says a lot of guys in my situation can't adjust to civilian life. Thinks maybe this is a good compromise. Get to save lives, but still get the kick of going on missions. Best of both worlds."

"You'll be good at it," she said.

"Do what I can," he replied. "You said you haven't been to our objective before."

"That's right."

"Any idea of the tactical picture?"

"It's an apartment," she said. "Studio, I think. You can check the street view on the computer. The address is already entered."

It was against procedure to allow a civilian to access an NYPD onboard computer, but just then, Erin didn't care. It wasn't like Ian was precisely a civilian in any case, and this was an unusual situation.

He studied the map and zoomed in for a street-camera view. "Tight sight lines," he said. "No cover approaching the front door, fire escape is exposed. Can't get close without risking sniper fire."

"Are you expecting snipers?" she asked incredulously.

"Always expect snipers," he said without a trace of humor. "Best chance is to park as close as possible, minimize time outside the vehicle. Assuming the bad guys will recognize your car."

"I guess so," Erin said. "It's in the Department motor pool with my name on it. Not too many black Chargers in the NYPD."

"I'll exit first," he said. "Check for threats. You take point with Rolf, I'll follow on and watch your six."

"Okay," she said. "You know, we don't really have any reason to assume there'll be trouble. Maybe relax a little?"

"This *is* me relaxed," he said in a perfectly calm voice. "Should see me tense."

"Jesus," she murmured. "Is this what it's always like inside your head?"

"Cass says I'm getting better these days."

"This isn't going to set you back, is it?"

"Only if we take fire."

Perry Street was quiet enough as they approached. Manhattan streets were never fully empty. There were always at least a few late-night pedestrians and motorists. But Erin's street-cop perception didn't pick up on anything out of the ordinary. A police spot was open at the corner, less than half a block from the apartment.

Ian was out of the car almost before it stopped moving. He glided several yards down the sidewalk into the cover of a parked Jeep, checking doorways and rooftops for anything suspicious. After a moment, he turned and waved her on.

The whole thing seemed a little silly to Erin. This wasn't Baghdad. It wasn't even a bad part of town. This was her home city and she was the police. The bad guys ought to be looking out for her, not the other way round. But Ian's caution was infectious. She popped Rolf's compartment and moved more quickly than usual to the front step of the apartment.

Kira's home was a five-story brick structure, unremarkable from the outside. The fire escape was bolted to the front of the building, flanked by window AC units. A half-height wrought-iron fence lined the lot, spruced up by a handful of small shrubs. A tiny foyer contained mailboxes and intercom buzzers for each apartment. 5B had the name JONES on it. Erin smiled to see that Kira had used multi-colored stickers to spell out her name.

She hit the buzzer for Kira's apartment and waited. And waited.

Ian pulled the front door open but didn't come in. "Can't stay there," he said without taking his eyes from the street. "Entryways are kill zones. Bottlenecks."

"I can't just kick the door down," Erin retorted. She pushed the buzzer again, holding it down long enough to wake Rip van Winkle, receiving no response. "Shit."

"Plan B?" Ian asked.

"Did you notice any lights on?" she asked.

"Fourth floor, left-hand window," he said at once.

Erin wasn't sure whether that was 4A or 4B, so she tried 4A first. Luck was with her. After a moment, a voice came on the line.

"Yeah? What do you want?" It was a crabby, female New York voice, but it didn't sound like the woman had just woken up. From the tone, Erin guessed it was a senior citizen with insomnia.

"Ms. Janklow?" she guessed, reading the name off the mailbox.

"I know who I am," the woman fired back. "Who're you?"

"Ma'am, I'm with the New York Police Department," Erin said. "We're doing a wellness check on one of your neighbors. If you could let us in?"

"Which neighbor?" Ms. Janklow asked, suspicion sharpening her tone.

"Kira Jones," Erin said. "Upstairs, in 5B."

"Oh, Kira," the woman said, softening somewhat. "Yeah, c'mon in."

There was a heavy clunk as the inner door's lock disengaged.

Erin had the door open in an instant. Five floors was a lengthy climb, but she took the stairs. Ian was always worried about elevators, and this time she shared his concern. An elevator was an uncontrollable way to enter an unpredictable situation. The doors might open onto literally anything, and then they'd be trapped in a kill-box.

Rolf loped beside her, taking the stairs easily. Ian was only a couple of strides behind. They raced past one landing after another. They saw nothing unusual, but each floor only increased Erin's disquiet.

Mrs. Janklow was on the fourth-floor landing, coffee cup in hand, clad in a floral-print robe.

"I ain't never had any trouble from Kira," the woman said. "She's a nice girl, even if she keeps odd company. And no girl ought to have hair that color. It attracts the wrong sort, if you know what I mean."

"That's her," Erin said, moving around her.

"Keeps unusual hours, though," Ms. Janklow went on. "It doesn't surprise me she's up. Are you here about that racket?"

"What racket?" Erin asked.

"That loud noise," Ms. Janklow said. "About an hour ago. I figured maybe somebody called you."

Erin felt a chill. "That's what we're here about," she said. It was almost the truth. "This is police business. Please go back inside and lock your door."

Erin paused a moment outside 5B and drew her Glock. She and Rolf were both panting. They'd gone soft after three months on vacation. Ian came up alongside, not even breathing hard. He'd been in superb condition before FDNY training and they'd only toned him further.

"Got a spare?" he asked.

"A spare?" Erin echoed.

He nodded to her Glock.

"No," she said. She'd left her backup piece, a snub-nosed .38, in the nightstand next to her bed. She hadn't imagined actually needing her guns tonight. "Aren't you carrying?"

"Not anymore," he said. "Trying to go without. Part of my therapy. Can't carry at the Academy anyway."

"Dammit," Erin muttered. "Okay, just stay behind me. If anything happens to me... I don't know. Figure something out."

She rang the doorbell. The chime was audible through the door. But there was no reply.

"Kira?" she called quietly. "It's me. Open up."

Silence answered.

Rolf's nostrils twitched. He lowered his head and sniffed at the crack at the bottom of the door, tail waving slowly.

Erin crouched down beside him and inhaled deeply. She caught a number of smells: old wood and brick, dust, rusty metal. Those were all things you'd expect in an old New York apartment. But overlying all of them were two smells she knew much too well: gunpowder and blood.

She grabbed the doorknob, twisted, and pushed. The door didn't budge. It was locked.

"Damn," she hissed. The thing to do here was call it in and wait for backup, but right then Erin didn't give a damn what the Patrol Guide said. Fear was rushing through her like a freight train, drowning out everything else. She drew back and kicked the door.

It was a good door, sturdy and solid. Cops tended to invest in high-quality locks. Erin knew how to break down a door, but she was lightly built and the door wasn't. It held firm. She kicked it again, then a third time.

The third kick did the trick. The door gave with a splintering crash. The lock tore out of the wood, leaving twisted screws behind. Erin launched herself into the room, clearing the doorway, pistol poised.

The apartment was small, just one room and an attached bathroom. It was nearly pitch-black. The smells became much stronger, almost overpowering. Erin groped for the light switch, found it, and flicked it on.

A golden bulb flared overhead. Erin caught a confused glimpse of a bed, a small desk with a laptop on it, and a two-seat couch against the far wall. None of that really registered. All she saw was Kira Jones, sitting on the left-hand sofa cushion, slumped over the armrest. Kira's hand rested on the couch. In it was her service pistol.

Kira's eyes were half-open. In that awful, endless instant, she seemed to be staring directly at Erin. But it was an illusion. She was looking at something much further away than Erin O'Reilly. The bullet hole in her right temple was tiny, almost insignificant.

Chapter 12

One of the first things you learned on the street was to separate how you were feeling from what you were doing. Erin O'Reilly was rooted to the floor in shock and horror. Erin's body was taking action. She watched herself, with an odd detachment, as she crossed the room in four running strides. She dropped Rolf's leash, shoved the Glock back into its holster, and pulled out her phone with the same motion.

Rolf sniffed at Kira's leg. He sat back on his haunches and barked sharply, which was part of his training when he located a body. Then he gave a low, anxious whine, which wasn't. He knew Kira. His tail swept the floor in a subdued, unhappy movement.

"Dispatch," came the answer in Erin's ear.

"This is O'Reilly," Erin said, marveling inwardly at how calm and level her voice was. "Shield four-six-four-oh. I need a bus to 100 Perry Street, forthwith. We have an officer down, GSW to the head. We're on the fifth floor, Apartment 5B."

"Copy that, O'Reilly," Dispatch replied. "Nearest officers are en route, ETA two minutes on Patrol units, seven minutes on bus. Is this a 10-13?"

"Negative," Erin said. She was feeling for a pulse as she spoke. "No perps on site."

"Do you have an ID on the officer?" Dispatch asked.

"Detective Kira Jones," Erin said, and her cool detachment shattered. She could barely force the words out through a throat that was suddenly very tight. "Internal Affairs, out of the Eight."

"Copy that. What is her status?"

Ian was beside Erin, looking at the fallen officer. He shook his head, but Erin didn't want to see it.

"Critical," she said. "Close-range pistol shot to the temple. Unresponsive. I can't... I can't find a pulse."

"Understood." The dispatcher's voice grew softer, more human. "O'Reilly, is the victim deceased?"

"Get that damn ambulance here," Erin snapped and hung up. She turned to Ian. "Kira's careful. She'll have first-aid supplies here. Check the bathroom. We'll need QuikClot for the bleeding and a pressure bandage."

"Erin," Ian said gently. "She's gone."

"You don't know that," Erin said. Tears were spilling down her cheeks as she spoke. She didn't even notice them. "You didn't see Phil Stachowski. He had a hole right through his head and he lived. And me. I got shot in the head and it didn't kill me. Get that goddamn aid kit!"

"Erin."

He laid his hands on her shoulders and squeezed hard, looking straight into her eyes. His focused, intense stare drilled through her panic and quieted her as effectively as a bucket of ice water to the face.

"Seen lots of head wounds," he said. "There's no chance. It's over."

"No," Erin said, but it was a reflexive denial that had no conviction in it. She felt herself beginning to shake. He held on, pulling her in close. It was an embrace without a hint of sensuality. He was holding her up, lending her his strength, keeping her upright on legs that threatened to give way.

"You've got another voice," he said. "A cold one. It's the one that tells you what you have to do. Keeps you going. Listen. What's it saying?"

"Secure the scene," Erin said numbly. "Looks like suicide, but isn't. Not a chance. Not Kira. I talked to her a few hours ago. She'd never do this."

"I believe you," Ian said. "We have other cops inbound. What do we do before they get here?"

Erin felt her instincts coming back on line, recovering themselves. It was like resetting the circuit breakers in the basement after a power surge. She felt new strength running through her. It was hot and tingly, a cocktail of adrenaline and distilled rage. Suddenly, her mind was completely clear.

"We need Levine," she said. "Before anyone else signs off on this. And the rest of my squad. We can't let IAB take over this case, no matter what. We don't know who's compromised. I shouldn't have called it in."

"Didn't have a choice," Ian said. "Cop gets shot, it's a big deal. Can't keep it quiet. Looks worse for you if you try."

"Go out to the landing," she told him. "Tell the uniforms there's a Major Crimes detective on scene. I'll give them their orders once they arrive, but try not to let them inside."

"Don't have any authority," he pointed out. "They can push right past me. Arrest me, even."

Erin nodded absently. She was already dialing Levine's number, glad she'd programmed it into her phone. "You'll figure something out," she said as the phone started ringing.

"You're interrupting a time-sensitive postmortem examination," Levine said in place of a greeting.

"This is Erin O'Reilly," Erin said. "I need you to do something for me."

"You wanted me to verify cause of death for William Ward," Levine said. "That's what I'm doing. I'll have the report by morning, as promised. Interruptions only delay the outcome."

"No," Erin said. "Drop everything and get to 100 Perry Street, Apartment 5B, Greenwich Village right now."

"That's physically impossible," Levine said. "I'm in the Precinct Eight morgue. Even at fastest speed, assuming I scrub out at once, I estimate between fifteen and twenty minutes."

"I meant, get started right away," Erin said, gritting her teeth. "This is a rush job. Everything else gets a back seat to this. And I mean *everything*."

"The morgue doesn't have seats," Levine said. "I do my work standing. The bodies are supine."

"Just get here as fast as you can. 100 Perry Street. Understood?"

"I can't say I understand something in the absence of all available information," Levine said.

Erin hung up on her and dialed Webb.

A very sleepy and grumpy Lieutenant mumbled "Webb," into his phone on the fourth ring, just a second or two ahead of his voicemail.

"Sir, this is O'Reilly," Erin said. "I need you in Manhattan, at Kira Jones' apartment. 100 Perry Street."

"Do you have any idea what time it is?" he asked. Then his voice abruptly sharpened as he belatedly picked up on her tone and engaged his detective instincts. "What's happened?"

"Kira's been shot," Erin said dully.

"By whom?" Webb was fully awake now.

"I don't know. She was holding her gun and it looks like she did it to herself, but—"

"You think it was staged?"

"Seems likely."

"Are those sirens in the background?"

"Yes, sir." Erin could see blue-and-red flashers through the curtains. A pair of Patrol cruisers had just arrived outside. A bunch of cops would be swarming upstairs in a matter of seconds.

"What's her condition?" Webb asked.

"She's dead."

Two simple words, but they brought it all the way home. Kira Jones with her brightly dyed hair, her piercings and tattoos, and her brand-new motorcycle was dead. She'd never go out with Dana, the cute bakery girl. She'd never know what had happened to her friend Bill Ward. She wouldn't go out with Erin and Vic to get drunk and celebrate Erin's engagement. And there'd be an empty seat at the wedding.

"Good Lord," Webb said quietly. "I'm on my way. Is Neshenko with you?"

"No, sir. Ian Thompson's here, and some of the local precinct boys are on their way up. That's it."

"What's Thompson—never mind, I'll get the story later. I'll call Neshenko. What else do you need?"

Erin clenched her fist around the phone. "I need to know what the hell happened," she said grimly. "And I'm going to figure it out."

* * *

The first arrivals were four uniformed officers. Ian stopped them outside, delaying them until Erin could step out and give orders. Erin set two of them to guard the door and sent the remaining pair back down to the lobby. Ian would have hung around if she'd let him, but she didn't want him getting tangled up in the investigation.

"You weren't here when it happened," she told him. "You didn't witness anything. And you're not with the NYPD. You should get out of here."

"Mr. Carlyle would want me to make sure you're okay," Ian said.

"Why wouldn't I be okay? I'm a cop, Ian, not some daycare brat. I carry a gun, I have a K-9, and I can call thirty thousand officers if I need backup."

"Trust all of them?"

She stared at him. "You think this is a coordinated attack?" she asked. "On all of us?"

"Don't know," he said. "Insufficient intel. Have to assume the worst."

"Okay. I'll be careful. But you need to get out. This is an active crime scene. Only perps, victims, and cops belong here."

"Affirmative," he said. "I'll report back to the Corner, brief Mr. Carlyle."

"Thanks."

He paused. "This the first one you've lost?" he asked.

"No. That'd be John Brunanski, back at the One-Sixteen."

"Partner?"

"We worked out of the same house. I was there when he got hit."

"This the first friend?"

Erin had to blink several times and clear her throat before she could answer. "Yeah," she managed to say.

He nodded. "Nothing I can say," he said. "Except I've been where you are. Know the terrain. You want to talk about it, find me."

"Thanks. You have a way to get back to the Corner?"

"I'll take the subway. Catch you on the flip-side."

The ambulance showed up a few minutes later and two paramedics rode up the elevator. They came in ready to do anything necessary, but it only took moments for them to come to the same conclusion Ian had reached with a single glance.

"Sorry, ma'am," the senior medic said, stepping back. "Headshot through-and-through. The body's already cooling. Even if we could get the heart going again, there's no point. There wouldn't be anybody home. I've seen plenty of these, more than I'd like. Self-inflicted GSW?"

"We'll see," Erin said, biting back a sharp retort. "If you can't do anything for her, don't disturb the scene."

"Of course," he said. "C'mon, Cooper, let's pack it in. This one's for the NYPD."

The medics passed Levine on their way out. The Medical Examiner was still dressed in her autopsy gear. Her lab coat was spattered with awful fluids, her hair was tied carefully back, and she had a pair of plastic safety goggles hanging by their strap from her neck.

"Thanks for coming so fast," Erin said.

"It was inconvenient," Levine said. "Interrupting an examination in the middle can compromise the data. It's also inefficient. UC Berkeley did a study on interrupted work and determined it takes fifteen minutes following an interruption to return to the necessary state of deep concentration to perform correctly. Where's the body?"

Erin pointed wordlessly.

Levine lost all interest in the living and approached the couch. She paused for a long moment, staring down at Kira. Her eyes went momentarily soft. The Medical Examiner took a slow, steadying breath. Then she knelt down and got to work.

"Female," she said. "Mixed ethnic heritage. Dyed hair, natural color dark brown or black. Age approximately thirty, subject to verification. Single gunshot wound, entry on right temple. Medium-caliber, probably handgun in nine-millimeter or .38-caliber diameter. Obvious powder marks indicate muzzle was in contact with temple. Exit wound on opposite side of cranium. Bullet appears to have passed directly through the brain. Preliminary cause of death is this bullet."

"Yeah," Erin said heavily. "I know."

Levine actually turned away from the body to look at Erin. This was so unusual and unexpected that the ME's sudden change of attention gave Erin a shock of surprise. "Then what was the point of pulling me away from my ongoing task?" Levine demanded.

"Doc, don't you recognize her?" Erin said. "That's Kira Jones. From the Eightball."

"You've also already made a positive identification?" Levine replied. "That further reduces the necessity of my immediate presence."

"You know her," Erin said. "Doesn't that matter?"

Levine looked back at Kira. "I fully apply myself to every victim," she said. "I'll do my best for her, as I would for everyone. I recognized her immediately, but my personal feelings aren't relevant."

"But you do have them, don't you?" Erin insisted. "Personal feelings?"

"Detective O'Reilly, do you *want* me to lose my focus?" Levine snapped with a surprising burst of anger. "Do you want me to be distracted from what I'm doing?"

"No. Of course not."

"Then why are you trying to amplify feelings which will distract me?"

Erin had no good answer for that. Instead, she said, "Doc, I have to know whether she shot herself or whether someone else did it to her. And I need to know as quickly as you can figure it out."

"That information will be in my report," Levine said, turning her full attention back to the body. "You will have the report as soon as I have compiled it. I don't waste time."

While Levine worked, Erin walked around the apartment, careful not to disturb anything. What she was most looking for was what she didn't see: a thumb drive. Kira's laptop appeared undisturbed, its lid closed, but nothing was plugged into its USB ports. Erin didn't touch it. The computer might contain critical evidence. She didn't want to mess anything up.

Heavy footfalls pounded their way down the hallway at a run. "Hold it! NYPD!" a Patrolman shouted.

"Me too," Vic voice replied impatiently. "Don't you see my goddamn gold shield? Outta my way before I shove your goddamn teeth down your throat!"

A moment later, Vic stomped into the room. He grabbed Erin and brought his face in close to hers.

"Are you hurt?" he demanded. "Why didn't you call me?"

Erin shook her head. "I wasn't here when... when it happened," she said, suddenly afraid she was going to break down and start sobbing. What was wrong with her? She was a professional. She'd seen death plenty of times. It was a part of life. More to the point, it was part of the Job.

Vic's eyes slid past her, taking in Levine and Kira. "Jesus," he said. "Jesus fucking goddamn crippled Christ in a wheelchair! What the fuck happened?"

"What did Webb tell you?" Erin asked.

"Just that Kira got taken out. I thought maybe you got hit, too."

"Why would you think that? I'm the one who called Webb! Didn't he tell you that?"

"Yeah, and he said you told him you were fine, but you'd say that if you were on your last pint of blood. Is this about our case, or is it a stupid damn coincidence?"

"We're Major Crimes," she said. "We don't believe in coincidence."

"Damn right," he growled. "If this was one of those Roadkiller punks, I'm gonna go into Evidence, check out that friggin' ice skate, and start cutting balls off assholes."

Vic trailed into a semi-coherent string of profanity. He couldn't seem to stand still, pacing back and forth in the apartment like a caged, agitated bear. He was looking at everything except the body on the couch, his hands clenching and unclenching. Erin had never seen a man who wanted so badly to hit something.

Vic was on his fifth or sixth circuit of the room when an overweight man in a shabby secondhand trench coat and battered fedora appeared in the doorway. The newcomer had heavy bags under his eyes and the expression on his face made Erin tired just looking at him.

"Thank God you're here, sir," she said.

Lieutenant Webb stepped inside. He took off his hat and rubbed his scalp where hair no longer grew. "Good to see you again, O'Reilly," he sighed. "I would've preferred just about any other circumstances."

"Me, too," she said. "Sorry to drag you out of bed."

"Don't apologize," he said. "You did exactly the right thing. If I hadn't been in CompStat all yesterday, I would've connected with you sooner. What do we know?"

"One of the neighbors, Ms. Janklow downstairs, heard a loud noise about ninety minutes ago," Erin said. "She didn't report it. I'm guessing it was the gunshot."

"Where were you?"

"At home, trying to sleep. I texted Kira about forty-five minutes ago. She didn't reply. I tried calling and it rolled to voicemail. I got worried and came over."

"Why?" Webb asked. "It was after one in the morning. She might've been asleep."

"She was working on something pertinent to the case," Erin explained. "I was expecting her to be up late."

"What was it?"

Erin glanced around the room. Levine was paying attention only to the body under her care and the uniforms were outside, but they'd be able to hear. She lowered her voice.

"We found something our shooting victim had in a safe-deposit box," she said.

"And you had a court order to open the box?" Webb asked.

Erin hesitated.

Vic stopped his pacing. "Of course we didn't have a friggin' court order!" he said. "What we had was the key. We don't even know if it was in Ward's name. Knowing that sly bastard, I'd guess it wasn't. We've been following a trail of dumbass clues all day, just to find something we don't even have anymore! The bad guys got it, unless Kira stashed it somewhere before she got nailed."

"You're assuming this was a homicide?" Webb asked.

"Aren't you, sir?" Erin replied.

"I'm not assuming anything," he said. "I see a dead body with a gun in its hand. I'm currently waiting for our Medical Examiner to determine whether the gunshot was self-inflicted."

"It's Kira!" Erin burst out. "She didn't shoot herself!"

"You're sure of that?" Webb fired back. "The night after one of her friends ate his own gun?"

"We don't know that's what happened," she said.

"In the time you worked with her, did she ever say or do anything that suggested she might be thinking about ending her life?"

Erin opened her mouth to say no. Then she remembered something, a conversation they'd had shortly after Kira had transferred out of Major Crimes.

"Listen to me, okay? That ambush with the Russians really fucked me up. I couldn't sleep for weeks. Nightmares, flashbacks, the whole works. I tried pills, I tried booze, I tried friggin' therapy. Then you know what? I ended up sitting in my bathroom at two in the morning one night, holding my service piece, wondering how it'd feel if I just shoved the thing in my mouth. That maybe it'd be worth it if it'd just make me stop being scared."

Webb saw the hesitation in her eyes. "We're detectives," he said. "We need to be open to all possibilities, however unpleasant."

"It was just words," she muttered. "And it was a long time ago. Hell, we've all thought about it. That doesn't mean a damn thing."

Webb nodded. "What was the item you recovered from the deposit box?"

"I never saw it," Erin said. "Kira told me it was a thumb drive, encrypted. She was trying to hack the password."

"That's not as easy as it is in the movies," Webb observed. "Neshenko!"

"What?" Vic asked. He'd commenced circling again.

"Stop that. You're making me nervous."

"Sorry," Vic growled. "I figured it beat the alternatives."

Webb raised a questioning eyebrow.

"Booze and fistfights," Vic said.

"You're right," Webb said. "It does. But right now we need to think and you aren't helping. If Levine rules this a suicide, there's no case here, whether we can find this mysterious drive or not. If it's a homicide, it means someone murdered an IAB detective. In either situation, Internal Affairs will be all over this."

"Can't we keep the Bloodhound away?" Erin asked.

"You're serious?" Webb asked. "You want Lieutenant Keane not to be involved in the investigation of the death of one of his own detectives? Just how likely does that seem to you?"

"We can't let him in," Erin insisted. "We have indications of a conspiracy in the NYPD."

"All the more reason to bring IAB into the loop," Webb said. "We can't investigate other officers' alleged wrongdoing."

"Bullshit," Vic said. "We do it all the time. Remember that crooked sergeant who got his rookie killed? And what about those Organized Crime Task Force assholes? And Stachowski's informant squad? We've taken down all kinds of bent cops. It's kind of a specialty for us."

"And every one of those was in violation of departmental policy," Webb said. "We're on thin ice here, people. One cop takes a bullet to the head, it's news. A second one twenty-four hours later makes it *national* news."

Erin gave him an unhappy look.

"I know," he said. "But we have a little time here. Keane's bound to be home and in bed. So we just need to use the time we've got here to steal a march. The first thing we need to do is—"

"You should tell O'Reilly about your coat, sir," Vic interrupted.

Webb and Erin both stared at Vic like he'd gone crazy.

"This is the first time she's seen it," he went on. "Seeing as how she just came back on duty and you were in that time-wasting meeting all day, sitting on your thumbs with all the other *lieutenants*."

Erin caught the emphasis on the final word, and saw where he was looking. She was still a little off-kilter from shock, but she understood enough to play along.

"I don't recognize the coat, sir," she said. "Replacement for your old one?"

"That's right," Webb said, obviously confused. "I bought a brand-new one after my old trench coat got blown up at the hospital after Christmas, but it didn't feel right. That new starchy fabric rubbed my neck and it was all stiff. So I went to a secondhand store and picked this one up. Do you like it?"

"It looks like something a child molester would wear, sir," Erin said, unkindly but truthfully. Then she turned, as casually as she could, and faced the doorway.

"Speaking of creepy guys," Vic said, "here's our very own Internal Affairs Lieutenant, looking like he means to do some police work for a change."

"A pleasure to see you, too, Detective Neshenko." Lieutenant Andrew Keane gave him a look most people reserved for dogshit and bread mold. "It looks like I got here just in time."

Chapter 13

"In time for what?" Vic asked. "This is an active crime scene, sir. CSU needs to be here. So does the ME, and the investigating detectives. I'm not quite sure what that leaves for you."

"I'm responding to a report of the death of one of my detectives," Keane said. "You say this is an active crime scene. What crime is alleged to have taken place?"

"Homicide, sir," Vic said, his voice dripping false politeness. "That's Latin. It's from the root *homo*, which means man, and the suffix *-cide*, which means to kill. We're using the term in the gender-neutral, of course, which makes sense since the deceased is female."

Erin, Webb, and Keane all stared at the big Russian. Erin realized her mouth was hanging open and closed it.

"Thank you, detective, for that dictionary diversion," Keane said coldly. "We're all extremely impressed with your unexpected mastery of dead languages. But it would seem premature to classify this as a homicide. I see a woman with a bullet hole in her temple and a gun in her hand. Surely suicide is at least a theoretical possibility, particularly when it isn't the first such incident in the NYPD within the past day? Or is it the practice of Major Crimes not to wait for the Medical Examiner's determination?"

"Neshenko?" Webb said.

"Sir?" Vic snapped to rigid attention.

"Impressed though I also am by your unexpected knowledge of Classical languages, shut up."

"Yes, sir. Right away, sir."

Webb turned his attention back to Keane. "My squad has responded to this call, Lieutenant," he said. "We will, of course, keep you in the loop with regards to what our investigation uncovers, but this is not yet an Internal Affairs case. We have no reason at this time to believe another NYPD officer is involved. As with the death of Officer Ward, if you wish to assign a liaison officer from your department, we will be glad to work with him or her. In the meantime, we have a lot to do, so if you'd care to give us some space to work?"

"I'm afraid not," Keane said. "I received word that the body was reported by Detective O'Reilly. Is that correct?"

"Yes, sir," Erin said.

"I see signs of forced entry on the apartment door," he said. "Was that you, Detective?"

"Yes, sir."

"I further understand you were investigating the contents of a safety-deposit box," Keane continued.

"How do you know that, sir?" Erin blurted, then silently cursed herself. That was exactly the sort of exclamation she hoped to get out of perps in interrogation rooms. She knew better than to sound off like that.

"I'll take that as confirmation," Keane said. "What was in the box?"

"I'm not at liberty to say, sir," she said.

"I'm ordering you to tell me," he said.

"I can't answer that question, sir," she said stonily. "Because I never looked inside it."

"I don't believe you," Keane said.

"That sounds like your problem, not hers," Vic interjected. Before Webb could say anything, he added, "Shutting up again, sir."

"I'm removing Detective O'Reilly from this case," Keane said. "Effective immediately."

There was a moment of absolute silence. A muscle in Vic's jaw twitched so violently it looked like he was having a seizure. He clenched his right fist. His knuckles popped, a startling sound in the stillness.

"On what grounds?" Webb asked quietly.

"Conflict of interest," Keane said. "And because she is a person of interest in the case."

"Like hell I am!" Erin burst out. "Just what are you accusing me of?"

"Quiet, Detective," Webb said.

"Did you hear what he said?" she demanded. "He's saying I shot her!"

"I'm saying nothing of the sort," Keane said. "Why would you say that? Is there something you'd like to tell me?"

There were a great many things Erin wanted to tell Keane just then, but she was angry, upset, still reeling from Kira's death. So many words wanted to come out that they got jumbled up and jammed in her throat. She felt like she was choking on her own rage.

"I don't like your tone, Lieutenant," Webb said. "Nor your insinuations. I'm asking you, as a courtesy, to leave this room."

"And as a courtesy of my own, I'm going to politely decline," Keane said. "You are not in a position of authority here. Besides, this posturing is premature. We still don't know the precise cause of death."

"That is incorrect," Levine said.

All heads turned her way. The Medical Examiner had stood up and was making notes on an old-school paper notepad. She didn't seem to be paying attention to the ongoing argument, and didn't look like she intended to say anything further.

"Please explain yourself, Doctor," Keane said. "You can't have completed your examination so quickly."

"I haven't," Levine said. "But my initial observation is sufficient to make a determination. This is homicide."

"I didn't think you were prone to snap judgments," Keane said.

"I have never made a snap judgment in my entire medical career," Levine said. "Powder stippling around the entrance wound indicates the muzzle of the weapon was in contact with the scalp. Blood spatter and singed flesh on the muzzle of this pistol suggests it was the weapon used to fire the shot. I expect to find gunshot residue on the victim, as well as elsewhere on the couch."

"That sounds consistent with a self-inflicted GSW," Webb observed.

"Correct," Levine said. "However, note the slightly fan-shaped pattern of powder burns directly beneath the entrance wound."

Webb and Vic leaned in to see what Levine was pointing at. Erin couldn't bear to look. Keane was continuing to stare at Erin.

"When combined with the location of the exit wound and probable path of the bullet," Levine continued, "the inescapable conclusion is that the weapon was held at a downward angle of approximately ten degrees."

"So?" Keane asked.

"So she means this was staged," Vic said. "The doc's right. Good spot, Levine."

"Explain, Neshenko," Webb said.

"Suppose I want to shoot myself," Vic said. He unholstered his Sig-Sauer.

"Hold on," Webb said sharply.

"Relax, sir," Vic said. He popped the clip out of the pistol and worked the slide, ejecting the bullet from the chamber. He held the now-empty gun against his own temple. "See how I'm holding it? The barrel's pretty much level. If anything, it's tilted a little uphill. The doc's saying this weapon was held like this."

Vic shifted his grip. He was now holding the pistol awkwardly high, angling it down toward his head.

"Nobody would hold their gun that way," he said. "I've seen plenty of GSW suicides. So have you. How many people fired *down* into their own head?"

"Not one," Webb agreed.

"You're right," Erin said. "She was sitting down and the shooter was standing over her."

"Unless she was trying to stage it to look like a homicide," Webb said doubtfully.

"Are you serious, sir?" Vic retorted. "This *looks* like a suicide! That's some double-think bullshit right there."

"You're saying someone broke in here and killed Detective Jones with her own sidearm," Keane said. "They then staged it to look like a suicide?"

"I don't know how the killer made entry," Levine said. "I am not qualified to determine other aspects of the crime. I am, however, certain this is a homicide, as my report will clearly state. Assuming I am freed from interruption long enough to complete it."

"How'd the bad guy get his hands on Kira's gun?" Vic wondered. "She's too good a cop to let some random schmuck get the drop on her."

"Unless the killer was someone known to her, and trusted by her," Keane said. "O'Reilly, you're suspended from duty, effective immediately. Give your shield and sidearm to your commanding officer and leave this crime scene at once."

Erin actually considered hitting him. She wanted to do it. She could have Rolf do it for her. The thought of the K-9's teeth sinking into Keane's smooth, calculating face was the only pleasant thing in her mind at that moment. She could feel her own pulse pounding in her head, especially in the tender spot on the left side of her skull where a bullet had glanced off the previous December.

"We'll straighten this out, O'Reilly," Webb promised. "I'm sure this is just a misunderstanding."

"I'm not misunderstanding a goddamn thing," Vic said, giving Keane a glare that in a just world would have killed him on the spot.

"We need to work," Webb said. "I'll need your gun and shield, O'Reilly. Don't worry, this isn't an unpaid suspension. It's just a vacation."

"You think *that's* what I'm worried about?" Erin said incredulously. "I just got back from vacation!"

"Just in time for two police officers to die," Keane said dryly. "You're not being detained at this time, Detective. But don't try to leave town. My office will be in touch."

"Is that a promise?" she couldn't help asking. "Or a threat?"

Keane didn't answer.

* * *

The Barley Corner was dark and silent when Erin let herself and Rolf in. The chairs were upended atop the tables, the televisions powered down. She entered the security code into the keypad beside the apartment door and climbed the stairs.

Carlyle was waiting for her in the living room, sitting on the couch. He had a book on his lap and a bottle of Glen D whiskey on the coffee table, two shot glasses ready to be filled. He stood up and came to her, opening his arms.

"You needn't say anything, darling," he said. "Ian's told me what happened. I'm sorry for your troubles."

Erin submitted to a brief embrace, but she was too angry to stay there for long. She pulled away and poured herself a stiff drink. Glen Docherty-Kinlochewe was a sipping whiskey, but she tossed it back in two deep gulps, drawing bitter pleasure from the burning in her throat and belly.

Carlyle got a drink for himself and nursed it more slowly. He watched her patiently and wordlessly.

"It's murder," she announced. "Some bastard barged into Kira's place, into her home, got her gun, made her sit down on her own damn couch, shoved the barrel into her skull and blew her away! And guess what? Lieutenant Keane says *I* did it!"

"That's absurd," Carlyle said.

"Tell him that!" Erin snapped. She poured another whiskey and drank it almost as fast. She couldn't even feel the effects from the first one. Did adrenaline counteract alcohol? She didn't know and didn't care.

"You've an alibi," he said. "You were here when the poor lass was shot. I'm not the only one can vouch for you. And you didn't even go there alone. Ian will swear to the truth."

"So what? I'm suspended! That son of a bitch Keane made me hand over my gun and my shield! I might as well not even be a cop right now! Kira's *dead!* She's dead and I can't even chase down the son of a bitch who killed her!"

"Suspended?" Carlyle was surprised. "So quickly? On whose authority?"

"Lieutenant Keane's," she said bitterly. "He didn't even care what happened. He was just looking for someone to hang this on. Now we've got two dead cops and I'm riding the bench! She was my friend, damn it!"

"You don't need a bit of gold on your belt to tell you you're a copper," Carlyle said. "And you've never needed permission to carry out your investigations. Don't you recall how you came to be made detective in the first place?"

"Yeah," she said. "I got suspended that time, too. Keane's the one who bailed me out. He's not going to step in to save me this time around. He'll fire my ass, and maybe throw me in jail while he's at it."

"For what? You've done nothing."

"And no innocent woman ever went to prison," she said hollowly.

"Come now, darling, you can't be serious." He shook his head. "You're a hero, practically a celebrity. If he tosses you in jail, it'll look dreadful for the Department and the city. We're worrying about your career and your pension, nothing more."

"Nothing more? This is my life we're talking about here! And Rolf! If I lose my job, I lose him!"

That silenced both of them for a few moments. Erin sat at one end of the couch, fumed, and had a third drink. Carlyle sat at the other, giving her space and time. Rolf settled on his haunches in front of Erin and laid his chin on her leg, giving her both barrels of his brown-eyed stare.

"Did the good Lieutenant ever mention why he saved you after your first major infraction?" Carlyle asked suddenly.

"Not really," she said. "What does it matter?"

"It struck me as curiously arbitrary," he said. "The same copper rewards you for one incident, of which you were guilty, and leaps on you for another, for which there's scarcely a scrap of evidence? Don't you find that odd?"

"If you're suggesting he had an ulterior motive, of course he did," she said. "Keane's always been an ambitious asshole. He's got ulterior motives coming out his ears. He thought I'd be useful to him in Major Crimes, especially owing him a favor. Aren't you always saying the world runs on favors?"

"I say it because it's true," he said. "Did he ever call in that favor?"

"No. In fact, I owe him another one for taking care of Lenny Carter."

"Whatever did become of Mr. Carter?"

"This is ancient history," Erin said. "Don't we have enough to worry about here and now? Cops are getting their brains blown out. For all I know, somebody's about to put a bullet in *my* head!"

"Humor me."

"I don't know, okay? We couldn't charge Carter normally. He was threatening to blow my cover to the O'Malleys. If that had come out, you would've been killed. I probably should've just blasted Carter myself before arresting him, but I had to be the good cop and take him in, so I palmed him off on Keane and asked him to handle it."

"And where's the lad now?"

"I told you, I don't know!"

"Is he breathing?"

"What?" Erin stared at Carlyle. "What the hell kind of question is that?"

"A pertinent one, I'm thinking," he said mildly.

"Of course he is! I mean..." Erin's certainty was a fragile thing. It melted away under Carlyle's calm, thoughtful stare.

"It seems you and Lieutenant Keane may be tied together," he said. "So why would the lad go suspending you?"

"He's pretty pissed at me," she said. "I kept him out of the loop on the Vitelli arrest. He chewed my ass off for that."

"Valentino Vitelli? The Lucarelli *capo* who was hauled in along with the O'Malleys?"

"That's the one. We had dinner at his house that one time, remember?"

"I've not forgotten it. Why should Lieutenant Keane care? Your lot arrested dozens of gangsters that night."

"I wondered about that," she admitted. "But I had kind of a lot on my mind at the time."

"Does the dear Lieutenant know you're innocent?"

The question brought her up short. "I don't know," she admitted. "Probably."

"If so, it rather raises the question why he wants you off this case."

She nodded. "It's not spite," she said. "And I don't think it's payback for keeping him out of the loop. Keane knows better than to get into it with a decorated officer without a good reason."

"You're a fine detective, Erin," he said. "Were I one of your superiors, I'd want you working. I assume Lieutenant Keane is aware of your good qualities. Therefore, unless he's cause to believe you really were involved in Miss Jones' misfortune, there's only one reason I can think why he'd want you otherwise engaged."

"Jesus Christ," Erin said. "You think Keane is involved?"

"Is it such an outlandish notion?"

She gritted her teeth. "No," she said. "I was suspicious of him once before. You remember that guy who had his throat cut in that restaurant last year?"

"I'm not likely to forget it either," Carlyle said. "Right after church, so it was. We watched it happen."

"We had the guy who did the cutting in Holding," she said. "Alphonse Luna, that was his name. We brought him in. He was actually glad to see us! He'd been wounded, you see, and thought he was going to die. Then we found him hanging in his cell."

"Suicide?" Carlyle asked with a wry twist of his mouth.

"That was the official verdict," Erin said. "But Levine hadn't finished her exam. Keane took it over and whitewashed the whole thing."

"Interesting," Carlyle said. "As I recall, both dead men in that particular incident were members of the Lucarellis."

"That's right," she said. "It was part of Vinnie Moreno's coup to take over the Family. He took out all the *capos* who weren't loyal to him. The only one of the old guard left standing was..."

"Valentino Vitelli," Carlyle said quietly.

The name hung in the air between them. Erin felt a tightness in her chest. For the first time in her career, she didn't enjoy the feeling as the pieces of a case started falling into place. This didn't feel like jogging onto the homestretch of a marathon. It felt more like teetering on a tightrope over a very deep pit.

"We figured the hitman was taking orders from Vinnie," she said. "But what if it was Vitelli instead? What if that guy was killed so he couldn't identify his boss? That hanging looked iffy to me, and I think Levine agreed. Luna didn't want to die. I think he was murdered."

"In the heart of a police station," Carlyle said. "In a locked jail cell, where only a copper would have access."

"Keane could have gotten in," she said. "He was disheveled, too, when he butted in on us in Holding. Unkempt. And he's *never* unkempt."

"Did you report your suspicions at the time?"

"No. It wasn't more than a gut feeling, and you can't go over an IAB Lieutenant's head on a gut feeling. All I did was ask Kira to keep her eyes open and see if she saw anything weird."

"This would be the same Kira who passed this very night?"

Erin closed her eyes. "Yeah. God damn it! If Keane really was working for Vitelli, everything makes sense. And if he thought

Kira was going to find that out, he'd absolutely be willing to kill her. If I'm right, he already killed Alphonse Luna to cover his tracks."

"And Leonard Carter," Carlyle added.

She winced. "Him, too, most likely. I didn't know that was what he was going to do with Carter, I swear! I just wanted him kept quiet, somewhere out of the way, until we took down the O'Malleys."

"I believe you, darling. No one's blaming you."

Erin blinked back angry tears. "So what am I supposed to do?" she demanded. "I don't have any proof! If I come at Keane now, it'll just look like I'm pissed about the suspension and looking for payback of my own. I'll sound like a raving lunatic if I start going off about the Mafia and murder and crooked Internal Affairs cops. And it's just a theory. Carter might not even be dead! What if we're wrong?"

"You're saying you need proof," Carlyle said.

"Yeah."

"Isn't that your job, darling? You're a detective, after all."

"Weren't you listening? I'm suspended! And he'll be watching me, whether he's guilty or not!"

"Then you'd best be careful," he said. "And choose your next move with particular care. Let's suppose, for the sake of argument, you're wrong and the Lieutenant is innocent. What ought you to do?"

"That's easy. Don't make waves, serve out my suspension, get back on duty as soon as I can."

"And what if you're right and he's guilty?"

"Then I take the bastard down," she said grimly. "No matter what it takes."

"Is it worth it?"

She stared at him. "What kind of a question is that? If I'm right, he murdered my friend! I can't walk away from that!"

He nodded. "Then you'd best start thinking how you're going to get him. I assume you're considering only legal recourses?"

"Carlyle, you're not going to put a bomb in his car."

His smile was gently teasing. "I had to ask, darling," he said. "You know I'd kill for you."

"And you know I don't want you to," she retorted. "No, we're doing this the right way if we're doing it at all. Once we have the proof, we nail his ass. Legally."

"What proof do you mean?" Carlyle asked.

"I have no idea," Erin said. "If I knew, I'd already have it."

Chapter 14

Sleep was no refuge. Erin woke from uneasy dreams to a dark bedroom and a heavy, furry weight on her stomach. Sometime after she'd dropped off, Rolf had climbed onto the bed and laid his head on her. He was trying to make her feel better, no doubt, but the main result was to leave her overheated and half-squashed.

The clock by her bedside informed her it was 5:25 in the morning. She'd only been asleep about three hours, but there was no chance whatsoever of snatching any more. She eased herself out from under the dog and away from Carlyle, who remained fast asleep. She tiptoed to the door and opened it as quietly as the best cat burglar.

She might as well have blown a whistle. When she emerged from the bathroom, Rolf was standing at the top of the stairs, leash in his mouth, tail wagging. He didn't care it was way too early, nor that there was no particular rush, given that Erin was on suspension. They were up, so it was time for a walk, or better yet, a run.

It was actually a good idea. Some exercise might calm her down and clear her head. She put on her running clothes, tucked her snub-nosed .38 into her fanny pack, leashed up Rolf, and set off for Central Park.

Most women would hesitate to go jogging alone in the park, especially before sunrise, but Erin had a handgun and ninety pounds of ferociously loyal K-9. God help any would-be muggers or rapists. She almost hoped somebody would make a play for her.

The park was fairly quiet, though she passed a few other early-morning fitness enthusiasts. She set a tough pace and was soon breaking a sweat. Rolf loped easily beside her, tongue flopping happily. He seemed to have completely forgotten what they'd seen during the night.

Erin hadn't. She kept thinking of Kira's face. Her thoughts were a stew of anger, horror, sadness, and confusion. Carlyle was right; Keane was up to something. But did that make him a killer? And if so, why? What had been on that damned thumb drive? And why had they been so eager to track it down? Come to that, what had happened to the fifty grand Kira had found in the deposit box?

They could have left the whole thing alone. If Ward really had killed himself, there was no case. They'd just been doing a freelance investigation, an ad hoc scavenger hunt. And at the end, the only prize was a bullet.

Damn William Ward and his goddamn mind games. If he'd had the guts to mail the thumb drive to the *New York Times*, it'd be out in the open right now and everything would be fine. If he'd wanted to be a whistleblower so badly, why hadn't he blown the damn whistle good and hard?

He'd been scared. Raving paranoid, in fact. But scared of whom? Lieutenant Keane? Keane was dangerous, true, but he wasn't all-powerful. Ward could've gone to a different IAB cop, or even done a run around the chain of command and taken his information upstairs.

Erin could think of only three reasons he wouldn't have done that. Either what he had was so explosive it would cause havoc no matter who looked at it, so he couldn't trust even the Commissioner himself; or what he'd found wasn't sufficient proof to convince someone up the chain; or Ward wasn't sure how high the corruption reached.

All three theories were scary, for different reasons. Erin didn't think it was the second option. Whatever Ward had hidden on the drive, it had apparently been dangerous enough that at least one person thought it worth killing for. That left two equally unappealing choices.

As Erin thought about it, she realized mailing an exposé to the *Times* wasn't a great idea. Not when you were dealing with people who might kill you. The really creepy thing, she decided, was that Ward had taken his own death for granted. He'd been completely sure he'd die if the bad guys found out what he was doing. So he'd been proactive and gone out in his own way.

Erin understood suicidal thoughts. She could empathize with someone who was traumatized, depressed, or despairing enough to take their own life. But to do it as a tactical decision was a new one for her. Kira's death actually reinforced the theory that Ward had been trying to send a message. The bad guys had thought so, too.

Erin was out of breath. She'd been pushing a little too hard and was fighting a stitch in her side. She slowed to a walk. Rolf circled her once and took up his usual place at her hip.

"How did they know?" she asked Rolf.

The dog had no answer. He didn't even know who she was talking about.

"If they've got ears in the Department, they'd know we'd busted those Roadkillers," she said. "But they wouldn't know about the safe-deposit box. The bikers thought the briefcase had real money in it. So how did they know Kira had been to the bank and gotten into the box? They couldn't have had the bank under surveillance.

"They were tracking *us*," she concluded angrily. "And we led them right to it!"

That was the ball game, then. The drive was gone and they'd never get it back. In all likelihood it had already been destroyed. Dumb crooks kept incriminating evidence around. Smart ones ditched it as soon as possible. Kira's killer wouldn't have left anything important.

Except that maybe he had. Erin stopped short and yanked her phone out of her fanny pack. She wiped the sweat from her fingertips and made a call.

"Webb," the Lieutenant answered almost immediately.

"I'm glad I didn't wake you," she said.

"Of course you didn't wake me," he replied. "Do you think I've been back to bed?"

"Kira's computer," she said.

"What about it?"

"Where is it?"

"CSU has it. One of our computer guys will take a crack at it in the next day or two."

"The hard drive's still in it, isn't it?"

"Yes. What're we looking for?"

"I don't know. But there'll be something."

"How do you know?" Webb's voice was sharp with sudden curiosity.

"This was staged as a suicide," Erin said.

"I know that," Webb said. "But Levine saw through it. She and Neshenko were right about the angle. It's not an impossible shot for a self-inflicted GSW, but it's incredibly improbable."

"That's right. It was murder. But the staging was a mistake. If the perp had made it look like a robbery, he could've stolen whatever he wanted. A crook would've swiped the computer, along with any loose cash or valuables."

"Right," Webb said. "But if we hadn't found Jones' computer, it would've told us someone else had been there."

"So they had to leave the computer," Erin said. "But they might've tried to delete files. We need someone good, someone very good, to go through that machine. And it needs to happen fast."

"What's the rush?"

"The perp's going to try to get at it as soon as he knows we're looking at it."

"How would our guy know that?"

Erin said nothing.

"Jesus," Webb said wearily. "You think it's another cop."

"I think I'd better not talk about suspects. I shouldn't even be discussing this over the phone. But we're in a hurry, like I said. And I can't come in."

"No, you can't. Because you're suspended from duty. You have a very unusual definition of suspension, by the way. I'm not complaining, I'm just making an observation."

"You don't think I killed her, do you?" Erin asked.

"Of course not," Webb said at once. "And neither does anyone else. If Keane really thought that, he would've pulled our whole squad off the case. Conflict of interest. Come to think of it, I'm surprised he hasn't. With one NYPD detective as a victim and another as a suspect, this really ought to be an IAB case through and through."

"You'll probably get yanked sometime today," she said. "That's another reason to hurry."

"Are you giving me orders, O'Reilly?" Webb sounded tired but amused.

"Suggestions, sir."

"I'll look into it. Enjoy your enforced vacation. Try to relax, and try really hard not to shoot anybody."

"Only if they shoot at me," she promised.

* * *

Erin walked Rolf back to the Charger. She loaded him into his compartment, slid behind the steering wheel, closed the door, and started crying.

She hadn't meant to, she didn't want to, but there was no stopping it. Anger and adrenaline could carry her for a while, but the weight of loss was pressing down; heavy and relentless. There was nothing productive for her to do, nowhere to rush off to. So she sat there, sweat and tears pouring down her cheeks, gulping in air with big, hiccupping gasps.

For all the senseless, tragic deaths she'd seen in twelve years wearing a shield, she'd never felt one the way she was feeling this. The cruel sadness of it was crushing the life out of her. She'd tried to ignore it, to push forward, but she'd run out of momentum. Kira's computer might give them what they needed to nail the bad guys, but so what?

All the times she'd promised to get the killers, to bring them to justice, seemed hollow now. What did it matter if she locked up Kira's murderer? Would it make Kira any less dead? What was the point of any of it?

When she'd been infiltrating the O'Malleys, she'd had Phil Stachowski to talk to in her weak moments. His calm, steady support had guided her through the treacherous obstacle course of undercover work. But now Phil was retired. The bullet that had nearly killed him had ended his career and left him a shattered shell.

But that didn't mean she couldn't talk to him. Hell, she was suspended. She could do whatever she wanted. Phil's disability made it difficult for him to talk on the phone. He'd still been in the hospital when she'd left for Hawaii, but she'd heard he'd recently been discharged. He lived across the river, in New Jersey, but that didn't matter.

"We've got all the time in the world," she told Rolf, sniffling and wiping her nose and eyes.

Rolf gave her a worried look. In his experience, when humans' faces started dripping, it was a sign things weren't going the way they ought to. He stuck his head through the hatch between the seats and licked her ear.

"Home first," she said. "Shower and breakfast. Then we're going to Jersey."

* * *

Frenzied barking answered the chime of the Stachowskis' doorbell. As Erin stood outside, she saw a golden, fluffy head bob into view through the window in the front door. Bradley, Phil's Golden Retriever, was trying his best to let her know that he'd love to let her in if he could just figure out the doorknob.

After a few moments, the dog's head was pushed to one side and replaced by Camilla Stachowski's face. She smiled when she saw Erin. The lock clicked back and the door swung open.

"Good morning," Erin said. "I'm sorry if it's a little early."

"It's fine," Camilla said. "Come in. Don't mind Bradley. I was just—Bradley! Stop that!"

The Retriever had noticed Rolf and, following an invasive sniffing of the Shepherd's hindquarters, was trying to climb on top of him for a friendly wrestling match. Rolf, being a professional, was ignoring the bouncing animal as well as he could. The K-9 gave Erin a long-suffering look.

Once Camilla had corralled her pet, Erin and Rolf went inside. Bradley reluctantly lay down at his mistress' command, but kept wagging his tail as he watched Rolf between his front paws.

"As I was saying, I was just about to go to work," Camilla said. "Phil's in the den. He'll be so glad you dropped by! We didn't know you were back in town."

"We got in over the weekend," Erin said. "I heard he'd come home. How is he?"

"He's doing really well," Camilla said. "The aphasia has gotten better, and he's got about eighty percent use of his hands. The doctor says he's making great progress."

Mrs. Stachowski was trying to sound upbeat, but Erin could see the deep lines on her face and the shadows under her eyes. Camilla remained a strong woman, but the past few months had added years to her appearance. She was obviously exhausted.

"That's great," Erin said, trying to match the other woman's tone. "Do you need anything?"

"No. Moira's moved in with us for now. She's been terrific. It's because of her that we haven't needed to get a live-in assistant. She won't even let me pay her. She just says, 'That's what family's for.'"

"She's a good sister," Erin said.

"The best," Camilla agreed. "Here we are. Phil! Look who's come!"

Phil Stachowski was sitting next to the window. His round, good-natured face, so different from what you'd expect from a seasoned police officer, broke into a warm smile. "Erin!" he exclaimed. "Didn't know you were coming. I'd get up, but you know how it is."

The blanket across his lap almost managed to conceal the wheelchair. Erin hurried to him, swallowing the lump in her throat. He did look much better than the last time she'd seen him. The horrible wreckage the bullet had left behind had been reduced to a puckered network of pink and red scars. The scars stood out brightly on the side of his skull, but he looked almost normal. His eyes were bright and attentive.

He held out his hand and she clasped it. He squeezed her fingers with a grip that was weak but capable. He patted the back of her hand as they shook.

"How're you doing?" she asked.

"Happy," he said. "Great to be home. Being retired aggrieves with me."

He paused and his brow wrinkled. "That wasn't quite it," he said, tapping the side of his head. "Still having some trouble. Words don't come out right. I can see them in here, but they get lost on the way out."

"Forget about it," Erin said. "I'm just glad to see you doing so well."

"Can't complain," he said. "I'm a medicinal miracle. Doctor said so. Ninety-five percent of people who get shot like I did don't even make it to hopscotch."

"The hospital?" she guessed.

"That's it," he said. "And the rest mostly turnips. No... you know, peas and carrots?"

"Vegetables?"

He nodded. "I still know who I am," he said. "I know my family. I'm still *me*."

"And it's a blessing," Camilla said. "Can I get you anything before I go, Erin? I think there's still a cup of coffee in the pot."

"That'd be great, thanks," Erin said.

"Cam makes great coffee," Phil said. "But that's not why you're here. And it's not just to tell me about that, either."

He pointed to her left hand. Erin followed the gesture to the ring on her finger.

"You're as sharp as ever," she said, smiling. "Yeah, he popped the question, so we're going to take the leap. You're invited, of course."

"Never been to a Mob wedding," he said. "Think maybe I'll wear my dress blues, make a statement. Congratulations. Happy for you. But like I said, not why you're here."

"No," she said, feeling the smile slide off her face. "Phil, something happened. Something bad."

He listened carefully as she explained, pausing only when Camilla brought a steaming cup of coffee. Camilla bent down and kissed him.

"I'll be back at five," she said. "The girls should be home by four. I love you."

"Love you, Cam," he said, and the look of quiet joy on his face as he looked at his wife brought fresh tears to Erin's eyes.

After Camilla had gone, and Erin had finished her story, Phil sat still for a few moments, thinking. Erin waited.

"Why come to me?" he finally asked. "I'm retired."

"You're retired," she agreed. "You're outside the Department now. IAB can't do anything to you. They're not watching you anymore."

"Unless someone followed you," he said.

Erin automatically glanced out the window. She saw nothing but the next door neighbor's house. "Yeah," she admitted. "But I don't think anyone did. I had my eyes open."

"Could have your car humbugged," he said.

"They'd just think I was visiting you," she said. "God, Phil, I thought I was done with all this. The creeping around, the secrets... I'm a cop, dammit! I shouldn't have to hide!"

"No," he agreed. "You think Lieutenant Keane is on the take?"

"It might be worse than that," she said. "At first I thought he was working for Valentino Vitelli. Now, I'm starting to think maybe Vitelli was working for *him*."

"Why do you think that?"

"The Roadkillers," she said. "And Los Cuchillos Locos. Those aren't Mafia organizations. One's an outlaw biker gang, the other is a Mexican drug operation. Neither one has Italian or Sicilian roots. And they hate each other. Keane's involved with all of them, I know it. But I can't prove it."

"You need to take this to the baseball," Phil said.

"The which?" Erin asked.

He waved his hand in frustration. "The big man. The boss."

"The Commissioner?"

"Yes."

"And what do I do when he asks why a suspended detective wants him to come down hard on the IAB Lieutenant who suspended her? He'll say I'm having a hissy fit because I got in trouble, and there'll be some bullshit about hysterical women."

"You're not historical," he assured her.

"I know that!" she snapped. "But some guys will think so anyway! You don't know what that's like, Phil. I'm not allowed to have feelings on the Job, or else I'm an oversensitive woman. It doesn't matter that I've closed all these cases, it doesn't matter that I've killed guys in gunfights. People still look at me and the first thing they see is a chick hiding behind a shield."

"Erin..." he began.

She stopped him with an upraised hand. "Besides, maybe the PC is in on it himself. You think of that? Ward thought it went pretty high up."

"How did he know?"

"I have no idea, because I don't have his files! The guy who shot Kira does. I have to solve this, and I don't know if I can!"

The tears overflowed, leaving angry lines on her cheeks. She was ashamed of the display of emotion, even though she knew he wasn't mad, wasn't judging her for it.

"Kira's my friend," she choked out. "And they killed her!"

"They?" Phil prompted. "Not 'he?'"

"I don't know if Keane pulled the trigger himself," she said. "But he had it done. I know it! That slick, smug bastard. And he's going to get away with it!"

"No," Phil said. "He's not."

"Why not?"

"You're going to stop him."

She swiped at her eyes with her wrist. "How?"

"Dig," he said. "Search. Be what you are."

"A cop on suspension?"

"A good detective. What do you need? To prove what you're saying?"

"That thumb drive," she said. "Or some physical evidence that puts Keane at Kira's apartment, assuming he was the triggerman."

"You won't get the drive," Phil said. "Not if Keane got it. He's too smart."

Her shoulders sagged. "Then I'm screwed," she said. "He doesn't have the weapon. It's still in the apartment. I bet he wore gloves, unless he hired some other sap to do the shooting."

Phil shook his head. "Had to do it himself," he said.

Erin thought for a moment. "You're right," she said. "Kira wouldn't have let some random guy get close to her. She didn't trust Keane, but she wouldn't have expected him to pull a gun on her either. She had to know the shooter. He was there!"

"Prove that," Phil said. "Then you've got him."

"No," she sighed. "Because he was there again. He could just claim any fibers or whatever were from his second visit. That's why he showed up in person. Damn it all, he contaminated our scene while we were standing right there watching him do it!"

"Then you need him to confess," Phil said. "On tape."

"Just how am I supposed to do that?" she demanded.

He smiled thinly. "You still have your tightrope? From the O'Malleys?"

"My tightrope? Oh, you mean my wire?"

"Yes."

"Yeah, it's in my underwear drawer." For her undercover work, she'd gotten a special bra with a recording device sewn into its underwire.

"Wear it. Talk to him."

"He won't admit anything," she said. "Like you said, he's too smart."

"You're smarter than he is."

"Yeah? How do you figure?"

"You're on to him. And he's scared of you."

"How do you know that?"

"He benched you. Besides, in his place, I would be."

Phil's words startled a smile out of her in spite of her frustration and sadness. "Thanks," she said. "That's actually really sweet of you."

"I believe in you," he said. "So should you. You've got this. You know what you have to do. Go do it."

Chapter 15

"At least somebody believes in me," Erin said as she aimed the Charger's nose back toward Manhattan.

Rolf licked her cheek. He'd always believed in her.

"Phil's in a wheelchair," she said. "And that asshole Keane has a corner office. Where's the justice in that?"

Rolf licked her again. He didn't think about justice, except when it meant he'd earned his rubber ball. Fairness was a very low-level, tangible thing for a dog. He wagged his tail. Car rides were great, but he hadn't bitten any bad guys yet. Surely there was something more valuable for them to be doing with their time.

She was about halfway under the Hudson River when her phone buzzed. Most tunnels blocked cell signals, but the Lincoln Tunnel had been rigged for wireless communication more than twenty years earlier, the first such setup in New York City. She saw Vic's name on the screen as she brought the phone to her ear.

"Don't you have better things to do than bug me?" she asked. "You're not suspended."

"Not yet," Vic said. "Where are you?"

"Right on the line between Jersey and Manhattan," she said. "In the Tunnel. Why?"

"I'll meet you where we ran into Dana yesterday," he said. "You remember the place?"

"Of course," she said. "You mean the—"

"Good," he interrupted. "Turn off your phone." He hung up.

"That was weird," she said into the dead phone. "I guess it's on our way anyway."

As he'd asked, she turned off her phone, though it went against everything she'd been taught as a police officer. Cops were supposed to always be reachable. She took 9th Avenue down to West 15th Street and parked outside Chelsea Market. She unloaded Rolf and led him into the building, keeping her head on a swivel. Vic had sounded a little strange on the phone and she didn't want to take any chances.

Vic was waiting for her outside the bakery. He was wearing a shoulder bag like a Wall Street guy would use for a laptop, which looked out of place strapped across his bulky frame. He had his arms crossed and was leaning against the wall in what he apparently thought was an inconspicuous posture. Market patrons were giving him a wide berth.

"Okay, Mr. Secret Agent," Erin said. "I got your creepy, cryptic message. What's the deal?"

"I needed to see you," he said. "But I didn't want to say where, in case the phone was bugged."

"Your phone? Or mine?"

"Either. Both. That's why I had you turn yours off. They can track our GPS."

"Who's 'they,' Vic?"

"That prick Keane, for one." Vic glanced around, as if Keane might suddenly materialize from a nearby doorway.

"So you think he did it, too," Erin said.

"Huh? Did what? What're you talking about?"

"He killed Kira."

Vic blinked. "Holy shit," he said. "You're serious?"

"Of course I'm serious!" she retorted. "Isn't that what this is all about? Why did you want to meet off-grid? Why the secrecy?"

"I wanted to meet away from the Eightball because that jerkoff shut us down," he growled. "As soon as I got into work this morning, Webb told me to go talk to the eggheads downstairs. He thought Kira might've had something important on her hard drive, so he wanted me to light a fire under the nerds and get the drive copied. But when I got there, they told me IAB had already laid claim to it. This little pencil-neck dipshit about half my age told me I didn't have permission to access the files!"

"So what did you do?" Erin asked.

"I said I'd exercise my back-door access to his colon with my size fourteen password," Vic said. "Then I said a couple things about his mom and left."

"Keane's got the hard drive," she said heavily.

"Yeah. Did he really shoot Kira?"

"Either he did it or he had somebody else do it."

"Jesus! I'm gonna friggin' kill him!"

"No, you're not."

"Oh, so you know what I'm not gonna do?" Vic's eyes had gone very cold and hard. "You think I can't? Or you think I won't? Because I guarantee I can, and I'm pretty damn sure I will."

"Stop it!" she snapped. "Quit it with the macho bullshit! You're not going to kill an Internal Affairs Lieutenant!"

"Say it a little louder, why don't you?" Vic suggested. "I think maybe some of the civilians might not have heard us."

Erin glanced around. Nobody was paying them the slightest attention except Rolf, who was watching her attentively.

"We have to be smart about this," she said in a lower voice. "Because Keane's smart, and he's a step ahead of us. If you go putting rounds in an IAB cop, you'll lose your shield for sure. Plus you'll end up in prison. Then you'll spend the next ten to twenty dodging shivs in the shower instead of watching your kid grow up."

"I'm gonna get him," Vic insisted. "Somehow."

"We'll get him together," she promised. "But we'll do it the right way, like cops. Not gangsters."

"You're one to talk," he said, but his eyes thawed just a little. "Okay, Miss By-the-Book. What's our next move?"

"That depends," she said. "What've you got in your bag? You said Keane took the computer."

"Keane took the computer we had at the Eightball," he said with a small, nasty smile. "He overlooked the backup unit."

"Backup unit?"

"Under Kira's bed. I found it in one of those fireproof boxes people use for their important documents."

"Wasn't it locked?"

"Yeah. Kira probably had the key on her, but I couldn't get into her pockets. Hank and Ernie had already carted her off to the morgue. So I took it home and crowbarred it open."

Erin stared at him, appalled. "You took evidence from an active crime scene? To your *house*?!"

He shrugged. "I didn't know what was in it. If I'd jacked the box open on the spot, CSU would've catalogued it and Keane could've grabbed it too. How do you know he's the one who killed her?"

"I'll explain later. Don't change the subject. That's not just against regs, Vic. It's a crime! You robbed Kira's apartment! I don't believe this!"

"And it's a damn good thing I did," he said. "Because otherwise we wouldn't have the drive. I put it in my personal laptop and got it the hell out of the office. I don't know what crap IAB has on our intranet, but I'm guessing they monitor our computer usage. This is some *1984* crap, I shit you not."

"What did Webb say about this?" she asked.

"He doesn't know."

"You didn't tell him? Oh, this gets better and better."

"It's for his own good. The poor guy's about to start collecting his pension. The last thing he needs is to get fired. What he doesn't know can't bite him in the ass."

"But you had no problem telling me about it and putting my ass on the line?"

The small, nasty smile was back on Vic's face. "None," he said.

"You haven't looked at the files yet?"

He shook his head. "I figured we'd do it together. I'm parked on West 15th."

"Me, too," Erin said. "Where do you want to go?"

"Public Library," he suggested. "And then you're gonna explain the part where our IAB boss is a friggin' murderer and how we're gonna throw his ass behind bars for the rest of his goddamn life."

Erin nodded absently. She was turning toward the exit and found their path blocked by a pair of men in off-the-rack suits. They were wearing sunglasses, but she recognized the one on the right. She thought the other one was also familiar.

"Sergeant Worthington," she said.

"O'Reilly," he replied. Cormack Worthington was in Precinct 8's Internal Affairs squad, a big guy with enormous shoulders. He'd played college football, and departmental rumor said he'd been involved in an iffy incident prior to his transfer to IAB.

"What's going on here?" Vic demanded. Neither he nor Erin believed for one second that it was a coincidence, running into a pair of Keane's guys.

"You tell me," Worthington said. "What's in the bag?"

"My computer," Vic said.

"Let's have a look," Worthington said.

"My *personal* computer," Vic clarified. "It's not NYPD property, which means you've got about as much right to see it as I do to check the color of your boxer shorts. They're pink, aren't they? Little hearts on them?"

"This is a stop-and-frisk," Worthington said. "Johns, check him."

"This is bullshit is what this is," Vic said. "You don't stop and frisk a Major Crimes detective. I'm warning you, buddy—"

"Don't make any sudden moves," Johns said. He was a smaller man than Worthington, but Erin figured him for the more dangerous of the two. He'd once been in ESU as a sniper. He had cool, calculating eyes that reminded her uncomfortably of Ian Thompson.

"Sergeant, you'd better explain yourself," Erin said.

"You keep out of this, O'Reilly," Worthington said. "You're on suspension and under suspicion. Back off, and keep control of that dog. We don't want this turning into anything unpleasant."

Johns stepped forward and held out a hand. "The bag, Detective," he said.

Vic sighed. "I always wondered how civvies felt when we stopped them for no good reason," he said. "I guess this is what it feels like. It kinda sucks."

"*Now*," Johns said. His left hand was still extended, but his right was hovering next to the grip of his pistol.

"Okay, okay," Vic said. "Sheesh." He pulled the strap of the shoulder bag over his head.

"I'm glad we could work this out," Worthington said.

"I'm gonna want a receipt for that," Vic said.

"I think we'll keep the paperwork to a minimum," Worthington said. "But you have my word, you'll get your machine back in perfect order. We just need to run a few routine—"

Erin never found out what lie Worthington was about to tell. Vic, in the process of handing the bag to Johns, abruptly flicked his wrist. The bag swung out and up, whipping around the back of the other officer's neck. Vic pulled and stepped forward.

Johns was quick on his feet. He reacted fast, but he lost a crucial half-second recovering his balance. His left hand wrapped around the shoulder strap about halfway up. His right snatched out his gun. But before he could bring the weapon in line, Vic looped the trailing end of the strap around the Glock's slide. The weight of the bag dragged the gun sideways as Vic let go of the strap. Then the big Russian got his hand around Johns' gun hand, twisting and flexing. The pistol clattered to the floor.

Erin couldn't believe what she was seeing. For once, her street instincts deserted her and she just stood there, gaping and watching a fight between a couple of New York's Finest.

Johns punched Vic on the shoulder with his free hand, which had no effect whatsoever. In response, Vic twisted Johns' right wrist harder. Johns went to his knees with a cry of pain.

"You pull a gun?" Vic roared. "You pull a goddamn *gun* on me?!"

Worthington extended his arms and charged Vic as if he'd been the opposing team's defensive line. He tackled the big Russian, sending the two of them straight through the doorway into the Fat Witch Bakery and leaving Johns on the ground.

Someone—it sounded like Dana Featherwood—screamed. Rolf, stiff-legged and bristling, started barking his head off.

The K-9's barking broke Erin's momentary paralysis. She saw Johns begin to recover, the man groping for his discarded Glock. Erin sprang forward and kicked the pistol. It spun away from Johns and into the bakery. She followed it in, Rolf right at her side.

They were just in time to see Vic struggle free and roll to his feet. Worthington gave a snort that reminded Erin absurdly of a bad-tempered bull and rushed him again. Vic was ready this time. The IAB Sergeant was a shade taller than Vic and much heavier, so Vic didn't try to match him strength for strength. Instead, he let his left shoulder fall back just before impact, grabbed Worthington's collar with his left hand and his belt with his right, and launched the ex-football player headlong.

Worthington would have gone an impressive distance, if not for the bakery's display counter. He got one arm up in the nick of time, which partially shielded his head and face. Glass shattered. The big man's upper body stuck halfway through the counter, face down in a tray of croissants. He lay there, stunned or unconscious.

There was a moment in which the only sound was the tinkle of broken glass as shards rained down onto the floor. Dana, behind the counter, had her hands over her mouth. Her eyes were very wide and she'd stopped screaming, too shocked to speak. Even Rolf had stopped barking.

"Holy shit," Erin breathed. "What did you just do?"

Vic cursed and ran back out of the bakery, not sparing Worthington as much as a parting glance. It took Erin a second to realize what Vic already had; Vic's bag had been left on the corridor floor, where he'd dropped it during his scuffle with Johns.

Erin and Rolf sprinted after Vic. Worthington was moving fitfully, so at least he wasn't dead. Erin wouldn't normally have left a fellow officer in such a state, but she had the feeling if she tried to help, she'd be likely to get a fist or even a bullet in return.

Johns was already halfway to the exit, running hard. Vic was trying to close on him, but the other guy had a substantial lead. Vic was in good shape, but he was a big guy who relied more on strength than speed. Johns was built like a runner and he moved like one. He'd easily make it outside before Vic or Erin could catch him.

However, they weren't the only pursuers available. Erin unclipped Rolf's collar. In a back corner of her mind she knew this was dangerous. Johns was NYPD, and it could be argued he was just doing his job. Siccing a K-9 on him wasn't just against the Patrol Guide. It could cost her shield.

"Rolf, *fass!*" she snapped, thrusting the fear aside. Reasons would occur to her later; in the moment, all she had to go on was instinct.

Rolf had none of Erin's compunctions. What he felt was the thrill of the chase. His breeding had molded him into what he was, and his training had forged and sharpened his raw material into a near-perfect instrument of pursuit. His claws scrabbled on the hard tile for an instant. Then he found purchase and was off.

A German Shepherd's running speed topped out at about thirty miles per hour. The fastest a human sprinter had ever managed was a shade under twenty-eight. That had been Usain Bolt, and Officer Johns might be fast, but he was no Usain Bolt. Rolf's paws ate up the ground between them. The dog shot past Vic like he was standing still.

Johns made it to the Market's entrance. He shoved one of the glass doors open on the fly. As he ran through, he looked back over his shoulder to see how close his pursuers had gotten.

What he saw was an open mouth full of fangs, airborne and inbound at high velocity.

Johns gave a startled gasp and covered his face with his right arm. That was a mistake. Rolf was trained to go for the right arm. He barreled into Johns and knocked him flat. The K-9's momentum carried him clean over the falling man, but he had a good grip on his target's arm and didn't let go. The result was ninety pounds of police dog yanking Johns' arm up and over his head with incredible force.

Erin wasn't close enough to hear the quiet pop of the shoulder joint as it dislocated, but Johns' scream was so loud it would have drowned it out anyway. Rolf did a full somersault and landed on his back. He twisted weasel-like back onto his paws, still holding his prize in his mouth, which did Johns' shoulder no favors. The dog crouched over the prone man, growling through a mouthful of arm.

Vic got there ahead of Erin, thanks to his head start. He unbuckled his bag from across Johns' chest.

"I oughta arrest you, jackass," he told the IAB guy.

Johns' reply was a moan. His face had turned sheet white from pain and shock.

"But I guess I can't," Vic went on, fastening the strap around his own body. "Next time I see you, though, I'm gonna kick your ass."

"Vic!" Erin gasped, joining him. "We have to get out of here."

"Great idea," he said. "Lead the way."

"Copy that," she said. "Rolf, *pust!*"

Rolf immediately released his grip. He grinned at her, wagging his tail and waiting to be told what a good boy he was. He already knew it, of course, but that didn't mean he ever got tired of hearing it.

"*Sei brav,* kiddo," she said. "We have to go. *Fuss!*"

Puzzled but loyal, Rolf padded alongside his partner. She'd forgotten to give him his Kong ball; a temporary oversight, no doubt.

Erin headed for her car. "Where are you parked?" she asked Vic.

"Doesn't matter," he said. "I'm ditching the Taurus and riding with you."

"How come?"

"We'd better stick together. Besides, they'll be looking for my car."

"Mine, too," she said. But she didn't argue the point. She popped the rear compartment for Rolf and slipped into the driver's seat. Vic climbed into the passenger side and Erin stomped the accelerator, earning an irritated honk from a New York driver on West 15th.

Rolf thrust his muzzle between the seats and panted at her, giving her a faceful of dog breath.

Erin pulled out his black rubber ball and flicked it over his head. He snapped at it like a striking snake, snagging it in midair. His head retreated back into his compartment, from which wet squeaking sounds began to emanate.

* * *

For a few minutes, Rolf's squeaking Kong was the only sound in the vehicle. Vic seemed content with the relative quiet.

"Jesus," she finally said. "You beat up a couple Internal Affairs cops."

"Yeah," Vic said. "That was fun."

"It was stupid," she said. "Do you have any idea how much trouble we're in?"

"You're telling me! You had your mutt take a chunk out of that guy! He's gonna need stitches!"

"He'll need his shoulder set," she said. "He'll be in a sling for weeks! And yeah, probably some stitches, too. What were you thinking?"

"I was thinking if they're so desperate for that evidence, we'd better make damn sure they didn't get it."

"Did it occur to you that those guys might've just been doing their jobs?"

Vic didn't answer.

"Vic?" she said.

"Yeah," he said heavily. "Shit, I'm sorry. I thought... I figured maybe this would help. You'd better take me back to the Eightball."

"What? Why?"

"So I can hand in my shield and sidearm. You take the computer and see what you can do with it. I'll tell the Captain it was all me, I picked the fight with those jerks. None of this needs to come back on you."

"Are you out of your mind, Vic?"

"I'm not letting you take the hit on this one," he insisted. "I'll swear I'm the only one who hit anybody. You were just a bystander."

"Shut up!" she snapped. "Stop being a goddamn martyr and think! Johns has Rolf's tooth marks on his arm! Unless you're ready to tell a board of inquiry that you ripped a man's arm out of its socket with your teeth, I don't think they're going to believe you!"

"That's... a good point," he admitted. "And I don't suppose those two assholes would go along with the story anyway. But it was worth a try."

"I appreciate the thought," she said. "Anyway, you're worrying about the wrong thing. Forget the inquiry; there won't be one."

"We kicked the shit out of two Internal Affairs boys," he said. "Keane's gonna be all over this. He's gonna want our scalps on his desk!"

"But it won't be official," she said. "Remember what Worthington said? He didn't want any paperwork. This is happening off the books. The last thing they want is attention. So stop worrying about your job. What you should be worrying about is getting shot in the head."

Vic considered this. "You're saying Keane's got people doing dirty work inside the Department?" he asked.

"And outside it, too," she replied.

"So he's some sort of crime boss now?"

"Looks that way."

"God, I hope Kira found something we can use."

Erin tried not to think of the alternative. "Me, too," she said under her breath.

Chapter 16

Erin switched on the car's police-band radio. The familiar patter of the NYPD poured out of the speakers. Vic drummed his fingers restlessly on his armrest. Rolf continued happily chewing his rubber ball.

"Jesus," Vic said. "I don't want to hear about friggin' traffic stops and purse-snatchers! Who gives a shit? Put on some music or something."

"Shush," Erin said. "I'm trying to listen."

"For what? You think Keane's gonna confess on air?"

"For a 10-13."

"Do we really have time to help out another cop? I hate to break it to you, Erin, but *we're* the cops who need help, and I don't think we can put out a call for backup just now."

"Not for us! For Johns and Worthington. Think about it. We just incapacitated two NYPD officers. Johns was still conscious and he must've at least had a phone. Even if he didn't, the Market was full of bystanders. There've been a dozen 911 calls by now, bet on it. So why aren't we hearing about it over the net?"

"Huh." Vic considered this. "One of those losers must've called Dispatch and shut things down. You were right. They're keeping it quiet."

"You know what that means?"

"It means we're not the only ones who've gone rogue," he said. "Shit, they really want to kill us."

"*Now* do you believe me about Keane and Kira?"

"Yeah. But how did you know?"

"She isn't his first murder." Erin quickly outlined her thoughts about the Lieutenant.

"Damn," Vic said when she'd finished. "We have to take this to somebody."

"Who?" she asked.

"Captain Holliday, I guess. He can send it up the line. Crap, that won't work. If he does it by the book, and Cap's gonna want to run this according to regs, that means an official inquiry. How long will that take? What happens in the meantime? Our sorry asses will get burned a long time before anybody puts the cuffs on Keane."

"Yeah," Erin said.

"And we can't arrest him ourselves," Vic went on. "If we had the evidence we could try. But we don't have either. I don't suppose you've still got an in with the Commissioner?"

She shook her head. "I think I burned that bridge when I turned down his promotion offer. It hurt his feelings. Anyway, for all we know, he'll be on Keane's side."

"You mean the PC is dirty?" Vic raised his eyebrows, but didn't immediately discount the idea. "If that's true, we're gonna have to tear the Department right down to the foundations. I gotta be honest with you, I don't think we're up for that."

"I don't know if it's quite *that* bad," she said. "But it's bad enough, if Keane can send his people out on jobs like this."

"That's for sure," Vic said. "I still can't believe Johns drew on me!"

"You nearly drew on me last year," she reminded him. "When you thought I'd killed that witness."

"Well, yeah, but that's different. In my defense, you were *trying* to make it look like you were a murderer! What was I supposed to think?"

"I'm still sorry about that. I should've told you the truth."

"Damn right."

"Vic?"

"Yeah?"

"You didn't know those IAB dicks wouldn't report you."

"That's true."

"You've got a kid on the way! You could lose your job!"

"We're talking about guys trying to kill us. If that doesn't stop me, you think threatening my paycheck is gonna even slow me down?"

"It was stupid of you."

"I never claimed to be smart. What's your excuse?"

"My partner needed backup."

"Thanks." Vic looked away. "Sorry."

"Forget about it," Erin said. "We're here. Let's see what's on that drive before anything else happens."

* * *

Once inside the Public Library, they went to a computer docking station, where Vic plugged his laptop in. Erin stood back while the machine powered up and took a few moments familiarizing herself with the terrain and its inhabitants. She marked every possible exit and made sure she knew where everybody else was. No one seemed to be paying them any attention, but she wasn't assuming anything. Rolf settled beside her, lying on his belly but with his hind legs under him and his head up. The dog wasn't resting; he was waiting for orders.

"You know, the last time I was here I got in a gunfight upstairs," Erin commented.

"I know," Vic said. "I'm still pissed you didn't bring me along."

"I wonder if they cleaned the bloodstains out of the carpet yet."

"Probably. Health hazard. Anyway, cold water takes care of those pretty well."

"How's it coming?" She leaned over his shoulder.

"Beats me. I'm a street cop, not a techie dweeb. I think I'm in. Here's what Kira had on her hard drive."

The computer screen was full of file folders and documents. Erin and Vic looked over the titles for a few moments.

"Try that one," Erin suggested, pointing at the folder labeled CHASE.

"Chase Bank?" Vic said. "Like the deposit box? Yeah, I like it." He clicked on the folder, then groaned. A password prompt glared out at them, the cursor blinking mockingly.

"This must be what we're looking for," Erin said. "But is it Kira's password, or Ward's?"

"Why would it be Ward's?" Vic asked. "This isn't his computer."

"Look at all the folders," Erin said. "They updated at the same time. That means this was an automatic backup drive. She probably had it back up everything daily. An encrypted file would be copied, same as the others. We'd just need the same password we'd need for the original."

"Great," Vic growled. "Good thing we're in a library. Should I grab a dictionary and start with the A's?"

"I wouldn't," she said. "It'll probably lock us out if we miss too many guesses."

"Then we're screwed," he said. "It's not gonna be some dumbass, obvious answer. Real people put shit like numbers and exclamation points in their passwords. The whole point is you're not supposed to be able to guess them."

Erin snapped her fingers. "That's it!" she said.

"If I'm right, why are you happy about it?" he demanded.

"You're wrong," she said. "I mean, you're right, but you're still wrong."

"Even if I am, I'm the one making sense here," he said. "Did you hit your head back at the bakery?"

"You're right about a normal password," she said. "But Ward wasn't trying to keep everybody out. This is part of the game. Ward *wants* us to be able to figure this out."

Vic groaned again and clapped a hand over his face. "Here we go again," he muttered.

"Remember his note? How'd it go? '*If you have the answer, you get more answers. The name you're looking for is the key that locks him away.*'"

"Okay," Vic said. "What the hell is that supposed to mean?"

"If we have the answer, we get more answers," she murmured. "I think he means we're already supposed to know what's in the file."

"What kind of sense does that make? If we did, we wouldn't need to get into the file in the first place!"

"I think it's his idea of a joke," she said. "What if he means the password has something to do with what's inside?"

"'*The name you're looking for is the key*,'" he said.

"And a password is a kind of key," Erin said. "Try 'Keane.'"

"Just that? Five lousy letters?"

"Humor me."

He sighed. "Okay, here goes." His keyboard clacked. He pressed ENTER.

The password prompt vanished and the file sprang open.

"Holy shit," he said. "I can't believe that worked."

The screen was packed with icons. Erin saw image files, spreadsheets, and word-processor documents. All of them had weird, cryptic headings.

"It's gonna take days to go through all this," Vic said. "Where do we start?"

"That one," Erin said, pointing to a text file called GAMEOVER.

He snorted. "Why not?" He opened the file. He and Erin started reading.

Quis custodiet ipsos custodes, qui custodes custodiunt?

I keep asking myself that. I'm the watchman. Internal Affairs watches me. But who watches them? And what about those watchman-watcher-watchers? At some point, is it just watchmen all the way down?

Tick tock. I have to keep focused. Not much time left. Go back and edit for clarity, if I can.

You're reading this. Of course you are, otherwise I'd be talking to myself, and that only happens if I circle back through it. Round and round. Focus, Bill. Focus. Good thing I'm typing, not writing longhand. Fingers are a little shaky from all the oxy.

Okay, where was I? You're reading this. Congratulations! You figured it out! You win the prize! An all-expenses-paid trip to where I live, where everybody's out to get you and yelling for help only attracts their attention. It's an awesome place. You'll love it here. You can have my spot. I won't be needing it much longer.

Fun fact: if the NYPD sacks you, you lose your pension. Do not pass GO, do not collect $200. But if you die on duty, your family gets full benefits, even if—wait for it—even if you eat a nine-mil sandwich you made yourself! Isn't that wild? No insurance company on Earth pays out life insurance for self-inflicted GSW, but the NYPD has you covered. I know, *because I triple-checked it. You have to know these things. They could save your life. Well, maybe the opposite of saving it. Ha ha. Get it?*

Maybe it's because of all the PTSD. They figure the least they can do is give your widow and kid a little something to make up for wrecking your life and your emotional stability. You're still out there doing it, tearing yourself apart a piece at a time. And I bet you think I'm *the crazy one right about now!*

How many times did I haul in some blubbering loser and he starts in about how he never meant any of it to happen, it wasn't supposed to go like this? But that joke's on me, because it's true. This wasn't plan A. This is more like plan AA. Get it? Because I'm a recovering... never mind. You get it.

I hope like hell you're the right person to get this. It's hard making a maze you intend to be solvable, but not too easy. It's almost impossible making a maze for one specific *person to solve. Are you the right one? No way to know.*

Anyway, this isn't my testament. That's in my will, properly notarized. My lawyer's got it, along with a bunch of other useful papers and stuff. That's family business, and none of yours. Please don't show this to my wife. She might not understand.

Damn, not much time left. Where was I? Oh yeah. I never meant it to go like this. I was just minding my own beeswax, making honey the old-fashioned way, pounding pavement, working the good old Task Force. Easy enough job, right? Get in with this biker gang, they're dealing smack, find out where they hang, give the Narcotics boys enough to shut the bastards down. Basic undercover gig.

But surprise! I get a call from this Internal Affairs jerk! He wants to meet, off-site and off the record. This is around New Year's. See attached spreadsheet. I got dates, I got times and places. It's all there. So I go to this skeezy bar and we talk. He's a slick son of a bitch. And he's not even in my AOS. What's he doing with me?

Turns out he knows everything about me. Sure, I got clean a while back, but that doesn't matter, y'know? He's got evidence. Hard evidence. That's it; goodbye job, goodbye pension. The booze is one thing; practically everybody hits the sauce sometimes. But the pills? It was on account of that knee injury, the one a couple years back. Took oxy for the pain, found out I couldn't kick the habit so easy. Get it? I couldn't kick, on account of having a bad knee...

Shit, I'm rambling again. So hard to focus. I'll be glad when this is over. So damn tired. Just gotta finish.

This guy... why can't I write his name? He says I'm in trouble, but he knows I'm solid, and he doesn't want me to lose my chance, doesn't want my wife to find out about any of it. If I go to work for him, I get to keep my shield and my pension. I figure he wants me to spy on my own guys. I tell him if that's what he wants, he can stick it up his ass.

He just smiles and says that's okay, that's not the job. I'm setting up something important, some kind of sting operation. I just need to make deliveries and take deliveries for the Roadkillers. Same deal as before, except now they know I'm a cop.

They know I'm a cop! What gives? I don't know, but I figure it's gotta be on the up and up, right? So I do as I'm told.

I was wrong. He was playing me. There's no sting. This is a private enterprise. Individual capitalism. He's investing in the private sector. It's what made this country great, right?

He's actually a drug dealer! You believe that? He's running a major criminal concern and he's doing it right in the heart of the NYPD! But he lost his supplier around the end of last year, so he's getting Mexican brown from the Roadkillers. And get this! He's also working with their competition, those Mexican Crazy Knives guys! Cuchillos Locos. *So I end up making deliveries to those guys, too. In for a penny, in for a dime bag.*

This is what he does. He gets cops who owe him, and he leans on them a little, and then he leans a lot, and then he owns you.

He owns me. I'm in too deep now. If I try to expose him, he'll drag me down with him. Either he'll have me killed, or he'll settle for trashing my career and sending me upstate. Either way, I'm toast. But what choice do I have?

Two days ago he ordered me to take care of a problem for him. He found out somebody's sniffing around his backside, like a friendly little dog. He wants me to arrange a little accident. It's that or I go down.

Here's the ironic thing. If it wasn't for that, I'd never have thought to take this to you. I would've assumed he owned you too, girl. After all, you're working for him. If he wants you out of the way, it means you're actually someone who can hurt him. Because he doesn't trust you, maybe I can.

Here's my one and only request. Hurt this son of a bitch. Make him squirm, make him scream. But don't say it was me who did it, okay? If I know, I'll know. If not, no harm done.

Keane.

There, I said it. That wasn't even so hard to do. He's the guy you want. I pulled the trigger, but he killed me. J'accuse! I accuse you, Lieutenant Andrew Keane!

KEANE!!!

God, I feel like William Shatner. You know the scene. Star Trek II, *when he gets marooned? And he screams "KHAAAAN!"*

If this ever gets made into a movie, don't have Shatner play me, okay? Too old, too hammy. Okay, that's two requests.

Crap, I used up my window. I was supposed to take care of the Jones problem in forty-eight hours. That was forty-six hours ago. I'll stash this in the box at Chase, as you know by now. That's the last of the breadcrumbs.

The birds ate the crumbs in that story, you know. People always forget that part. Breadcrumbs are shitty signposts. Next thing you know, you're lost in the woods and there's a gingerbread cottage in front of you. Either you or the witch ends up getting cooked.

Throw this goddamn witch in the oven where he belongs. Burn him to ashes.

"Wow," Erin said as Vic scrolled to the end of the note.

"This guy was not okay," Vic said.

"He was supposed to kill Kira," she said. She almost choked on the words.

"Yeah," Vic said. "But he didn't. He wouldn't. He'd rather die than kill one of ours. I gotta respect that."

"You don't get it," she said. She could feel sobs trying to climb up her throat and rip their way out of her. She swallowed, trying to force them down.

"What don't I get?"

"Keane found out Kira was spying on him."

"I guess so. That was pretty ballsy of her. And it gives us our motive."

Erin was shaking her head. "No! I told her to do it! I persuaded her. Both these cops are dead because of me!"

"I oughta smack you!" Vic snapped with sudden, startling anger.

Erin reflexively shied back. "I'm sorry," she whispered. "It's all my fault." She wasn't going to be able to hold back the tears much longer.

"Stop it! We don't have time for your bullshit! You self-indulgent brat!"

Vic had insulted Erin plenty of times, but this was different. This was white-hot, righteous anger. She'd only had it aimed at her once before, when Vic had thought she'd killed Teresa Tommasino. Vic was always an intimidating guy, but his rage was straight-up terrifying.

"You think this is about *you?*" he demanded. He was keeping his voice pitched low, since they were in a library and he didn't want to attract attention, but that only intensified him, like the thin beam of a blowtorch.

"If I hadn't—" she began.

"Bullshit!" he interrupted her. "That's like saying a girl deserves to get raped because she walks down the wrong alley or wears the wrong friggin' shirt! You and Kira were investigating a criminal! If you're gonna blame yourself for that, you'd better let Webb hang onto that precious gold shield of yours, because you should never go after another bad guy! I can't believe this crap! You didn't make Ward shoot himself and you sure as shit didn't make Keane kill Kira! You know why we carry weapons? Because when we corner the bad guys, sometimes they fight back! Does that mean we let them walk? Then we might as well hand guys like him the keys to the friggin' city, because they'll own it!"

Vic finally ran out of breath and stopped. He was breathing hard, nostrils flaring. He reminded Erin of a pissed-off bull moose she'd once seen on a nature program. Suddenly, oddly, she felt like laughing instead of crying. Or maybe doing both.

"You finished?" she asked, not entirely trusting her own voice.

"Yeah, pretty much. You done being an idiot?"

"I think so."

"Good. Now, we don't know how valuable the evidence on this drive is. We need to go through it."

"The first thing we need to do is make copies," Erin said. "And we need to get them to Holliday and Webb. But we need to spread this out."

"You really think that's a good idea?"

"It's the only idea," she said grimly. "As long as this is the only copy outside Keane's possession, he'll think he may be able to keep a lid on this. And that means he'll probably try to kill us and take it."

"I hope he does," Vic said. "Then I can blast his friggin' guts out."

"You told me once you didn't like killing," she reminded him.

"There's exceptions," he said. "But yeah, you're right. These files are too big to e-mail, and we'd better keep them off the network, in case Keane's got some sort of monitoring software. We'll need some thumb drives. Let's stop by a Best Buy and pick up a few. Then I can copy the data while you drive, and we can deliver them to the Captain and Webb at the Eightball."

"Sounds like a plan," Erin said. "But we need to do it discreetly."

"I'm discreet," Vic said.

"You're loud and aggressive. That's the opposite of discreet. And I'm suspended, remember?"

"Does Holliday have the authority to arrest Keane?" Vic wondered as he shut his laptop lid and they started for the exit.

"If the evidence is solid enough," Erin said. "Hell, you or I could do it in a pinch. At least, if I wasn't suspended I could."

"I'm still on active duty," he said. "Can I just walk up into his office and cuff him?"

"It'd be risky," she said. "If this evidence doesn't hold up, that'd be it for your career."

"I could always become a stay-at-home dad," he said. "I could spend my time cleaning house and teaching Mina how to castrate would-be date-rapists."

"You really think that'd work?" Erin asked.

"Sure!" he said. "What you gotta do is, you come in with a low thrust with your knife—"

"That wasn't what I meant," she said. "Now let's go to the Eightball. But first, I need to swing by home."

"Why?"

"I have to change clothes."

"Erin, that's the girliest thing I've ever heard you say."

"Oh, and do you have a spare gun I could borrow? This snub .38 is better than nothing, but not much."

"Okay, that's more like it. Here, I'll swap you my Sig for the AR-15 you have in the car. If the shit goes down, I wouldn't mind the rifle."

"Jesus, Vic, we're going to our station, not Fallujah. This isn't going to turn into a war zone."

"Says the girl who just asked me for a bigger gun."

Chapter 17

While Vic waited in the car and copied Ward's files to the external drives they'd picked up en route, Erin ran up to her apartment. She found Carlyle sipping coffee and reading the newspaper.

"Everything all right, darling?" he asked as she blew past him into the bedroom.

"That's a complicated question," she replied, stripping off her shirt. She changed into her special bra, the one with the hidden microphone, and put on a fresh blouse.

"Anything I ought to be fretting over?" he asked from the doorway.

"Maybe," she said. "Vic and I are about to go deliver some evidence that'll probably put Lieutenant Keane behind bars."

"So he's the one who did for poor Miss Jones?"

"Among others, yeah." Erin grabbed a handful of spare cartridges for her revolver and stuffed them into her pocket, just in case. "Once we get the stuff to the Captain, I think we'll be okay. But things might get a little hairy. Keane has guys working for him."

"What sort of lads?"

"Both kinds," she said. "Cops and mopes."

"I'll have a talk with Mr. Mason downstairs," Carlyle said. "I hate to close the doors again, so soon after our grand reopening, but if you're thinking it's necessary…"

"No," she said. "We need to keep up appearances as much as we can. Vic, Rolf, and I beat up two of Keane's guys, but he may not know what we've got yet. If we can keep him in the dark another couple of hours, it'll help."

"Anything else you're needing?"

She leaned in and gave him a quick kiss on the cheek. "A little luck and a little time," she said. "Oh, and keep tabs on this."

She handed him one of the thumb drives. It had been the first one Vic had copied. Carlyle turned it over in his hand.

"What's this?" he asked.

"Insurance," she said. "If anything happens to Vic and me, I want you to leak this all over the city. Newspapers, TV, whoever. Call that blonde bimbo from Channel Six, Holly Gardner, and everyone else you can think of. The password is 'Keane,' K-E-A-N-E. Got it?"

"Aye. Be careful, darling."

She gave him a half smile. "I'll try, but you know I can't promise anything."

* * *

From the Barley Corner it was only a short jaunt to the Precinct 8 station. Erin drove the Charger into the basement garage, distinctly aware that when she scanned her NYPD ID at the entrance, a computer somewhere was logging her.

It was the middle of the day shift, just before lunch, so the garage was almost empty of squad cars. Erin squeezed the recorder in her underwire, activating the microphone. Then she popped the Charger's trunk and grabbed Rolf's Kevlar vest. After she'd strapped the Velcro fasteners around him, she put on her own body armor. Then she pulled her jacket over it, concealing the protection.

"Shit," Vic muttered. "I left my vest in my car. You really think anybody's gonna shoot at us?"

"I never expect it," she said. "But I try to be ready for it. Now, this should be quick and easy. Up to the second floor, straight into Holliday's office. Don't stop, don't talk to anybody else. We'll get Webb afterward."

"Copy that," Vic said. He had Erin's AR-15 in his hands and was running a quick check on the rifle. "Stairs or elevator?"

"Stairs," Erin said.

They jogged up the concrete steps, Rolf's tongue hanging out. The K-9's tail wagged eagerly. The vest meant work, and work was *fun*. He could hardly wait to see what would happen. He just wished his partner would run a little faster.

"It's gonna be fine," Vic said out of the side of his mouth. "The Captain's got our back. So does Webb."

They spilled out of the stairwell onto the second floor. Erin was thinking what she'd say to Captain Holliday. To tell him this was an irregular situation was putting it mildly. But Vic was right. Holliday was a fair-minded, reasonable man who'd always done his best for the officers under his command. If they could trust anyone in the Eightball, it was Holliday.

Several people were in Major Crimes. Zofia Piekarski was sitting at her desk. She was wearing a complicated system of straps and buckles, like the sort of thing the ESU door kickers used for their gear, but instead of extra ammunition and radios, she had a baby strapped to her chest. Tiny arms and legs dangled. The baby had a pacifier in its mouth.

Captain Holliday was standing in his office doorway. Lieutenant Webb was beside him. They were talking to a trio of men who had their backs to the stairs. The right arm of the one on the left was in a sling. The man in the middle was clad in a very nice suit, freshly pressed and laundered. His hair was black, slicked down, and perfectly combed.

"Oh, shit," Vic said under his breath.

Piekarski was the first to spot them. "Look, Mina!" she said in the high-pitched tone people used on babies. "There's Daddy!" She held the tiny wrist between her thumb and forefinger and gave a little wave. But Piekarski's smile froze on her face when she saw the look in Vic's eyes and the rifle in his hands.

The conversation stopped short. Holliday and Webb glanced toward the newcomers. Webb looked tired. Holliday's face was inscrutable, screened by his mustache, but his eyes were very serious. The other men turned to face Erin, Vic, and Rolf.

Sergeant Worthington's face was a mess. Little cuts crisscrossed his forehead and cheeks, which were puffy and swollen. Erin counted six Band-Aids. A particularly nasty gash, missing his left eye by less than half an inch, was held shut with a butterfly bandage. Johns' face was unmarked, but his sling was a clear reminder of Rolf's teeth.

Lieutenant Keane, flanked by his battered henchmen, regarded the detectives coolly, giving nothing away.

A few very awkward seconds passed. Johns drifted to one side, opening an angle. His left hand dropped to his belt. He'd shifted his sidearm to that hip to compensate for his injury. Erin wondered idly whether he was as good a shot with his left as with his right. Not everyone practiced off-hand shooting.

"Detective O'Reilly," Keane said. "I must say, I'm surprised to see you here, given your suspension. But I'm glad. Maybe you can help us clear up some troubling information that has just come to light."

"That's why I'm here," Erin said grimly. "Captain, I've got something you need to see."

"We'll get to that in a moment," Keane said. "First, would either of you like to request a Union lawyer?"

"What?" Erin said.

"You have the right to have an attorney present," Keane said. "Do you wish to waive that right?"

"I don't need a friggin' attorney," Vic snapped. "How about you, Lieutenant?"

"Detective, please," Holliday said, raising a hand. "Let's keep this civil. Lieutenant Keane has been making some serious allegations. Before we do anything else, I'm going to need you to put that rifle down."

"I'll do that the minute these guys disarm," Vic said. "Did Jigsaw over there tell you how he got that pretty face?"

Worthington flushed darkly. "Listen, jerkoff," he growled, taking a step toward Vic.

"Everyone knock it off!" Holliday said. "We need to discuss this more calmly, in a controlled space. Neshenko, I'm ordering you to safe that gun and put it on the desk in front of you."

"Sir, we didn't do a damn thing wrong," Vic said. "They're the guys you want!"

"*Now*," Holliday said, ice in his voice. "Then we'll talk."

Jaw quivering, Vic flicked the safety switch on the AR-15 and laid it on Erin's desk. "Zofia," he said quietly. "Maybe you'd better move."

Piekarski looked back and forth between the two groups of cops. "Will someone please tell me what's going on?" she asked, but she stood up and moved toward the restrooms, out of the line of fire.

"Captain, this is important," she said. "We have evidence of a conspiracy within the Department, headed by Lieutenant Keane himself."

"I told you they'd do this," Keane said. "Once they were uncovered, they'd try to deflect the blame onto someone else, probably me."

"Of course we would," Vic said. "Because you're *guilty*."

"Detective O'Reilly went to Detective Jones' apartment last night," Keane said. "She was in the company of Ian Thompson, the former Marine sniper and Mob associate. Thompson has killed no fewer than four men in the past year. The DA declined to bring charges in each case, because Detective O'Reilly was able to manipulate each situation into the appearance of self-defense or justifiable homicide, but in point of fact, former Sergeant Thompson has been serving as O'Reilly's personal assassin for several months."

"That's a lie and you know it," Erin interrupted.

"Oh, my mistake," Keane said. "Next you'll tell me Thompson didn't kill those men? Two of whom were murdered directly outside your brother's home?"

"They were kidnapping my sister-in-law!" Erin shot back.

"How convenient that the dead were members of a faction opposed to that of your lover—I'm sorry, your fiancé—in the O'Malleys," Keane continued. "Michael Connor was the greatest threat to Morton Carlyle, wasn't he? He tried to kill Carlyle at least once, in fact."

"Someone set Carlyle up," Erin said. "They planted a bomb in Mickey's car and made him think Carlyle had done it, so Mickey tried to kill us."

"And failed," Keane observed. "You killed Connor, without witnesses, while he was unarmed."

"Unarmed!" Erin echoed. "Did you *see* that guy?! He was the size of a truck! He killed people with his bare fists!"

"If Connor was such an innocent, helpless victim," Vic said, his voice dripping sarcasm, "maybe you can explain how Erin ended up in the hospital with a concussion and her dog got his ribs broken. I pulled her out from under that guy, and she was practically dead. Not to mention the half-naked woman I found tied to a chair in his hideout! I can't believe this crap!"

"This is just one incident in a pattern of behavior," Keane said. "O'Reilly has flouted the law at every step of her career, from her disregard of procedure and direct insubordination during the investigation of the Queens Museum art heist and Brunanski killing to the use of Mob associates to 'safeguard' witnesses and the reckless use of explosives in urban areas."

"I personally approved the staged bombing at the JFK Hilton," Holliday said mildly. "Nobody was hurt."

"You were not in possession of all the facts, Captain," Keane said. "Nor was I. I've been running an investigation into Detective O'Reilly's operations for some time, and I've concluded that she is attempting to build a criminal organization within the NYPD itself."

Erin's mind went completely blank from sheer outrage. It was as if her thoughts had frozen up, like a computer whose hard drive had crashed. Lame rebuttals wandered through her head. *He did that, not me,* she thought, wincing at the whiny tone of her own inner voice.

"What about me?" Vic demanded. "You saying I'm a criminal, too?"

"You are definitely implicated in some of O'Reilly's activities," Keane said. "And your prior record of excessive force is, to say the least, problematic. And then there's the question of the money."

"What money?" Vic predictably retorted.

"Fifty thousand dollars, found in your NYPD-issued vehicle," Keane said. "In cash. Drug money, in all likelihood."

Erin hoped the shock she was feeling didn't show on her face. Engrossed in the mysterious data file, she'd completely forgotten about the money Kira had found in the safe-deposit box. That money had found its way to Keane's hands, and then to his goons. They must have planted it in Vic's car outside Chelsea Market.

"I've never taken a dirty dollar in my life," Vic growled. "And you're a goddamn liar."

"I have the evidence," Keane said.

"I bet you do," Erin said. "Because you planted it there!"

"Captain!" Piekarski burst out. "You're not seriously listening to this, are you?"

The petite blonde was standing just outside the bathroom doors, hands on her hips, baby dangling from her harness; the image of angry motherhood. Give her claws and fur, Erin thought, and she'd be an undersized grizzly bear.

"This is such complete bullshit!" Piekarski went on. "Vic would never be a gangster. He always does the right thing. He's the best goddamn man I know!"

"Thank you for reminding me of another infraction against NYPD policy," Keane said. "Two lovers, serving in the same unit even while having a child together?"

"When we got together we weren't even in the same precinct, numbnuts," Vic snarled. "And neither of us requested her transfer."

"That's correct, if insubordinate," Holliday said.

"Sorry," Vic said. "I should've called him *Lieutenant* Numbnuts."

"Lieutenant Webb requested additional personnel for his unit, through proper channels," Holliday said, ignoring Vic's latest outburst. "I approved the request. Sergeant Logan in the Five agreed to transfer Officer Piekarski. He thought it would be a good stepping-stone for her toward her gold shield, and it was never intended to be anything but a temporary assignment. Neshenko had nothing to do with it, nor did Piekarski herself. She's been an exemplary officer and an asset to the squad. I have a glowing fitness report for Officer Piekarski in my office as we speak, and I would be more than happy to forward it for your review."

"That's all very well," Keane said. "But now you have a pair of rogue detectives running amok, leveling baseless accusations at Internal Affairs in a desperate bid to camouflage their own misdeeds. One of my officers is dead, Captain. I have reason to believe she was murdered either by O'Reilly, Thompson, or both. That's why O'Reilly was suspended from duty. Now I find her here, in the company of a suspected drug dealer, trying to sneak behind my back to peddle their cock-and-bull story in the hopes your dislike for IAB will cloud your judgment."

"What I like or dislike is my own business, Lieutenant," Holliday said coldly. "And I am not in the practice of allowing it to affect any of my professional duties. I'm hearing quite a few accusations coming from both sides. What I would appreciate is some evidence to back up those accusations."

"Whatever they've been able to fabricate—" Keane began.

"We didn't fabricate a damn thing, sir," Erin interrupted, speaking to Holliday. "What we've got is a collection of files compiled by Officer William Ward immediately prior to his death; files naming Lieutenant Keane as the head of a conspiracy inside the NYPD."

"Of course you do," Keane said, rolling his eyes. "And I suppose you're going to say I killed the late Officer Ward, too?"

"No," Erin admitted. "He did shoot himself."

"Then we're to take the posthumous word of a disgraced, morally compromised, suicidal street cop as gospel?" Keane asked. "An officer who was running drugs through multiple violent street gangs?"

"How did you know about the Roadkillers and the Crazy Knives, sir?" Erin asked.

"Since Jones was shot, I took over her investigation into the circumstances surrounding Ward's death," Keane said smoothly.

"You've familiarized yourself with the details of the case very quickly, sir," Erin said. "I didn't think the gang names had been filed in any reports yet. We didn't have time."

"Detective O'Reilly," Holliday said. "Why don't you tell us your version of what happened?"

"Captain—" Keane began.

Holliday silenced him with a look. "You've made your accusations, Lieutenant," he said. "O'Reilly has the right to defend herself. Detective?"

"Bill Ward was like a lot of officers in the NYPD," Erin said. "He was a good cop, but he had a problem with drinking. He went to AA meetings and managed to get sober. But he'd also gotten hooked on oxycodone after a knee injury a few years ago. That habit was harder to kick, but Ward stuck with it and got clean.

"However, around New Year's he was approached by a fellow NYPD officer. This other cop knew about Ward's substance-use history, and had enough evidence to ensure he'd get thrown off the Force if it came to light. Ward had a young kid and a wife. He needed his job. But the other officer said he'd keep quiet, if Ward did something for him. He'd even make some extra cash on the side.

"All he had to do was facilitate drug deals with a couple of biker gangs. The crooked cop needed Ward because he had contacts with the Roadkillers, and the previous distribution network had dried up."

"Why?" Holliday asked.

"His previous underworld contact was Valentino Vitelli," Erin explained. "We arrested Vitelli right after Christmas."

"Fun times," Vic commented.

"Ward went along with it," Erin said. "What choice did he have? But pretty soon there were other requests, as he got in deeper. And now he knew his blackmailer would have evidence of his drug dealing, too. He wasn't just looking at losing his job, but at jail time. Still, Ward was a good man, and he had a line he wouldn't cross. But then he was ordered to kill another NYPD officer, one who was sniffing around and got too close to the truth. And he had to do it fast.

"Ward was stuck. He wouldn't do it, couldn't. But what were his choices? He could confess, spill all the beans and hope, but his best-case outcome was dismissal from the Department. Even if he could hand his boss to the higher-ups, he'd never be able to put on a shield again. Goodbye salary, goodbye pension. And he also knew if this man would order him to kill another cop, his own life was worth just as little.

"He found a loophole in NYPD policy. If he died while he was still a cop, even by suicide, his family would still get his pension. If he went to prison, they'd get nothing. So he decided to take one for the team.

"But not only that, he wanted to give one big middle finger to the guy who'd wrecked his life. So he put together everything he had on the man and hid it somewhere safe. Then he left a trail of cryptic hints that would lead the one cop he trusted to the truth."

"Why not just drop his evidence in the mail?" Webb asked, entering the conversation for the first time. "Why make a game out of it?"

"Ward loved logic games," Erin said. "And he was pretty paranoid by that point. He didn't know how many officers were compromised. Plus, he'd started using again. Being around drugs, coupled with his guilt and the stress of his situation, made him fall off the wagon."

"So we're taking the cryptic, garbled dying words of a drug addict," Keane said. "Better and better."

"Ward spent his last night leaving messages around Hell's Kitchen," Erin said. "Kira, Vic, and I have been following them. We found a thumb drive in a deposit box at Chase Bank, along with a bundle of cash. That'd be the cash that was taken from Kira's apartment and planted in Vic's car. The drive was encrypted, but Ward gave enough hints to guess the password."

She took one of the remote drives out of her pocket and held it up. "Here's the evidence," she said.

"That's impossible," Keane snapped. "That's a different drive."

Everyone looked at him.

"I'm curious how you could possibly know that, Lieutenant," Holliday said.

Erin had to give Keane credit. He didn't flinch, or stammer, or show any of the usual tells of a man caught saying more than he should. He would've fit right in at Evan O'Malley's poker table.

"CSU recovered a remote drive from Jones' apartment," he said smoothly. "It was password-encrypted. Our technicians haven't cracked the password yet. I assumed it was the one O'Reilly was referring to in her brazen attempt to bluff me."

"You don't have to bluff when you're holding good cards, sir," Erin said. She walked across the room and extended the drive to Holliday. "We haven't had time to thoroughly examine the contents, but it's all there. Dates, times, pictures, videos, accounts. The password is 'Keane.' K-E-A-N-E."

Holliday raised an eyebrow. "I'd better not take that," he said. "We'll have it properly logged as evidence and examined. In the meantime, bag it and put it in my office."

"Captain!" Keane exclaimed. "I know you're partial to your own detectives, but are you seriously giving any credence to this story?"

"I said I'd be happy to listen to your version of events," Holliday said. "Now's the time. What is your rebuttal, Lieutenant?"

"First off, I categorically deny everything of which she has accused me," Keane said. "Although I can't quite believe I have to say it. I am not a drug dealer. I am not in league with incarcerated gangster Valentino Vitelli, or with any other member of the Lucarelli Mafia family. I am not currently engaged in any illegal operations with the Roadkillers, nor any other gang. I certainly did not order the late Officer Ward to kill Kira Jones."

"I didn't say that," Erin interrupted.

"You didn't attach my name to your slanderous little story," Keane said. "But everyone knows you were talking about me."

"No, sir," she said. "I didn't say Kira Jones was Ward's target."

Keane blinked. "Yes, you did," he said.

Erin smiled coldly. "I didn't," she said. "I just said Ward had been ordered to kill a cop. But you don't have to believe me. We can check the recording."

"What recording?" Keane demanded.

"I've been recording this conversation," she said. "I have a low-profile microphone from when I was infiltrating the O'Malleys. I'm wearing it now. It's picked up every word of your lies."

Holliday was giving Keane a stare that would have done Doc Holliday, the famous gunslinger, proud. "There's only one way you'd know that," he said quietly. "Ward was telling the truth. And so is O'Reilly."

"Nobody move."

Officer Johns was off to the side, in a perfect position to cover the rest of the room. He was holding a Glock nine-millimeter in his uninjured hand. It was pointed at Holliday and Erin.

Chapter 18

"You need to think very carefully about what you're doing," Holliday said. He sounded no more upset than if Johns had filed an unsatisfactory set of DD-5s.

"It's a little late for that," Johns said. "Don't try it, Neshenko!"

Vic froze in the act of reaching for the AR-15.

Erin stayed still, sizing up the situation. Johns was standing against the west wall, by himself. Worthington, Keane, Holliday, Rolf, and Erin were in a tight cluster next to Holliday's office. Vic was near the stairwell to the south, a few yards from Piekarski, who was at the restroom entrance. Everyone was armed, with the exception of baby Mina and maybe Piekarski, but only Johns had a weapon in hand. Erin considered Vic's Sig-Sauer, resting on her belt. She was confident she could draw and fire, but the weapon's weight would be unfamiliar. She might miss, and whether she did or not, Johns would certainly get a couple of shots off.

"What are you doing, Detective?" Holliday asked.

"Cleaning up his mess," Johns said, flicking an eye Keane's way.

"This situation was under control," Keane said.

Johns snorted. "You lost control the moment you popped Jones," he said. "How did you think that was going to end? You never should've done that, especially without clearing it with the rest of us."

"Making an accusation like that in the absence of evidence is a serious mistake," Keane said.

"Ditch the lawyer talk, boss," Johns said. "Everybody knows what happened."

"Why'd you have to do it?" Worthington interjected. "Kira was good police. She was just doing her job."

"He was saving himself," Johns said. "Same as he always does. It's always about looking out for Number One, isn't it? She got a little too close. What I can't figure is why he didn't do what he usually does and bring her into the game. Everybody's got weak spots."

"That's how you work," Erin said to Keane. Out of the corner of her eye she saw Piekarski take a slow, careful step toward Vic and the stairs. She didn't react, keeping her focus on Keane and Johns, willing them to look at her. "Being in charge of the Eightball's Internal Affairs gives you a window into all the officers assigned here. You can sift through their infractions until you find the vulnerable ones. Then you recruit them into your little ring. How many dirty cops do you have on your roster?"

"You're paranoid," Keane said. "Johns, holster that weapon right now and let's discuss this like reasonable people. We can find a solution."

"Oh, I'm being reasonable," Johns said. "But I'm done taking your orders, Lieutenant. Don't pretend you were doing anything but using us. All we could ever be was tools for you. I've done some awful shit, and I didn't even want to. You've got it all in a nice, neat file somewhere. If the shit goes down, you always figured you'd burn everyone else and get off clean. But that's not going to happen. Not this time."

"I don't know what this man is talking about," Keane said.

"I killed for you, you son of a bitch!" Johns snapped. "If you lie to me one more time I'll blow your goddamn brains out."

Piekarski took another cautious step. She was about ten feet from the stairs now. Vic drifted toward her, keeping his hands empty and open, being as nonthreatening as possible. Holliday stood very still, barely blinking as he regarded Johns.

"So what's your plan?" Holliday asked. "I understand your beef with Lieutenant Keane, but I don't see how that applies to the rest of us."

"As of right now, the only people who know the whole story are in this room," Johns said. "And until we can work out a solution, that's where we're all going to stay."

"This is an active police station," Holliday said. "You used to work ESU, Johns. You know how this is going to go. Once you barricade with hostages, there's only two outcomes. You leave in handcuffs or you leave in a body bag."

"Then we'd better figure out a third one," Johns said. "Because I'm not going to jail, and I don't mean to die here."

"You can give us Keane," Erin said. "Flip. Testify against him. We can get you immunity. You won't go to prison."

That promise was beyond her power to keep. It would be up to the District Attorney whether or not to charge him. But Erin was prepared to say whatever was necessary to keep everyone alive.

"You expect me to believe that?" Johns demanded.

"I hope not," Keane said. "Because it's nonsense. O'Reilly won't settle for partial victory. She'll want to take everyone down."

"You're burned whatever happens," Webb said to Keane in obvious disgust. "Shut up. The grownups are talking."

Erin had never expected to hear Webb suggest Lieutenant Keane was a spoiled brat. It gave her less pleasure than she would have thought.

"If you start shooting, you might get one or two of us," she told Johns. "But somebody's going to get you, I guarantee it."

"That's a good point," Johns said. "One at a time, you're going to take out your guns and put them on the floor, starting with you, O'Reilly."

"That's not going to happen," Holliday said. "If you want my sidearm, you're going to have to work for it."

Johns' finger was inside his trigger guard. It tightened slightly, the muzzle of his pistol aimed directly at Holliday. The Captain didn't flinch.

"For God's sake, man," Webb said. "There's a little kid here!"

Johns' eyes went toward Piekarski, just as the woman got close enough to the stairwell. The blonde made a break for it, sprinting toward the stairs. And everyone started moving at once.

Johns' first bullet went wide as he swung his Glock Piekarski's direction. Vic lunged between the gunman and Piekarski, grabbing Erin's desk and flipping it onto its side. The rifle tumbled to the floor, along with Erin's computer monitor, file tray, and coffee cup. The monitor screen splintered and the coffee cup shattered. Shards of ceramic spun across the room. Vic reached for his ankle and came up with a pocket-sized automatic pistol.

Piekarski took the stairs two at a time, hurtling downward as Johns' second bullet screamed by a whisker from her face, blasting a shower of plaster out of the wall just over Mina's head.

Erin snatched out Vic's Sig and racked the slide, chambering a round. Keane, Worthington, and Webb were moving too, drawing their own guns. Johns pivoted back in the direction of the group, firing as he turned. Holliday flinched but didn't go down.

Another pistol went off right next to Erin. Holliday had his gun drawn, though Erin hadn't seen him do it. His piece was a Colt .38 Special, an old-school revolver, as cool and reliable as the Captain himself. The first slug punched into Johns' upper right torso, the impact spinning him partway around. The second slammed into his left side as he spun, catching him under the arm.

Erin took aim, but Johns was already falling. She held her fire.

Keane shot her twice from a range of just under six feet, directly in the chest.

It was like being pummeled with a baseball bat. Erin went over sideways, the breath knocked out of her in a vicious one-two punch. She flopped to the floor like a stranded fish and gave a sobbing gasp, trying to draw breath that wouldn't come. Dimly, she saw Keane, Webb, Worthington, and Holliday all firing.

"*Fass!*" she croaked out.

Rolf needed no further encouragement. His partner had been hurt and that was completely unacceptable. He coiled and sprang.

The Shepherd was attacking from a standing start. He had no room to build up to a run. It didn't matter. He hit Keane with the full force of his ninety-pound body, jaws snapping. He caught Keane's arm in his teeth and raked the man with his hind claws as he dragged the Lieutenant down.

Erin tried to sit up and more or less succeeded. She sucked in a breath that burned as it entered her lungs. She saw Keane lying on the floorboards in front of her, Rolf on top of him. Blood was pooling beneath him and his left leg was bent all wrong. A short distance away, Johns lay at the center of another splash of blood, twitching and moaning.

Holliday, Webb, and Worthington were still standing, though Holliday's upper right sleeve was turning dark. The Captain and Webb were pointing their guns at Worthington, who tossed down his pistol and raised his hands.

"I didn't shoot at you," Worthington said.

"I know," Webb said, nodding at Keane. "You shot him. But you're still under arrest."

Erin saw Keane's pistol lying between them. She reached out and batted it out of his reach.

"You good, O'Reilly?" Webb asked.

"I don't know," she whispered, taking in another painful breath. "I think so." Her ribs felt crushed, but she didn't feel any wetness or see any blood on her clothes. *God bless Kevlar*, she thought.

Vic stalked past her, gun in hand. He aimed the weapon at Johns. "You bastard," he said in a low, deadly voice. "You goddamn bastard. That's my *kid* you shot at!"

"Neshenko!" Webb shouted. "Stand down right now!"

Vic paid no attention. He sighted along the barrel, drawing a bead on Johns' sweating, blood-streaked face.

"Vic," Erin said. "Don't. He's not worth it."

He hesitated. His breathing was harsh and ragged. The muscles on his neck and jaw quivered.

Half a dozen uniformed officers stormed up the stairs, guns drawn. A chorus of voices announced the obvious information that they were the NYPD, and ordered all the bad guys to drop their weapons.

Holliday holstered his revolver. "Sergeant Malcolm," he said to the first uniform. "We need two buses, forthwith. Three if they're available. And get a message to the Deputy Chief. Tell him I'll need to meet with the top brass immediately. You understand?"

"No, sir," Malcolm said honestly as he stared at the chaos in Major Crimes. Then, recovering a little, "Yes, sir. Copy that. Right away."

Erin's breath was coming more easily now. She thought she might even have escaped any broken ribs. She'd definitely have bruises, but those were par for the course. She looked warily at Vic.

He slowly crouched and returned his backup pistol to its ankle clip. Then he stood up, took five strides across the room to the first-aid box on the wall, popped it open, and carried the kit to Johns' side. He began tending to the wounded man with brisk, angry movements.

Erin stood, bracing herself on Webb's desk, and found she could remain upright. Keane was unconscious at her feet, Rolf remaining latched to his arm. The Internal Affairs Lieutenant been shot at least three times, though Erin wasn't sure who'd fired. She didn't even remember whether she'd gotten a shot off. She sniffed the Sig's barrel. It was cold and smelled only of oil, not gunpowder.

"*Pust,*" she told Rolf, who immediately released his victim and panted at her, ready to be told what an exceptional dog he was.

She fished out his toy and handed it to him. He took it in his jaws and trotted happily to his blanket next to the wreckage of Erin's desk.

Webb had been handcuffing Worthington. He thrust the big man in the direction of the uniforms. "Get this punk down to Holding," he said. "But make sure he's in his own cell. Don't put him with any other prisoners."

"Yes, sir," one of the Patrolmen said.

"Sir," Erin said to Holliday. "You've been shot."

"Oh," Holliday said, seemingly noticing the spreading bloodstain on his sleeve for the first time. "Twenty years on the street and I catch my first bullet two steps from my own office. How about that."

"It's been a weird day, sir," she said. She was still having trouble catching her breath, so she sat down in Webb's chair and pressed a hand to her aching ribs.

"That it has," Holliday agreed. "Officer Polikowski?"

"Yes, sir?" one of the uniforms said.

"I think we'll need additional medical supplies. Please see what you can scrounge from other departments."

"Copy that, sir." Polikowski made himself scarce.

"You don't seem to be bleeding to death," Webb said, walking over to Erin.

"Not yet," she said. "Vest caught both rounds. I think I'm okay."

"Did you get all that on your microphone?"

"Yeah, unless the bullets broke it. Keane shot me!"

"I know. That's why I shot him. So did Worthington."

"I know why you shot him. Why did he?"

"I'm planning to ask him," Webb said. "Just as soon as we clean the rest of this mess up."

Chapter 19

"Bruised ribs," was the paramedic's verdict. "You'll be fine. Ice packs, ten to twenty minutes at a time. In two or three days, once the swelling goes down, you can apply warm heat packs. You won't need prescription painkillers. Over-the-counter stuff should work. As the pain subsides, you can resume normal activities."

"Like getting shot at?" Erin suggested wryly.

"I wouldn't recommend it," the EMT said. She grinned. "You're lucky you were wearing your vest."

"That's how I feel," Erin said. "Lucky, lucky, lucky." It still hurt to breathe.

She was in the women's restroom next to Major Crimes. She could hear a lot of activity outside. On the plus side, she reflected, CSU hadn't had very far to travel. They hadn't even needed to load up their van.

"Am I good to go?" she asked, buttoning her blouse. She felt tempted to put her vest back on, for the sense of security it offered, but decided against it. The extra weight pressing against her bruises was something she could do without.

"Unless you want to go to the hospital for some X-rays," the medic said.

"Thanks, but no." Erin hopped down off the counter where she'd been sitting. Rolf scrambled to his paws and padded out of the room beside her.

Captain Holliday was sitting at Vic's desk. It was the first time Erin had ever seen the Captain not wearing his suit coat. Holliday was stripped to his undershirt. Another medic was finishing wrapping a bandage around his upper arm. Holliday looked more annoyed than in pain.

Piekarski and Mina were back at Piekarski's desk. Piekarski was playing a game with the baby which consisted mainly of holding her index fingers in front of Mina's face. Mina would reach out, grab the fingers, and try to put them in her mouth.

The rest of the room was a shambles. CSU had the area in front of Holliday's office taped off and was in the process of labeling and photographing bloodstains and cartridge cases. Erin's desk still lay where it had tipped over, surrounded by debris.

As she surveyed the scene, Vic hurried up the stairs. He went straight to Piekarski with the look Erin had only seen on his face a couple of times: soft-eyed concern. He looked like a completely different man in those rare moments.

"You sure you guys are okay?" he asked.

"I told you, Vic, we're fine," Piekarski said. "We didn't get hit."

"Those bullets were only a couple inches away," he said.

"Yeah," she replied. "Which means they *missed*. I thought you detectives had training in ballistics."

"It's not funny." He put out his hand. Mina grabbed a big, meaty finger and wrapped her own little digits as far around it as they would go. In spite of himself, Vic smiled.

"What's going on?" Erin asked.

"Keane and Johns are on their way to Bellevue," he said. "Would you believe it, the medics think both of them are gonna make it? There's no justice in the world."

"Really? How many times did they get hit?"

"The Captain tagged Johns twice," Vic said. "Damn good shooting, too. Collapsed one of his lungs, broke his collarbone, probably messed him up some other ways. Keane got it worse. I hit him once. So did Worthington and Webb, I think. That's not counting the busted wrist your mutt gave him. I gotta spend more time on the range with that little backup sissy-pistol. It's got no recoil. I overcompensated low and took out his kneecap. I swear, I didn't do it on purpose. I was trying to gut-shoot the son of a bitch. Those other two did better. I'm surprised he's still breathing."

"Maybe they aimed for the heart," Erin suggested. "He doesn't have one."

Vic snorted. "That's a thought."

"What about Worthington?"

"Webb and I stashed him in Interrogation Room One. We're letting him stew for a bit while we figure out what the hell to do with him. Webb's downstairs filling out some paperwork."

"And my desk?"

Vic had the decency to look a little ashamed of himself. "Sorry about that. I needed cover."

"You destroyed my computer!"

"The Department's computer."

"Whatever."

"They'll replace it. I said I was sorry!"

Erin sighed. "Forget about it."

"O'Reilly," Holliday said. He'd put on his shirt and was fastening his vest. "Glad to see you standing."

"You too, sir," she said. "I hope that's not bad."

"Just grazed me," The Captain said. "I expect it'll hurt more tomorrow. Are you fit for duty?"

"Ready and willing, sir."

His mustache twitched in a hint of a smile. "Good woman. Make sure that drive is logged properly. Do you have copies?"

"Yes, sir."

"Good. Until we know how far the rot goes, we need to be careful. Don't tell me where the others are. That way I can't reveal it, accidentally or under duress."

"You're good at this cloak-and-dagger shit, sir," Vic said. "Did you used to be a spy?"

"That's classified," Holliday said, deadpan. "I'd like to talk to you two in my office, if you have a moment."

Vic looked at Piekarski.

"I told you," she said. "We're fine. Nothing's going to happen to us."

"I'm looking online, first chance I get," he said. "I swear they make bulletproof vests for babies. Maybe a onesie?"

"Vic, we're not swaddling our kid in Kevlar."

"You can't be too careful."

"Vic!"

"Fine, fine. But as soon as she's old enough I'm teaching her guns, knives, and Krav Maga."

Piekarski rolled her eyes. "You were going to do that anyway," she said.

* * *

Holliday's office, in contrast to Major Crimes, was pristine with the exception of the glass panel in the door. This sported a pair of bullet holes. The bullets had embedded themselves in the brickwork on the opposite wall, narrowly missing one of the windows.

"Shut the door please, Neshenko," Holliday said. The Captain motioned the two detectives to the chairs across from his desk. Erin and Vic sat, Rolf taking his accustomed spot next to Erin. Holliday sat in his black leather swivel chair and regarded them for a few moments.

"I never thought I'd be in this position," he finally said. "IAB is supposed to investigate us, not the other way around. Do you two have any idea what you've stirred up here?"

"We didn't exactly mean to, sir," Erin said.

He waved a hand. "I'm not looking for an apology. I'm just trying to understand what happened. Let me see if I've got this straight. You were assigned to look into Officer William Ward's death, an apparent suicide. It has since been ruled as such by our own Medical Examiner. I have Dr. Levine's report in my inbox as we speak. However, in the course of your investigation, you determined that Officer Ward was involved in criminal activities."

"That's correct, sir," Erin said.

"These included, but may not have been limited to, the transportation and traffic of narcotics with at least two gangs, as well as conspiracy to commit murder of an NYPD officer."

"Yes, sir."

"Officer Ward was coerced into these activities, on the basis of a prior narcotics addiction, by Lieutenant Keane of Internal Affairs. It is your determination that Lieutenant Keane has been systematically blackmailing vulnerable officers into following illegal orders."

"Yes, sir."

"You further believe Lieutenant Keane murdered Kira Jones upon learning of her efforts to investigate him."

"He also killed Alphonse Luna in a holding cell last year," Erin said. "He staged that to look like a suicide, too. There may have been others."

Holliday sighed. "Here's the problem, Detective. CSU may be able to determine from fiber evidence that Keane was in Jones' apartment, but we already know he was there. He showed up while you were examining the scene. We can check him for gunshot residue, but we already know he has that on his hands, since we all saw him discharge his sidearm about ten feet from where I'm currently sitting. I don't think we can make a murder case against him for Jones."

"He also tried to kill Erin," Vic pointed out.

Holliday nodded. "That's true. Though that was a confused situation, I think I can get the DA to charge him with attempted Murder Two. However, that's going to be a very messy prosecution."

"Sir, we can't let him walk!" Vic exclaimed. "He's a friggin' cop killer! Not to mention a grade-A douchebag!"

Holliday held up a calming hand. "I'm not disagreeing with you, Neshenko," he said. "You're correct on both counts, though the latter is not punishable under the law. I'm not suggesting we let him walk. I'm looking at the situation from a practical perspective. This will be a delicate case and we need to make sure whatever we throw at him sticks. I'm open to suggestions, preferably ones which will leave this disgrace of an officer behind bars well into my retirement."

"There's Ward's file," Vic said.

"We don't yet know what's on it," Holliday said. "But I agree, we'll go over it with the finest-toothed comb we have."

"Worthington," Erin said.

"What about him?" Holliday asked.

"He turned against Keane at the last minute," she said. "I think he wants to save himself. He may know some things about Keane. He shot him, for crying out loud!"

"Excellent idea," Holliday said. "Of course I shot Keane, too. I know a great many officers fantasize about shooting Internal

Affairs cops, but I haven't heard of it actually happening before. Normally, all of you would be on modified assignment while your precinct Captain investigates. However, in this unique situation, I expect to be in the same boat as you by the end of the day, so what happens next will probably be up to whichever high-ranking IAB officer comes in to take over."

"Goody," Vic muttered.

"We do not, of course, know whether Lieutenant Keane has compromising material on high-ranking members of the Department or not," Holliday continued. "And regardless of whether or not, speaking hypothetically, Lieutenant Keane has dirt on the Commissioner or the Chief, they might prefer to keep this as quiet as possible. So it would be in all our best interests if you could give me some ammunition I could use to prevent the entire affair from being swept under the metaphorical rug."

"Translation," Vic said. "Lean on Worthington and get the goods before you get replaced by some bureaucratic hack."

"Precisely," Holliday said. "We'll try to flip Johns as well, but considering he's in critical condition at present, it's probably unwise to count on his testimony. Was Keane really working for the Lucarellis?"

"Maybe," Erin said. "Or they were working for him. You could take a trip up to Riker's and ask Valentino Vitelli, but he's old-school enough to still believe in *omerta*. I don't think he's interested in being a rat."

"I suppose not. It does help explain why Keane was so eager to bring down the O'Malleys. As I recall, it was his suggestion to turn Carlyle and Corcoran and use them as a wedge to get inside the Irish Mob."

"Yeah," Erin said. "He was getting rid of the Lucarellis' competition."

"Too bad he was too late," Vic said. "There's not much left of the Lucarellis, either. Just bits and pieces. This is like one of those movies where everybody's dead by the time the credits roll."

"Not quite all of us," Holliday said, his mustache ruffling in a hint of a smile. Then the smile subsided. "I know you were both close to Detective Jones. My sympathies."

"Thank you, sir," Erin said.

"She was a damn good cop," Vic said. "They don't make them any better."

Holliday nodded. "The best way we can honor her is by seeing she didn't die for nothing," he said. "Also, I know this is short notice, but when we hold the Departmental funeral, I think she'd have liked the two of you to be pallbearers."

"Of course," Erin said, startled. She hadn't even been thinking about that. "We'd be honored."

"Absolutely, sir," Vic said.

"But for now, you have work to do," Holliday said. "Dismissed."

Erin and Vic stood and moved to the door, Rolf hopping up to accompany Erin.

"One thing more," Holliday said.

Erin flinched. She couldn't help it. That was exactly the sort of thing a detective said right before nailing a suspect with that armor-piercing question that would reduce him to a quivering blob. She forced herself to turn and look her Captain in the eye.

"I understand congratulations are in order," he said, his eyes flicking down to the ring finger on her left hand. "I wish they could come under happier circumstances. Oh, and your suspension is rescinded. Obviously. Collect your shield and sidearm from Lieutenant Webb at your convenience."

"Thank you, sir," she said. She'd been expecting something much worse.

"That went well," Vic said in an undertone as they walked across the ruined office.

"You think any meeting with the brass goes well as long as you don't get fired," Erin replied.

"That's because it's true," he said. He glanced at the gun on her hip. "Why didn't you turn in my Sig?"

"I don't have to," she said.

"Erin, just because those bastards are still breathing now doesn't mean they're gonna survive," he said. "This is still an officer-involved shooting, of other officers! I can't believe I gotta be the one to remind you of the rules."

"You don't understand," she said. "I never fired a shot."

He stopped short. "Really?"

She nodded. "Really."

"An absolutely insane close-quarters gunfight, half a dozen guys blasting each other at contact range, and you didn't get a single round off?"

"Not one. Johns was already on his way to the floor when I threw down on him, and then Keane knocked me over. By the time I got my breath back, Rolf was on him and it was all over."

Vic shook his head. "I dunno about you, Erin. You're going soft. You get what's probably your one and only chance in your whole career to waste an Internal Affairs dick and you blow it."

"C'mon, Vic," she said. "Do we ever seriously complain about *not* having to shoot anybody?"

"I guess not. Thanks, by the way."

"For what?"

"Reminding me not to smoke that jerk when I had him down. I really, really wanted to. But if I'd done it, I guess Webb would be looking to fill a vacancy in the squad. So I appreciate it."

She put a hand on his shoulder. "Anytime," she said. "You want to be in the room when we talk to Worthington?"

"I better not," he said. "I'm still a little keyed up. We don't want me banging his head on the table. I'll stay with Zofia and start getting Major Crimes up and running again. We're gonna have to do some more legwork to close this one."

"Vic Neshenko," she said. "Are you turning into a responsible detective?"

"God, I hope not," he said. "The problem with being responsible is, people give you responsibilities."

"Like fatherhood?"

"Something like that."

Chapter 20

Vic took custody of Rolf and stepped into the observation room. Erin and Webb sat down opposite Worthington next door. The big IAB man looked somehow shrunken, sitting there with his hands cuffed to the table and his face still showing the marks from his close encounter with the bakery display.

"Do you want—" Webb began.

"Screw the Union lawyers," Worthington interrupted. "Screw all of it. I don't give a crap anymore. Just tell me one thing."

"What's that?" Webb asked.

"Is that little weasel dead?"

"You mean Lieutenant Keane?"

Worthington nodded.

"Not yet," Webb said. "If you're lucky, he'll pull through."

"Lucky?" Worthington echoed. "How exactly is that lucky?"

"You won't be looking at a murder charge."

Webb and Erin had agreed that the Lieutenant would play "good cop" for this interrogation, since Erin had gotten in a fight with Worthington and that tended to damage the rapport she would have tried to establish. That was fine with Erin; she wasn't feeling particularly charitable or empathic at that moment. Her ribs hurt like hell and she kept thinking about Kira. She was also pissed at Keane, all his people, everything he stood for, and even Vic for wrecking her desk. She understood Vic's concerns about bouncing this jerk's head off the tabletop. It was awfully tempting.

"Murder?" Worthington exclaimed. "I was protecting other cops! Or did you miss the part where he shot O'Reilly?"

"I'd be more touched by your concern if you hadn't tried to beat the shit out of me at Chelsea Market," Erin said dryly.

"You got the better end of that one," Worthington said, actually cracking a wry smile. "You've got a rep, you and Neshenko both. I should've remembered it. You're a lot tougher than you look."

"Why did you and Johns come after us?" she demanded.

"Keane told us to."

"Officially?"

He smiled again. "Not exactly."

"What did he tell you?"

"He said Neshenko took something from the Jones crime scene. Important evidence."

"Hold on," Webb said. "That's a serious accusation. Why didn't Lieutenant Keane pursue this through official channels?"

"Isn't it obvious?" Worthington replied. "He didn't want it on record. The whole point was to keep it quiet."

"Why?" Erin asked. "Kira's computer was already logged into Evidence. All we had was the backup."

"Keane had the computer," Worthington said. "He could keep it locked up as part of an IAB investigation, probably forever. Either he could've kept it, or it could've quietly disappeared. It wouldn't be the first time. I think he wanted to know how much you knew."

"So he could decide whether we were a threat or not," she said grimly.

He nodded.

"You told him you weren't happy about what happened to Kira," Erin said.

Worthington wasn't smiling anymore. "I wasn't. She was a friend, for Christ's sake! He had no right to take her out like that!"

"But you had no problem doing other dirty work for Keane," she growled.

"I never killed for him. No way. That's over the line!"

"What did he have on you?" Webb asked gently. "I've seen your service record. You're a decorated officer. You've never been in serious trouble."

Worthington hesitated.

Webb sighed. "Look, Cormack," he said, deliberately using the man's first name. "If you were coerced, here's your best chance of getting out of this relatively clean. You don't have to tell me, but here's the thing about blackmail: Keane's going to use it against you one way or another. You can get out in front of him, but only if you talk to me now."

It was Worthington's turn to sigh. "I never should've done a damn thing he asked," he muttered. "I knew it was only gonna get me in more trouble. It's just so easy, you know? And the way he played it at the start, it didn't seem so bad."

"That's how the Mob gets you, too," Erin said.

"You know about my incident?" he asked.

Webb nodded. "Four years ago," he said. "Right before you transferred to IAB. You interrupted an armed robbery in Central Park and killed the perp when he tried to stab you."

"Yeah," he said. "Except that's not how it went down. I screwed up. It was just a purse-snatching, some junkie trying for some cash for his fix. There was a foot chase. My partner was this old-timer carrying fifty pounds extra, so I left him way behind. I caught the perp on a bridge. He tried to get free. I dunno exactly what happened, but I took him down hard and he hit his head on the railing. Stupid bastard died at the scene."

"And the knife?" Webb asked.

"The guy was just a kid, y'know? About sixteen, skinny as shit. I weighed about three of him. And he was black. How do you think that'd look in the paper? They run pictures of him and me side by side? So I panicked. I had this knife on me, folding blade. I quick jabbed myself in the vest a couple times and gave myself some of those, y'know, defensive wounds on the arms. Then I wiped it down and stuck it in the kid's hand. But I swear to God, I was trying to arrest him. I didn't mean to kill him, you gotta believe me."

"I do," Webb said soothingly. "What did Keane do?"

"He met with me outside the station, off the record. I dunno how, but he knew the knife was mine. He said I was a good cop and he didn't want me getting jammed up, so he'd take care of me. He's the one who suggested I transfer to IAB."

"He hadn't been running Internal Affairs at the Eightball very long," Webb observed.

"Yeah, he'd just made Lieutenant," Worthington said.

"I guess he was already building his little empire," Erin said.

"He had the knife," Worthington said unhappily. "If I didn't play ball, I'd be looking at termination from the Department for sure, and maybe manslaughter charges. Even if those didn't stick, the kid's family would hit me with a wrongful-death suit. I didn't know what else to do. And I didn't know who to talk to. I mean, normally if you're getting blackmailed you go to Internal Affairs, right?"

"I see what you mean," Webb said. "Will you testify against Keane?"

"If you can get that thing with the kid knocked down," Worthington said. "Jesus. Keane was killing cops! I knew it was bad, but I didn't figure it was *that* bad!"

"Did you know about Valentino Vitelli?" Erin asked.

"I'd heard stuff about him," Worthington said. "Nothing definite."

"Why did you decide to shoot Keane?" Webb asked.

"He and Johns were gonna shoot everyone there," Worthington said. "Taking cops hostages? I didn't sign up for that. I figured, screw it. I was gonna do the right thing for once. I thought maybe it was my last chance. When the Captain took Johns out, I made my move."

"Did you profit from your extracurricular activities?" Webb asked.

"Indirectly, I guess," Worthington said. "I wasn't getting envelopes full of cash, if that's what you mean. I got good fitness reports. I made Sergeant on Keane's recommendation. I got good assignments and my pick of cases. It was one of those whaddaya call them, those Latin things. Like, you scratch my back, I'll scratch yours."

"*Quid pro quo*?" Webb guessed.

"That's it," Worthington said. "And he always had that stick in case I stepped too far out of line."

"One more thing," Erin said. "William Ward."

"What about him?"

"How were you connected with him?"

Worthington spread his hands as far as the handcuffs allowed. "I wasn't," he said. "Keane kept things divided, so none of us really knew what the others were up to, or even exactly who was working for him. Once we started looking at you guys, I started figuring some of it out, but until then I didn't know."

"And to be completely clear," Erin said. "You had nothing to do with Kira Jones' death?"

"Not a goddamn thing!" Worthington said angrily. "I told you. Hell, I told Keane! That was over the line."

"Do you know why Keane wanted her dead?"

"Only what I heard from you. You'd better ask him."

"I plan to," Erin said.

* * *

"He won't say anything," Webb predicted.

"Maybe not," Erin said.

"He's too smart."

"I'm not arguing."

"But you're still standing in this hospital waiting room."

"So are you, sir."

Webb smiled. "That's true," he said. "Maybe I thought you and Neshenko needed some adult supervision."

"I'm not gonna kill him," Vic said. "If I was, I had plenty of chances back at the Eightball. I should've stayed there and kept helping Zofia."

"She's fine, you know," Erin said. "So is Mina."

"I know," he said unconvincingly. "You know what they don't tell you about being a dad? How scary it is."

"Tell me about it," Webb said. "I have two teenage daughters. In Los Angeles."

"We're cops," Vic said. "We know the world is dangerous. But when it's your own kid... shit. I have nightmares about stuff happening to Mina. I can't believe that asshole Johns *shot* at her!"

"I think he was shooting at Zofia," Erin said.

"Whatever. Let's talk to Keane and get out of here."

"As soon as the doctor clears us," Webb said. "Here he comes now."

"I should've guessed," the ER surgeon said. "Multiple GSW and my kid sister. They go together like ham and eggs."

"Don't look at me, Junior," Erin said. "I didn't shoot him."

Doctor Sean O'Reilly Junior nodded doubtfully. "Whatever you say, kiddo. All I do is patch them up. I don't care who they are or where they came from."

"What's Lieutenant Keane's status?" Webb asked.

"Serious but stable," Sean said. "He's lucky. The abdominal shot was near the surface and just tore up the muscle wall on his left side, and the shoulder was too high to clip his lung or his brachial artery. The knee is bad, but not life-threatening. He'll walk with a limp for the rest of his life."

"Good," Vic said with vicious satisfaction.

"This man's a police officer," Sean said, confused. "You're happy he's crippled?"

"Damn right I am," Vic said. "It means even if he weasels out of taking the rap, he'll be out on disability so we'll be rid of him one way or another."

"Is this man a cop or a suspect?" Sean asked. "Right now he's in a recovery room handcuffed to a bed with an armed officer babysitting him."

"He's both," Erin said. "Can he answer questions?"

"He may be a little groggy from the anesthesia," Sean said. "But as long as you keep it short and don't agitate him too much, I don't see the harm. I'll need to be present, of course. If you'll follow me?"

"They've done a good job fixing up Intensive Care," Erin commented as they walked into ICU. No visible sign remained of the explosion caused by a certain disaffected Irishman. She could still smell the fresh paint on the walls.

"You were also involved with that incident, if memory serves," Sean said.

"It would've happened whether I'd been here or not," she said. "I was able to save the patient."

"And destroy half the ward."

"You're a real glass-half-empty guy, Doc," Vic said. "Think of it as an opportunity to renovate your facilities and upgrade your equipment."

"By that line of thinking," Sean replied, "if you ever get brought in with a double load of buckshot in your abdomen, you should think of it as an opportunity to rearrange your internal organs and efficiently resection your bowels."

* * *

Erin had seen a lot of patients lying in hospital beds. No matter who they were, the sight always stirred at least a little pity. To be so broken and helpless, completely at the mercy of doctors and nurses, unable even to control your own body and its private functions, was a cruel punishment that ought to be more unusual than it was.

This was the first time she'd seen Andrew Keane without his suit on. Clad in a one-size-fits-all hospital gown, he was no longer the formidable Internal Affairs Lieutenant, the feared Bloodhound. Now he was just a man about Erin's own age, shorter and slimmer than average, bloodied and battered. An IV tube ran from a saline bag into his left forearm. Electrodes were plastered to his chest, connecting him to the inevitable mysterious beeping medical machines. His right wrist was handcuffed to the bedrail.

Erin reminded herself that this man had murdered two people she knew of, and probably more. One of those had been a friend. He'd amassed personal power and wealth through blackmail, extortion, and manipulation. He'd done it from a position of public trust, which only made it worse. She hated him.

But she also felt the tiniest bit sorry for him.

Webb cleared his throat. "How are you feeling, Lieutenant?" he asked. Since Keane had tried to kill Erin just a couple of hours earlier, and Vic hated him, Webb had defaulted to "good cop" once more.

"Remarkably well, considering," Keane said to Erin. "I am enjoying the fruits of the American pharmaceutical industry. And your brother does excellent work. It runs in the family, apparently."

"You know why we're here?" Erin asked.

"Of course," Keane said. "You're interviewing suspects. You're hoping for a confession, which would eliminate any serious need for a trial. The Commissioner would agree, obviously. This sort of thing is damaging enough for the Department without the public spectacle. I can practically hear the reporters sharpening their pencils in anticipation."

"I don't know anything about that," Erin said. "And I don't care. I'm here for the truth."

"Only that?" Keane chuckled politely, an artificial little chortle that grated on Erin's ears. "Whose truth? Mine? Yours?"

"There's only one kind of truth," she said.

"If only that were the case," he replied. "But we all know better. There's no black and white here in the real world. It all runs together into gray. Colors bleed."

"So do people," Vic growled. "I guess even you do when somebody pokes a few holes in you. I hope every step you take on that bad knee hurts like hell, and I hope you think of me every time it does."

"I'm not going to trial," Keane said. "Nobody's going to let that happen."

"The DA will be happy to discuss your plea bargain," Webb said. "If you have something to offer, you might even manage not to die behind bars."

"Yeah," Erin said. "You can look me up in the retirement home in fifty years or so. I'm curious. Major Crimes was full of guys with guns. I wasn't even pointing one at you. Why'd you shoot me?"

"Isn't it obvious?" Keane replied. "In a gunfight you target your most dangerous opponent first. I admit to having made the mistake of underestimating you in the past, Detective O'Reilly. I wasn't going to do it again. You should be glad you were wearing a vest."

"You should too," she said. "It's one murder charge fewer."

"Come now," he said. "We both know I'll never be charged with murder. Your evidence is circumstantial at best, barring a confession, which I'm not about to give you."

"We still have you on all kinds of conspiracy," Vic said. "Not to mention attempted murder of a cop. You're going down, buddy."

"Maybe," Keane admitted. "But not for life. Particularly once District Attorney Markham hears what I can offer him."

"And what's that?" Webb asked.

"That's between the DA and myself," Keane said. "Though I'm sure he, and others, are more than a little curious what became of an unpleasant detective by the name of Leonard Carter. I may be able to shine some light on that man's disappearance."

Erin felt a sudden chill. Keane was looking directly at her. She steeled herself to give nothing away. "I'm sure you do know where he went," she said. "Because I handed him into your custody—alive. What happened to him after that, you know better than anyone else."

"If that's your story," Keane said. "We'll see. In any case, I'm certain the DA will also be interested in the identities of certain corrupt officers within the Department, not to mention what I may be able to do with respect to damaging a few major criminal organizations in this city. I think I've been dealt a fairly strong hand, in spite of everything."

"You son of a bitch," Vic snarled. "I should've shot you right in that smug, lying face. If you do get out, you'd better make damn sure you get witness protection, because if I ever see you on the street, I'm gonna take out your other kneecap and leave you in the goddamn gutter."

"Are you recording this conversation as well, Detective O'Reilly?" Keane asked. "Because I believe Detective Neshenko just made a threat of unlawful violence against me."

"Oh, you understood?" Vic said. "Good. I hate having to explain a threat because the perp's too dumb to get it the first time. That's just embarrassing."

Erin was, in fact, recording the conversation, but she didn't say so.

"We've had a number of unfortunate encounters," Keane said to Erin. "I'm sorry things worked out the way they did. You may not believe me, but it's true. I'm also sorry for what happened to Detective Jones."

"Don't you say her name!" Erin snapped. "You killed her!"

"Let's assume, for the sake of argument, that you're right," Keane said. "If that were true, which I don't admit, it would have been because she was conducting an illicit investigation into her superior officer. My opinion of Detective Jones is that she was loyal, hardworking, and competent, but no braver than the situation required of her. She was, to put it bluntly, gun-shy. It seems extremely unlikely to me that she would have undertaken an off-the-books investigation on her own initiative. Someone more courageous must have put her up to it; someone with experience in clandestine operations and in toeing the fuzzy line between legality and criminality. That person, I think we'd be forced to agree, would bear a certain moral responsibility for what happened to her. Wouldn't you say?"

Erin stared at Keane. Her previous feeling of pity was completely gone. In its place was loathing and disgust. How dare he suggest it was *her* fault? She wanted to scream the words in his face. But that was what he wanted. He was trying to wrest some power, some sense of moral equivalency and control, back into his own hands. The worst of it was, he was succeeding.

She couldn't handle it, couldn't be in the same room with this man one second longer. She spun on her heel and marched out without another word to anybody.

Chapter 21

Vic found Erin in the parking lot a few minutes later. She was sitting on the curb, staring at the asphalt between her shoes. Rolf was beside her, chin resting on her knee.

"What an asshole, huh?" Vic said, settling on the curb on the other side of her.

Erin nodded. She didn't trust herself enough to say anything.

"I wish we smoked," he said after a moment. "Then I could offer you a cig, and you could smoke it, and we'd both feel better."

"Why stop there?" she replied, trying to control the tremor in her voice. "If we were tweakers, you could give me some crystal meth."

"Or I could hook you up with heroin, crack, fentanyl..." he said. "You name it. Zofia has friends on the Street Narcotics squad. Or we could raid the pharmacy right here at Bellevue and get you some oxy or morphine. It's a real smorgasbord."

"There'll be whiskey at home," she said dully.

"Yeah," he said. "Vodka for me. Shit, I really could use a drink."

"I don't know what I was expecting," Erin said. "Keane's been in this for himself the whole time. He's not going to change now. He'll say or do anything to get out of this mess. Absolutely anything, and he'll bring us all down with him."

"He won't get out of it," Vic said. "He can't."

"Are you sure about that?" she shot back. "Suppose he talks to Markham and offers to serve up the Lucarellis on a platter, with the Roadkillers and the Crazy Knives on the side?"

"He's a cop killer," Vic insisted. "He's gonna burn."

"*Alleged* cop killer," she said wearily. "Weren't you listening to him and Holliday? That won't stick. All we have for sure is him shooting me, and those rounds didn't even break the skin. You really think the DA won't trade that for taking down three major gangs? He gave Carlyle immunity in exchange for the O'Malleys, remember? And Carlyle did some pretty bad shit."

"How bad?" Vic asked.

"Bad enough I'm not going to tell you about it," she said. "You already hate him."

"No, I don't."

Erin was surprised enough at that to turn and look Vic in the face. "You don't? You hate practically *everybody*."

"Nah. I'm not saying I'm gonna ask him to be Mina's godfather or anything, but he's not so bad. At least he's trying to do right, and that's more than you can say for a lot of punks out there. Hell, he's better than half the cops we've been dealing with. He's out of the game, right? For good?"

"Right," Erin said. "He's completely legit now. The Barley Corner's just a pub these days. It's become a tourist attraction, did you know that?"

"Really? I'll have to go back sometime. But I tend to get in fights when I show up there."

"As I recall, the big fistfight you got in at the Corner was with another cop," she said. "And Corky came in on your side."

Vic chuckled. "You're right. Am I still allowed to hate him?"

"If you want."

He stopped laughing. "I guess our case comes down to what we can find," he said.

"Worthington can give us a little leverage," Erin said. "And we'll be able to go through Keane's files. Maybe we'll find something incriminating there, a smoking gun, but I wouldn't bet on it. He's too smart to store anything sensitive where we can get at it. So what we've got is Ward's dossier."

"Which was compiled by a raving paranoid who was about five hours away from eating his own gun," Vic said. "I wouldn't bet my career on that. Well, maybe *my* career, but that's not saying much. I sure as shit wouldn't bet *yours*. I wish we had something else for support. I wish they hadn't planted that drug money in my car. What I really wish, though, is that Kira hadn't gotten shot."

"You and me both," Erin said bitterly. "Did you hear that bastard? He tried to blame *me* for getting her killed!"

"Yeah," Vic growled. "I wanted to yank his IV tube out of his arm, ram the needle up his goddamn nose, and stir his friggin' brains for that. So Kira was looking into him? That's because he was dirty, dammit! And it's not like she found anything on him anyway, right?"

Erin didn't answer. She stared at Vic.

"Right?" Vic repeated. He cocked his head and raised an eyebrow. "Hello? Erin? Anybody home?"

"We went looking for Ward's file on Kira's computer," Erin said quietly.

"Yeah," Vic said. "And we found it on her backup drive, which I took. At the risk of my job, I might add."

"But that wasn't the only thing on the backup drive," she said. "It has all Kira's stuff on it."

"I guess so," he said. "Hold on, what do you mean?"

Erin stood. Rolf's ears perked toward her, picking up the sudden change in her energy.

"Keane would've been pissed if he found out she was spying on him," she said. "But that wouldn't be enough for him to kill her. To take a risk like that, he had to know she found something. Something big."

"Kira would've told us if she had anything like that," Vic objected. "Especially if she was looking because you asked her to."

"She tried," Erin said. "Damn it, we put it off! We thought we had more time! We need to get Webb. Then we have to go!"

"Where? Back to the Eightball?"

"No. The Barley Corner. You said you wanted to go there again. Here's your chance."

"What's there?"

"Another copy of the backup drive," she said. "And that drink you want."

* * *

"You go looking for a break in your case," Webb said. "So the Irish cop and the Russian cop decide to walk into a bar. Could you be any more stereotypical?"

"Well, we *were* reminiscing about bar fights," Vic said.

"This case started in a bar," Erin said. "It makes as much sense to end up here as anywhere."

Webb looked around the refurbished pub. "I like it," he said. "It's still got that Old World charm, but it looks like the plumbing is up to code now."

Carlyle had been talking with Ken Mason under the big-screen TV. When he saw the detectives, he excused himself and walked over to meet them.

"What's this I'm hearing about a shooting in your station house?" he asked Erin, taking her hand in both of his.

"It wasn't that big a deal," she said. "Nobody got killed."

"That's technically true," Webb said.

"I'm pleased to hear it," Carlyle said. "And here I'm thinking there was a great shoot-out, bullets and bodies littering the premises. It's all over the news, so I'm glad to be mistaken. Lieutenant, it gives me great pleasure to welcome you to the reopened Barley Corner. I'd be delighted to offer you the drink of your choice, on the house. That goes for you as well, Detective Neshenko. Erin already drinks free of charge, of course."

"Sorry, we're on duty," Webb said.

"I'll have a headshot," Vic said at the same time.

Webb glared at him. "Neshenko," he said in quiet, warning tones.

Vic's face was the picture of round-eyed, broken-nosed innocence. "What? Who's gonna get mad? Internal Affairs?"

Webb started to say something, changed his mind, started to say something else, and changed it again. "Bourbon for me," he said instead. "Wild Turkey."

"I'll have a Glen D," Erin said.

Vic shook his head. "Forget that," he said. "She wants what I'm having."

"Oh, I do, do I?" It was Erin's turn to put menace in her voice.

"You'll thank me in a minute," Vic said.

Carlyle waved to the daytime bartender. "Matthew," he said. "Two headshots and a shot of Wild Turkey."

Erin studied the drink the bartender slid into her hands. "What is this?" she asked suspiciously.

"Vanilla vodka, raspberry vodka, standard-issue vodka..." Vic began, ticking items off on his fingers.

"Jesus," she muttered. "You're going to have to carry me out of the bar."

"...and orange juice," he finished.

"So, basically a fancy screwdriver?" Webb asked.

"Yeah," Vic said. "If you want to be boring about it."

Erin tried a sip. "Not bad," she said.

"Told you so," Vic said.

"But Glen D whiskey is better," she said.

He rolled his eyes. "This is why nobody respects the Irish. You've got no taste for the finer things in life."

"We didn't come here just to run down your booze supplies, Mr. Carlyle," Webb said. "Though I'm starting to suspect my detectives' motives."

"We need to look at the drive I left with you," Erin said.

Carlyle nodded. "It's upstairs in my office," he said. "Shall I fetch it down?"

"No," Erin said. "We'll all come up. We wanted to look at it somewhere private."

"Besides," Vic said. "This way I get to snoop around your digs."

"You'll find no contraband, Detective," Carlyle said. "I'm a good citizen now."

"Contraband, hell," Vic said. "I just want to see how Erin's living these days."

* * *

Vic's verdict on Erin and Carlyle's apartment was that it needed more gun cases and diapers. He also insisted on checking the bathroom, on the bizarre theory that there might be a dead guy in it.

"It's happened before," he said.

"I'm wounded, lad," Carlyle said. "I may not be a gangster any longer, but I've been around enough of them to know how to properly dispose of a body, should the situation require it."

After Vic's housekeeping critique was complete, and he'd raided Carlyle's personal liquor stash, they all trooped into Carlyle's office and clustered around his computer. Carlyle plugged in the thumb drive and brought up Kira's files.

Anticipation gradually dulled to determination, then to boredom as one file folder after another showed nothing of interest. They took turns sitting at the computer, opening files and checking them one by one.

"She doesn't even have any decent porn," Vic complained after an hour. He'd given up on mixing cocktails and was pouring himself straight shots of raspberry vodka.

"Decent porn is a contradiction in terms," Webb said. He clicked on another folder, scanned its contents for a moment, sighed, and closed it again.

"Well, yeah, but she was into both guys and girls," Vic said. "So there's gotta be some complicated, interesting shit here somewhere."

"Speaking of decency, I'd appreciate it if you'd show a bit," Carlyle said. "We're going through an unfortunate lass' personal effects without her permission. Should we find anything inappropriate, I trust we'll set it aside."

Vic rolled his eyes. "Look, buddy," he said. "If I ever kick it, feel free to go through my computer for the good stuff. I guarantee you'll find some."

"Whatever's here would have to be something recent," Erin said, ignoring Vic.

"That doesn't help us," Webb said. "These files were all backed up simultaneously. They all have the same date-stamp."

"Except this is a backup drive," Erin said. "Aren't there older copies of her data? Can't we compare them with the most recent one?"

"Grand idea, darling," Carlyle said.

"Let's see," Webb said. Kira's backup had updated weekly. He found the previous week's files and opened them side by side.

"Don't you have an automated way of doing that?" Vic asked.

"Probably," Webb said. "But I don't know how. When I first put on my shield, home computers were hardly a thing yet. I've never really gotten the hang of them."

Several long minutes passed.

"This is damn good vodka," Vic said, hoisting the bottle. "Thanks."

"You're quite welcome," Carlyle said dryly. "It's from my private store. It should be good. It's rather expensive."

"Try not to get too sloshed," Webb said. "You can get drunk off the clock."

"I'll have you know I can function better now than I can when I'm stone-cold sober," Vic said. "Want me to recite the alphabet backwards? I can do it. In Cyrillic."

"I don't know Cyrillic," Webb said. "I wouldn't know if you were doing it right."

"Even better," Vic said. "Okay, listen up. Modern Russian has thirty-three letters: twenty consonants, ten vowels, a semivowel…"

"Knock off the language lessons," Webb said. "I think I've got something."

Four pairs of eyes eagerly glued themselves to the screen. Rolf, curled up next to the desk, had gone to sleep half an hour earlier.

"It's a medical report," Erin said after a moment.

"And it's under Sarah Levine's name," Webb said. "But it's incomplete. No autopsy, no bloodwork. That's weird."

"It's not like Levine to file an incomplete report," Erin said.

"She didn't file it," Webb said. "Look. No countersignature, either. Is it a rough draft, or what?"

"Who's it for?" Vic asked.

"Alphonse Luna," Webb said.

"The Mob hitman who died last year in our holding cell," Erin said.

"Levine didn't do the postmortem on him," Webb said.

"Yeah," Vic agreed. "IAB kicked her off it and brought in their own guy."

"Looks like Levine filled out what she knew anyway," Webb said. "I wonder why."

"Because she's thorough," Erin said. "She'd done part of the examination, so she wrote up what she had. She never filed it, because she wasn't administering the autopsy. It's like if one doctor gets another's patient at the hospital. The first doctor doesn't have any further responsibility, but Levine is big on habits and patterns. She'd write down what she knew, even if nobody else would ever see it."

"Why didn't she tell us?" Vic demanded.

"Tell us what?" Webb retorted. "An incomplete examination for a body no longer in her care? For a case that wasn't assigned to us? We never asked for her findings. Looks like she forwarded this report to the doctor who finished the autopsy to help that guy."

"The real question is what those findings were," Erin said.

"'Results of preliminary examination strongly suggest homicide,'" Webb read aloud. "'Ligature marks appear inconsistent with hanging. While lack of defensive wounding indicates subject did not offer significant resistance, subject had suffered recent penetrating gunshot wound to right upper shoulder region, and would not have been able to offer effective resistance. Additionally, possible skin cells were observed beneath fingernails of left hand. Recommend taking scrapings of fingernails to obtain tissue samples.'"

"They got tissue samples from the dead guy?" Vic said. "That's big."

"Look here," Webb said. "Jones got her hands on the official postmortem from the other doctor. It's right here. Does the name Petrucelli ring any bells?"

"He's not familiar to me," Carlyle said. "He wasn't affiliated with the O'Malleys."

"He sounds Italian," Vic said darkly.

"And all Italians are affiliated with the Mafia," Webb said, rolling his eyes.

"I knew if I kept being sarcastic around the Lieutenant, it'd rub off on him eventually," Vic said. "My work here is done."

"Shut up, Neshenko," Webb said.

"I think I've heard the name before," Erin said. "But I can't place it."

Webb nodded. "I have, too. It was in connection with a Mob case, if that jogs your memory. Unfortunately, Neshenko's stereotyping is right this time."

Erin snapped her fingers. "That crooked doc who signed the bogus certificate on that Mafia guy, Lorenzo Bianchi. Is this the same guy?"

"I'd be surprised if it wasn't," Webb said. "I didn't know he was working for the City."

"He's working for Keane, not New York," Erin said. "I bet he's on some sort of temporary contract. And if he's written one bad death certificate, he's done others."

Webb opened Petrucelli's report. "Let's have a look," he said.

"Damn," Vic said after a few moments. "No autopsy. No fingernail scrapings. No nothing. And they cremated the son of a bitch, so we can't dig him up."

"A rubber-stamp job," Webb agreed. "He just lists 'suicide' as cause of death."

"Keane wanted this swept under the rug," Erin said. "Because he killed Luna himself."

"Levine would've tied him to it," Vic said in tones of absolute conviction. "That girl doesn't miss a thing."

"Petrucelli acknowledges Levine's report," Webb said. "He'd have to, if he wanted to keep her quiet. Otherwise she might have made a stink. But he didn't take any of her recommendations. It's like he didn't even look at her report."

"How good is this?" Erin asked. "Can we use it to burn Keane?"

"Not by itself," Webb said. "It looks bad, but it's circumstantial. He could always just argue the doctor was incompetent or lazy, or there was a miscommunication somewhere."

"We need the doc," Erin said. "Is he still at Bellevue?"

"No," Webb said. "Looks like he has a private physical rehab practice in Lower Manhattan."

"Which just happens to use lots of prescription painkillers, I bet," Vic added. He checked the address. "Hey, that's not far. We can be there in ten minutes."

Chapter 22

The detectives walked into a very ordinary-looking Manhattan lobby and consulted the usual floor plan.

"Eighth floor," Vic said, poking the elevator call button. The left-hand elevator opened and they trooped in.

"Now remember," Webb said, "we need him to talk."

"That'll be easy," Vic said. "I'll just hang him out his window by his ankles."

"No," Webb said wearily. "That's police brutality."

"I won't drop him!" Vic said indignantly. "He won't have a mark on him! What's brutal about that?"

"Does the word 'inadmissible' mean anything to you?" Webb asked.

"How about if I grab a syringe of whatever's lying around and tell him I'll inject it into his tear ducts if he doesn't come clean?"

"No," Webb repeated, even more wearily.

"I don't know why you even brought me along," Vic pouted.

"You volunteered," Webb said. "Also, it's your job. And I thought you might need adult supervision."

"Zofia's an adult," Vic replied.

"She's thirty," Webb said. "You're older than she is."

"Age doesn't make you an adult," Vic said.

"How right you are," Webb said. "I think you should let O'Reilly and me do the talking. You just lurk in the background and look menacing."

Vic brightened. "I'm good at that!"

The elevator disgorged them into a clean, professional-looking medical office, complete with a perky blonde receptionist.

"Hello!" she chirped. "Do you have an appointment?"

Webb laid his shield on the counter. "My name's Lieutenant Webb," he said. "I'm with the NYPD. We've consulted with Dr. Petrucelli in the past. I was hoping to talk to him."

"Let me see if he's available, sir," she said. She picked up the phone and punched in a number. "Yes, Doctor, it's Britney. I have a Lieutenant Webb here from the police. He needs a consult. Okay, thank you!"

Britney hung up and gave Webb a bright smile. "It'll just be a few minutes," she said.

They settled in the waiting-room chairs. Erin, to her own astonishment, started paging through a bridal magazine. She hadn't really given much thought to what she'd be wearing for her wedding; "white dress" was as far as she'd gotten. She'd considered putting on her dress blues, but had figured Carlyle the traditionalist wouldn't approve. Neither would her own mother, and Erin anticipated several skirmishes with Mary O'Reilly on wedding topics. It was important to pick her battles.

"No *Guns and Ammo*," Vic complained. "No *Soldier of Fortune*. Not even *Maxim*. Do guys come here at all?" He was forced to settle for *Sports Illustrated*, and not even the Swimsuit Issue, as he loudly bemoaned.

After about ten minutes, Britney told them the doctor would see them in his office. "End of the hallway, on your right," she added.

Petrucelli was behind a big, heavy-looking desk which made his slight build look even smaller. He blinked at them through wire-rimmed glasses that perched above a pitiful little mustache.

"Thank you for seeing us on such short notice, Doctor," Webb said, offering his hand. "Harry Webb. These are Detectives Vic Neshenko and Erin O'Reilly."

Petrucelli blinked again at Erin's name. He shifted in his chair and cleared his throat. "Yes, hello, Detectives. What can I do for you?"

"We've met only once before, but it was only a short conversation," Webb said. "I wouldn't expect you to remember it. That was when you were still at Bellevue."

"I'm afraid I don't recall," Petrucelli said. His eyes shifted and Erin suspected he was lying. "Now, I do have a full slate of appointments this afternoon, so we'll have to keep this brief."

"Of course," Webb said. "I just have a few questions about your postmortem consultation regarding the death of Alphonse Luna."

"I'm sorry, the name isn't familiar," Petrucelli said.

"Do you do a lot of postmortems, Dr. Petrucelli?" Erin asked. "It seems like an unusual sideline for a rehab doc."

"I'm happy to assist the City of New York in whatever capacity is required," Petrucelli said.

"I'm glad to hear it," Webb said. "Because we represent the City. I'd just like to know why you didn't perform an autopsy on Mr. Luna."

"I'd have to look up the report," Petrucelli said. "I'd be happy to check my records and get back to you as quickly as possible."

"That won't be necessary," Webb said, laying a printout of the report on the doctor's desk. "I have it with me, as it happens. I also have this other report, which contains several recommendations. If you wouldn't mind?"

Petrucelli bent forward and squinted through his spectacles. "Where did you get this?" he demanded. "This is an internal document."

"Internal to the NYPD," Webb said. "I did properly identify myself at the beginning of this conversation, didn't I? I'm with Major Crimes. We're investigating the murder of Mr. Luna, among other interconnected crimes."

"It wasn't a murder," Petrucelli snapped. "It was clear-cut suicide."

"Oh, good," Erin said. "You remember it after all."

Petrucelli glared at her. "Young lady," he said. "I wouldn't dream of telling you how to conduct a police investigation. Are you telling me how to conduct a postmortem examination?"

"I don't see how that's relevant," she replied. "Since you didn't. All you did was sign off on the official narrative."

"The man was a professional criminal," Petrucelli said. "He was also a murderer! Why do you care that he hanged himself? It's a net gain for society."

"That's an unusual view for a physician to take," Webb said.

"And a very detailed recollection of a case you couldn't remember a moment ago," Erin added. "I wonder what else you'd remember if you put your thinking cap on. You might recall being paid off in exchange for your report, for instance."

"This conversation is over," Petrucelli said. "I saw you as a courtesy. You come into my office and insult me in return? You accuse me of taking bribes? Get out."

"We know all about Andrew Keane," Erin said quietly. "We know he strangled Luna and posed his body. We know you helped him cover it up."

"That makes you an accessory to Murder One," Vic said. "Funny thing about first-degree murder. If you're an accomplice, you get the same penalty as the guy who did it. That means you're looking at twenty to life. And we're talking hard time, not one of those country-club prisons they send you to for screwing around with your tax returns."

Petrucelli flinched. "I don't know what you're talking about," he said weakly. "Are you threatening me?"

"Me? No," Vic said. "I'm not allowed to threaten people. Lieutenant Webb was real clear on that when we were on the way up to see you. He even said I can't dangle you out your office window, if you can believe it. I'm just telling you what the law says. The Manhattan District Attorney, now, he's another story. *He's* gonna threaten you with what I just said. Cops don't put people on trial, you know. That's the DA's job. We just slap the cuffs on you and haul your ass downtown."

"There's no evidence," Petrucelli said. "No proof of anything!"

"Because you whitewashed the report and cremated the body?" Webb said. "That's true. But there's the little question of this other report. It was written by Dr. Sarah Levine. Have you ever met her? No? There's some things you should know about her. Dr. Levine, unlike you, actually *is* a Medical Examiner. She's truly exceptional at her job. In the past week, she's examined two apparent suicides. One was genuine, one was staged. She knew which was which immediately, without even needing to take the bodies back to the morgue. And she has an unusual brain. I have the feeling when we talk to her about this case, she'll remember every detail. We may not be able to bring criminal charges against you, not immediately. But we'll certainly have enough to take to the OPMC."

"The which?" Vic asked.

"He knows," Webb said. "Would you care to enlighten my colleague, Doctor?"

Petrucelli said nothing. He licked his lips nervously.

"It's the Office of Professional Medical Conduct," Webb explained. "They enforce misconduct which can result in loss of license to practice medicine in New York."

"You can't do that," Petrucelli said.

"I can and I will," Webb said, his voice suddenly losing its genial, conversational tone. It was hard and cold now. He leaned forward, planting his hands on the desk. "Andrew Keane is a murderer. He's killed at least twice. One of his victims was a police officer. One of *my* officers. He's in the hospital now, under guard, after he tried to kill another of my detectives earlier today. He's badly wounded and prison-bound. Once he's had a little time to think things over, he'll start wondering what sort of deal he can make. Charles Markham, our District Attorney, is going to want his pound of flesh. Keane will be delighted to give the DA someone else's. Every other criminal he can betray will lighten his own sentence. Do you really think he's going to stay loyally silent about you if he can throw you the wolves in exchange for, say, a five-year reduction?"

Petrucelli shrank back in his chair. He looked even smaller than he had a moment ago. Webb wasn't a tall man, but his anger gave him presence.

"This is your chance, your one chance, to save yourself," Webb said. "You can talk to us, or you can take the fall."

"We know how Keane operates," Erin said. "He blackmails people. If you were coerced, you can get off easy. We don't need to know whatever dark secret Keane has on you. Just tell us what happened with Luna. We won't even ask you about the other fake death certificates you've signed, like the one for Mr. Bianchi. I'm sure you remember him."

Petrucelli squirmed, pinned to his chair by three pairs of eyes. He seemed like he was still trying to decide what to do, but Erin knew better. She'd already seen him crack, and those cracks would only get wider. They owned him.

* * *

"Did you get all that?" Webb asked as they rode the elevator back down. It was forty-five minutes later. Petrucelli had rescheduled his appointments. He'd proved talkative and cooperative enough in the end.

"Every word," Erin said. She was still wearing her hidden microphone.

"We'll get his signed statement," Webb went on. "But that should be just a formality now."

"What an asshole," Vic said.

"Petrucelli?" Erin asked.

"Keane," he said. "That bastard's poisoned the Department! It's gonna take friggin' *weeks* to clean up his mess!"

"Months," Webb said. "Maybe years. On the bright side, I'll be retiring soon, so it won't be my problem much longer."

"What're we going to do with Petrucelli?" Erin asked.

"We'll get his testimony," Webb said coldly. "After that, OPMC can have him. I expect he'll lose his medical license, and good riddance. As for the rest, the DA will decide."

"Amen to that," Erin said.

"*Now* do we have enough to nail Keane?" Vic demanded.

"I think so," Webb said. "With the good doctor's testimony, we know he falsified his report on Luna's death. Together with the attempt on O'Reilly's life, and Worthington being able to tie him to the efforts to retrieve Jones' hard drive, we have a pattern. I think once we get all the pieces tied together, the DA will be glad to finish the job."

"He'd better not offer Keane a deal," Erin said.

"Whatever deal ends up being struck, it'll include prison time and dismissal from the Department," Webb said.

"He deserves to die in prison," Erin said angrily.

"That's not up to us," Webb reminded her.

"Think positive," Vic added. "He's screwed so many people over, he's bound to be locked up with some of them. And if he somehow manages not to get shanked in the showers, if he ever hits the street, there'll be more guys waiting for him on the outside. And I'll be one of them. That's the problem with operating through fear. Once people aren't scared of you anymore, they'll be lining up to kick your ass."

"I was hoping for more," Erin said.

"Take the win," Webb advised her. "Don't get greedy."

"What now?" Vic asked.

"We go to the Eightball and fill out a ream or two of paperwork," Webb said.

Vic groaned.

"Then, at five o'clock, we go to a bar," Webb continued. "First round's on me."

"Who are you?" Vic asked, feigning astonishment. "What'd you do with our commanding officer? And why didn't you do it sooner?"

"We'll have a Departmental funeral in a few days," Webb said. "We'll all have the chance to pay our respects. But I think we ought to do a little something today, just us, to remember Kira."

Erin nodded. "I think that's a great idea, sir."

Chapter 23

"I love what you've done with the place," Piekarski said.

"Thank you, Miss Piekarski," Carlyle replied.

Mina reached out from her harness and made a play for Vic's shot glass. The Russian slid it further down the bar, out of reach.

"Not till you're older, kid," he said.

Piekarski sipped at a glass of Glen Docherty-Kinlochewe. "God," she said. "I missed that. Women talk about swollen feet and weight gain and hormones and labor pains, but it's the lack of booze that really gets to you."

"I wouldn't know," Erin said.

Piekarski winked at Carlyle. "You will," she said.

"Hold on," Vic said. "Did I miss something here?"

"No!" Erin almost shouted. Her expression of shock set Carlyle to chuckling.

"Sorry," Vic said. "I just missed the signals last time something like this happened, so I didn't want to be the last guy to know this time around."

"Is Mina going to be a cop?" Erin asked, holding out a finger. Mina dutifully grabbed it and started sucking on the fingertip, gurgling happily.

"Jesus, I hope not," Vic said. "The world's plenty dangerous as it is."

"It'll be up to her," Piekarski said. "New York's Finest can always use another good officer."

"There's a few openings in IAB," Webb commented.

"Any word on who we'll be getting to replace Keane?" Erin asked.

"Some asshole or other," Vic muttered. "It doesn't really matter which. All assholes are the same, and they all stink."

"I don't think they've settled on anyone yet," Webb said. "But I heard the name McDowell getting batted around."

"Fiona McDowell?" Erin said, surprised.

"You know her?" Vic asked.

"I know of her," she replied. "Dad used to run into her on the Job sometimes."

"I think I've heard of her, now you mention it," Vic said. "Isn't she the one they call the Cast-Iron Bi—"

"That's her," Erin interrupted.

"Great," Vic sighed. "We get rid of a crooked IAB dick and replace him with a nut-buster."

"What's wrong?" Piekarski asked, sliding a hand up his leg. "A big, strong guy like you insecure about saluting a lady?"

"I'll salute you any time," Vic said. "Nobody can make me stand to attention like you do."

Nine long, awkward seconds of silence followed.

Webb coughed. "Nothing's decided," he reminded them. "Regardless of who comes in, he or she will have a tough job rebuilding trust in IAB at the Eightball. There's going to be more investigations. More heads are probably going to roll. It's going to be tough and it's going to be messy. I expect all of you to support the new Lieutenant, and to exemplify proper police behavior and adherence to regulations."

"You know us, sir," Vic said. "Why would you ever expect that?"

"Wishful thinking, I suppose," Webb said. "Joking aside, I have something to say, so listen up."

Everyone turned toward Webb, with the exception of Rolf, who only had eyes for Erin.

"This was a tough case for all of us," Webb said. "It hit way too close to home. We've all lost brothers or sisters on the Force before, but Kira Jones was one of *ours*. Major Crimes is a small family, but that's what we are—family. I don't have to remind you, my life is terrible. I have two ex-wives and two teenage daughters on the other side of the country. I work long hours so I don't have to spend so much time alone in my lousy apartment. We bitch at one another, we complain, we break some rules, but at the end of the day, I know you would run through fire for each other. It's probably this excellent whiskey talking, but I just wanted to say how proud I am of each and every one of you."

"It's *definitely* the whiskey," Erin said, but she smiled as she said it.

"To be fair, it's very fine whiskey," Carlyle said.

"Shut up, O'Reilly," Webb said. "I'm trying to make a point here. Some of us are rising stars, on their way to bigger and better things."

He nodded at Piekarski, whose ears went pink.

"The rest of us have black marks on our records and skeletons in our closets," he went on. "I left LA because it was turning me into a burned-out has-been gumshoe. I killed a man who didn't deserve to die, because I was trying to impress a woman I should never have trusted."

"I've never heard that story," Vic said, perking up. "Sounds like a good one. Do tell?"

"I'm not nearly drunk enough for that," Webb said. "Neshenko, you basically got kicked out of ESU because your CO was afraid you'd do something stupid and get thrown off the Force. O'Reilly, do you know why you're here?"

"I used to think it was because I caught those cop-killers down in Queens," Erin said, staring at the whiskey in her glass. "And recovered that stolen painting. I acted like a detective before they ever gave me a gold shield. But I know better now. Keane saw the complaints the detectives at the One-Sixteen filed against me. He figured I was a loose cannon he could get leverage on and control. After I took that contract for Valentino Vitelli, to kill the witness to the murder Vitelli's son committed, he thought he had me under his thumb. The whole thing was a setup. I probably shouldn't be here."

"And yet you've proved a remarkable detective," Webb said. "Keane couldn't have been more wrong about you. Captain Holliday and I know what sort of officer you are. And that goes for the rest of you, too. We've taken this bunch of misfits and forged you into an unbreakable team."

"I'll drink to that," Vic said, hoisting his glass.

Webb stopped him with an upraised forefinger and an eyebrow. "Just a moment. Kira Jones was part of this team, too. I know she transferred, but you can't transfer out of a family. She proved she was still one of us. Practically the last thing she did on Earth was give us the ammunition we needed to take down her own killer."

"She avenged herself," Vic said. "Like Brandon Lee in *The Crow*. What do you call that? The spirit of vengeance that comes back to Earth? Isn't it a revenant or some shit?"

"Beats me," Erin said.

"I don't know," Webb said. "Paranormal avengers weren't covered at the LAPD Academy."

"Whatever," Vic said. "She stuck it to Keane even with a bullet in her head, and that makes her a friggin' legend in my book."

"And that's who we're toasting," Webb said. "I think we should have a drink in memory of Kira Jones, without whom a killer would still be loose and doing mischief."

"Cheers," Vic said, with feeling.

"What's a good Irish toast?" Erin asked Carlyle.

"Are you wanting something sentimental, or something more humorous?" he replied.

"We'll take both," she said.

"Very well," he said. "I'll give you the Blessing of Saint Patrick first:

> *May the road rise up to meet you,*
> *May the wind be always at your back,*
> *May the sun shine warm upon your face,*
> *May the rains fall soft upon your fields,*
> *And until we meet again,*
> *May God hold you in the palm of His hand.*"

They clinked glasses and drank. Erin blinked away tears.

"What about the humorous one?" she asked hoarsely.

"It's one of Corky's favorites," Carlyle said. "May our dear friend Kira have found her way to Heaven a full half hour before the Devil knew she was dead."

Sometimes, Erin thought, laughter and tears made a damn good cocktail.

Here's a sneak peek from Book 27: Vino Blanco

Coming 3/24/2025

"Who was that punk?" Sean asked quietly.

"He's nobody, Dad," Erin said. "Forget about it."

Sean grunted and rubbed his mustache. He was sitting at the bar on the opposite side of Erin from Carlyle. The three of them were sipping Guinness, the chardonnay abandoned, and watching the final acts of the engagement party.

Most of the guests had left. Corky had gotten three Patrolmen very drunk and the four of them had formed an impromptu quartet. All were attempting to sing "Dublin Pub Crawl," but only Corky was succeeding. Sean Junior, who was not on good terms with Corky, was on the opposite side of the room, chatting with Jasper Ackermann. Both men were surgeons, so Erin supposed they had plenty to talk about. Jasper's fiancé, Sarah Levine, was drawing a diagram on a napkin to demonstrate an autopsy Y-incision for Anna and

Patrick O'Reilly. Their mother, looking on, was less than thrilled.

"I told you a long time ago, kiddo," Sean said. "If you're going to be a cop, you can't bring the Job home with you. Thirty-nine years of marriage and I never did."

"It's different for you, Dad," Erin said. "The Barley Corner *was* part of the Job. But that's all in the past now."

"Richie thinks differently," Sean said. "Whoever he is."

"He's Evan O'Malley's son," Carlyle said quietly.

Sean blinked. "Why isn't he in jail?" he demanded. "I thought you locked all those bastards away!"

Carlyle cleared his throat.

"I didn't mean you," Sean muttered. "Or Corcoran over there, though God knows he deserves it."

"All right, lads," Corky was saying. "Once more, with me:

> *We all went in to Lannigan's pub for we're a jolly crew.*
> *We all went in to Lannigan's for a final drink or two.*
> *Lannigan's, Flannigan's, Milligan's, Gilligan's, Rafferty's, Cafferty's, Dillon's, McQuillan's,*
> *McCleary's, O'Leary's, O'Hegarty's, Kitty McGee's, in Dublin town upon the crawl,*
> *A hell of a time was had by all, down where the beer and whiskey flew!*"

"He probably does," Carlyle admitted. "But we don't all get what we deserve, and thank the good Lord for that. Richard's the one who slipped through the cracks."

"How come?" Sean asked.

Erin shrugged. "He was clean," she said. "We couldn't tie him to any of the O'Malley rackets. We thought he was going to take over the drug business, but that whole thing got derailed, and we shut the gang down before anything could happen with Richie. As far as the law goes, he's a civilian. We can't touch him."

"But is he?" Sean asked. "A civilian?"

"So far as I know," Carlyle said. "He's never killed a man, nor done anything else of note to the underworld. He's always been a bit of an embarrassment to his da, truth be told. His chief distinction's been a lack of it. When Erin described him as nobody, she was being unkind but scarcely inaccurate."

"All Evan's muscle guys are behind bars," Erin said. "Anything Richie wants to do, he'll have to do himself, and I don't think he's got the balls for it."

"He had the stones to walk into a pub full of cops and threaten you to your face," Sean said. "Don't underestimate a dumb kid with nothing to lose."

"Vincenzo Moreno made that mistake once," Carlyle observed. "But young Richard's a husband and father. He may have lost his family's fortune and the power Evan accumulated, but he hasn't a wish to spend the rest of his own life in prison. The very fact he turned up in person like that is a sign of his weakness. If he was truly intending to take action against Erin or myself, he'd hardly advertise it like that and put us on our guard. In the Life, if a lad wants you dead, the first inkling you'll get is when he sets his revolver behind your ear."

"Seriously, Dad," Erin said. "It's not a big deal. We've won. The O'Malleys are finished. The Lucarellis are smashed to pieces and they're fighting one another over scraps. We even broke up Keane's little operation inside the Eightball."

"Yeah," Sean sighed. "I kind of wish you hadn't done that."

"Why? Because he was a cop? He was as dirty as they come!"

"I know that!" Sean snapped. "And I've got no time for scumbags like him. It's the look of the thing. You know how things go in the Department. If they didn't already think you were a snitch for Internal Affairs, your coworkers are pretty sure of it now."

"Not the ones who matter," Erin said, giving a fond glance to Vic's table. The big Russian was sitting with Zofia Piekarski and Lieutenant Webb, all three giving their attention to little Mina Piekarski. The baby was lying on her back on the tabletop, wiggling her feet in the air.

"Everyone matters," Sean said. "When you're on the street and you call in a 10-13, you need every boy in blue to have your back—and every girl, too."

"He killed my friend," Erin said quietly.

"And you had to burn his ass for it," Sean said. "I get it. But there's a price you have to pay."

"You're worrying too much," she said. "On the list of guys I need to worry about in New York, Richie O'Malley is about third from the bottom."

"Who's at the top these days?" Sean asked.

Erin shrugged. "That's a good question. Most of my enemies are locked up or pushing daisies. But I'm more scared of Evan than his son, even if Evan's in jail. The same goes for Kyle Finnegan and Valentino Vitelli."

"When are the trials set to begin?"

"God only knows," Erin said. "Even picking the venue's going to be a nightmare. This case covers all five Boroughs, plus Jersey. There's even an international component, what with all the smuggling from Great Britain. It's going to take months to even empanel a jury, let alone finish trying the cases. There's dozens of defendants."

"I hope none of the bastards get out on bail," Sean growled.

"No fear of that," Carlyle said. "The charges are murder and conspiracy. The only lads who might post bail are the wee harmless ones who're only looking at a handful of years. They're the small-time earners, not the hardened killers."

"If you say so," Sean said. "How about Keane and his goons?"

"Keane's in the prison infirmary at Riker's," Erin said. "So is that douchebag Detective Johns. Keane had other guys, but I'm not worried about them."

"Why not?"

"Because they all hate him," Erin explained. "He coerced and blackmailed all these guys. They were scared of him, but now he's been busted, they know he's going to sell them out to save himself. They're not going to help. They're running for cover."

Sean nodded. "Glad to hear it."

* * *

An hour later, Erin sank onto Carlyle's couch. She kicked off her high heels and stretched out, sighing with relief.

Carlyle paused in the doorway, two whiskey glasses in his hands, and took a moment to savor the sight of her stocking-clad legs.

"Enjoy the view," she said. "Because I'm not wearing nylons and heels very often. You men think you have it rough with your dress shoes and ties? My feet are killing me."

He sat down beside her, setting the glasses on the coffee table. He took hold of her left foot and began massaging it.

Erin closed her eyes and sighed again. "Careful," she said. "I might think you were trying to get me in bed with you."

"Are you saying this would work?" he asked, gently kneading her flesh.

"Mmm," she murmured. "Yeah, probably."

He shifted to her other foot after a moment. Then, ever so gradually, his skillful fingers worked their way up her calves. Erin lay back, enjoying the twin warmth of good whiskey in her belly and her lover's hands on her skin.

An annoying, persistent buzzing sound intruded on her. She gave an irritable wave with her hand, as if it was a fly she could brush away. But the buzzing continued. It was coming from her handbag, on the floor next to Rolf. The K-9 had his chin between his paws. He gave the bag a look of mild curiosity but didn't bother to raise his head.

"Damn it," she muttered, levering herself upright and thrusting a hand into the bag, feeling for her phone.

"You're off duty tonight," Carlyle reminded her.

"Never completely," she said, fumbling the phone up to her face. Webb's name showed on the screen. "*Damn* it!" she said again, with feeling.

Carlyle leaned back, letting her swing her feet around onto the floor. She cleared her throat and thumbed the phone.

"O'Reilly," she said, trying not to sound as grumpy as she felt.

"I'm sorry to disturb you," Lieutenant Webb said. "Especially this late at night, on a day off."

"You should know, sir," she said. "You were at the party. I saw you half an hour ago!"

"And it was an excellent party," he said. "How much have you had to drink?"

She had to pause and do a quick internal count. "Two glasses of wine," she said. "Then two pints of Guinness at the bar after. And I just had a shot of Scotch. But that's spread over a few hours. I'm good."

"Are you okay to drive?"

"Absolutely. Where are we going?"

"I was taking the subway to Brooklyn," he said. "But I'm on my way back now. If you could pick me up on the way, I'd appreciate it. We're going to Riker's."

Erin felt a tingle of anticipation that had nothing to do with the alcohol in her bloodstream. "What happened?" she asked.

"Someone broke into the infirmary," he said. "They put a shiv in Detective Johns' throat."

"What's his condition?"

"He's dead."

Ready for more?

Join Steven Henry's author email list
for the latest on new releases, upcoming books and
series, behind-the-scenes details, events, and more.

Be the first to know about new releases in the Erin
O'Reilly Mysteries by signing up at
clickworkspress.com/join/erin

Now keep reading to enjoy

Zombie
A Dr. Sarah Levine Story

Zombie
A Dr. Sarah Levine Story

Steven Henry

Clickworks Press • Baltimore, MD

Copyright © 2024 Steven Henry
Cover design © 2024 Ingrid Henry
Cover photo © 2024 under license from Shutterstock.com (Credit: Josiah_S/Shutterstock)
Additional cover photo © 2024 under license from Shutterstock.com (Credit: boommaval/Shutterstock)
NYPD shield photo used under license from Shutterstock.com (Credit: Stephen Mulcahey/Shutterstock)
Author photo © 2017 Shelley Paulson Photography
Spine image used under license from Shutterstock.com (Credit: Vlad Ageshin/Shutterstock)
All rights reserved

First publication: Clickworks Press, 2024
Release: CWP-EORSL1-INT-P.IS-1.0

Sign up for updates, deals, and exclusive sneak peeks at clickworkspress.com/join.

This is a work of fiction. Names, characters, places, organizations, and events are either the products of the author's imagination or used in a fictitious manner. Any resemblance to actual persons, living or dead, is purely coincidental.

Zombie

Combine 1.5 oz. Jamaican rum, 1.5 oz. Puerto Rican gold rum, 1 oz. 151-proof demerara rum, 4 dashes Pernod, .75 oz. fresh-squeezed lime juice, .5 oz. "Don the Beachcomber's Mix," .5 oz. falernum, 1 tsp. grenadine, and a dash of Angostura bitters in a blender with 6 oz. crushed ice.

Blend at high speed for 5 seconds. Pour into a tall glass or Tiki mug and fill with additional crushed ice, if necessary. Garnish with a mint sprig.

"Don the Beachcomber's Mix" AKA "Don's Mix"

Crush 3 cinnamon sticks in 1 cup water. Add 1 cup sugar and bring to a boil, stirring until sugar is completely dissolved. Simmer 2 minutes, then remove from heat and let stand for at least 2 hours. Strain into a glass bottle. Add 1 part mixture to 2 parts fresh grapefruit juice. Cover and refrigerate. Will keep for up to 2 weeks.

Chapter 1

The one thing never to forget when handling human remains was respect. In many ways it was like operating heavy machinery or firearms, or working with dangerous pathogens. The most hazardous legal occupations in America were commercial fishing and logging, because of the inherent risks of powerful machines.

The most dangerous illegal occupation was probably prostitution, though those numbers were harder to come by. It was estimated to have a fatality rate of around 200 per 100,000 workers, as opposed to 114 per 100,000 for fishermen.

The body on Sarah Levine's table was one of those two hundred unfortunate working women. Levine had finished the postmortem examination and was finalizing her report. The clinical phrases marched across her computer screen.

Body found by chance by an NYPD Patrolman in a dumpster behind a tobacco shop. Female, mixed ethnic background including Caucasian and African ancestry, age approximately nineteen years. Black hair, brown eyes. Tattoo of a butterfly on lower back. Three piercings in left ear, one in right.

Earrings catalogued, inexpensive gold-plated hoops. Cause of death: blunt-force trauma to maxillofacial region. Blows consistent with cylindrical object. Trace metallic residue indicates steel pipe (note photograph of left cheek showing clear marks of threading at end of pipe; may aid in identifying weapon). Evidence of recent sexual activity. Bruising and tearing to genital area suggests nonconsensual encounter. Bloodwork shows moderate quantity of opiates. Fingerprints not a match to any on file in Tri-State area. Dental records pending possible identification. No papers, licenses, or other identification found on body. Clothing consistent with occupation of worker in sex trade.

Preliminary conclusion: Unidentified subject, "Jane Doe," is a streetwalker who has been raped and beaten to death with a pipe. She might be identified in the future, but there is a high likelihood nobody has reported her missing.

Levine knew all the data, had memorized it. That was her job and she was good at it, possibly the best Medical Examiner in New York City. That wasn't ego-driven exaggeration. Levine prided herself on her objectivity, particularly with respect to her own abilities. But the data were only half the job.

Levine believed the dead deserved respect. Whatever their path in life, everyone ended the same way. From dust they were made and to dust they were doomed to return, but while they remained recognizably human, Levine honored their remains as best she could. The dead could not speak, so Levine had to coax their stories from their cold flesh. She owed them the truth.

This nameless girl lying on Levine's slab might never be identified, her killer never brought to justice. That was a job for the Homicide detectives. But their case would not fail due to an oversight or error by Sarah Levine. As long as Jane Doe was under Levine's care, Levine would do her absolute best.

She added the date and time to the report, glancing at the clock. Her shift technically ended at 1700 hours, five o'clock in the evening. It was now 2036 hours, 8:36PM. Nonetheless, she took ten more minutes to carefully reread the report, ensuring everything was clear, concise, and free from spelling or grammatical errors. Then she sent the report, being sure to copy all appropriate recipients.

After that, she secured Jane Doe's body. She had already replaced the organs removed during the autopsy and had stitched up the Y-incision. Now she carefully slid the body onto a gurney and wheeled it to the shelf where it would rest until transferred out of the Precinct 8 morgue for burial or alternative disposal. Some examiners had orderlies take care of this part of the procedure, but Levine preferred to do it herself. She didn't particularly like orderlies. She worked best alone, in the absence of interruptions. The whispers of the dead were very quiet, easily drowned out by the chattering of the living.

Only after she had given Jane Doe as much peace and privacy as circumstances allowed, after she had thoroughly washed her own hands and forearms, after she had cleaned and put away her instruments, did Levine take a moment to check her phone. She didn't bother with her e-mail, knowing that if she saw something requesting an answer she'd be here all night, fielding one question after another. Levine couldn't leave a question unanswered once she had seen it. That didn't really bother her, but she did occasionally need to leave the lab for things like food and sleep.

Her phone told her she had a voicemail from Jasper, received at 8:05. She'd had the phone with her, but silenced, and his call had rolled through without her noticing the subtle vibration. When Levine was conducting an autopsy, she tended to block out minor distractions. She accessed the message while she waited for the elevator.

"Sarah," he said. "To confirm your caller ID, it really is me. If you hear this before four in the morning, please contact me and come to Mount Sinai Beth Israel Hospital. After that I'll be at home, probably asleep. I'd like a consultation on an unusual case."

Jasper was a clear communicator who understood how her brain worked. She knew he was working the overnight shift at Mount Sinai Beth, but he'd still specified which hospital she should go to, in order to avoid potential confusion.

She'd made a good choice with Dr. Jasper Ackermann. It was a relationship founded on mutual respect, professional admiration, and basic compatibility. Also, though Levine thought this was borderline irrelevant, he had very attractive brown eyes that gave her an oddly warm feeling when he looked at her, and his features were pleasingly symmetrical.

Levine had been planning to go home and catch up on some medical journals. She hadn't anticipated seeing Jasper before morning. It would be interesting to visit him at work. Jasper was a skilled cardiologist. If he was looking for her input, it meant someone had died, most likely of causes other than cardiac arrest. Of course, every cause of death eventually resulted in cardiac arrest, Levine reminded herself. Heart stoppage had formerly been the primary criterion for determining when life had ceased. In medicine it was important to be as specific as possible, to avoid misunderstandings.

The elevator arrived and she climbed in. While it glided up out of the basement, she sent Jasper a text message.

"I am in the elevator leaving the morgue now. I will meet you in your office unless otherwise notified."

Levine had a car, but she didn't usually drive it to work. The subway offered many excellent opportunities to study interesting pathogens and abnormal psychological cases.

* * *

For some reason, most people did not like hospitals. Levine had never fully understood why. It probably had something to do with fear and repression. From conversations with other people, she had gradually come to realize that many humans were not reconciled to their own mortality. The average person apparently got through his or her day without thinking about death or serious illness. Hospitals dredged up those deep-seated fears.

Levine had no illusions whatsoever about mortality. Carbon-based lifeforms were inherently impermanent. The human body constantly changed, renewed itself, and deteriorated. Eventually, inevitably, the forces of entropy triumphed over the body's regenerative capabilities and the organism died.

Hospitals were comfortable for Levine. They were beacons of light and knowledge, places where skilled, dedicated professionals applied all their powers to pushing entropy back into the shadows. The struggle was doomed to eventual failure, but that only increased its nobility in her eyes. To persevere in the face of destruction was courageous. Every vaccine, every successful surgery, every recovery from illness was a small victory. Where most people saw sickness and death, Levine saw healing and hope.

Even the exterior of the building shone like a lighthouse in the Manhattan night. The emergency room entrance positively glowed. Levine was drawn to it by an impulse she recognized as primordial, the longing of primitive humanity for the warmth and security offered by a campfire.

She wondered, in passing, why humans were so entranced by fire while most animals instinctively shunned it. There was probably an adaptive advantage handed down from Neolithic tribes. She made a mental note to glance through one of the online anthropology journals later, if she had time.

Levine walked briskly into the hospital and pressed the elevator button. Jasper's office was on the fifth floor. While the elevator hummed into motion, she took a moment to smooth her hair. It had become slightly disarranged on the subway platform by the close passage of a train. Jasper was her fiancé, but he was also a fellow medical professional and she was here in her official capacity. She needed to maintain a basic standard of appearance.

Jasper was standing in front of his desk when she arrived outside his door. That was extremely unusual. Doctors had to stand for prolonged periods, particularly when performing surgical operations, so in their offices they tended to sit. Also, Jasper was twitching slightly. His right knee bounced in a rapid motion, moving so quickly it seemed to vibrate. His hands were clasped behind his back, but Levine noted the tension in the tendons above his shirt collar.

In short, though his face was impassive, Levine easily diagnosed him with an acute stress reaction. A purely psychological cause was unlikely. Jasper had successfully performed, by Levine's count, sixty-seven open-heart operations. Only two operations had been unsuccessful, resulting in fatality to the patient. He had complete control over his muscular functions, which was vitally important in his occupation.

"What's your temperature?" Levine asked at once.

Jasper started violently. Even though he had been facing the door, and she had told him she would be there, he was still surprised. Hypothesis number one was that he was acutely uncomfortable or otherwise mentally compromised, either by pain or illness. Hypothesis number two was that he had simply been deep in thought and had not noticed her arrival. The obvious first step was to rule out serious illness.

"Normal," he said, recovering quickly. Levine was pleased to see his eyes focus on her with a normal pupillary response. He appeared fully awake and alert.

"Are you sure?" she asked.

"Yes, I took it just a few minutes ago," he said.

"Other symptoms?"

"Of course not," Jasper said. "I would have isolated myself."

There was a momentary pause. Levine mentally reviewed what they had just said and realized she had made some underlying assumptions which Jasper had not contradicted.

"But you have been exposed to something?" she asked. He wouldn't have checked his temperature unless he had been.

"I don't know," Jasper said quietly. "That is—we've had a minor containment breach."

"A containment breach is a binary event," Levine said. "Either it has occurred or not. If it has occurred, it is by definition not minor. How would you define a 'minor' breach?"

"We have a body downstairs," Jasper said.

"I know," she said. "Your text informed me of that."

"Here's the file," Jasper said, reaching back onto his desk and picking up a manila folder, which he extended toward her.

"Should I take precautions touching you or anything you've handled?" Levine asked, making no move toward the folder.

"Not necessary," Jasper said. "That is—I've been vaccinated against yellow fever. Have you?"

"Yes," Levine said. "I traveled to Puerto Rico five years ago for the tropical disease seminar. Everyone in attendance received the full battery of immunizations against local pathogens."

"Oh, right," he said. "I'd forgotten."

Levine's eyes narrowed. It wasn't like Jasper to forget something like that. He knew perfectly well she'd gone to the seminar and he was well acquainted with her medical history.

"Jasper?" she asked, disliking the unprofessional tone that crept into her voice. "Are you all right?"

He ran a hand through his hair, which gave him a pleasantly disheveled look, though it went directly against Levine's view of proper meeting etiquette.

"I don't know," he said. "Take a look at the file, please, and tell me what you see."

Levine took the folder and flipped it open. She quickly scanned the document with eyes well accustomed to harvesting medical information.

"Rodney Young," she read aloud. "African-American male, age sixty-seven years. Deceased yesterday, time of death 2356 hours."

"Just before midnight last night," Jasper confirmed. "He was Weinberg's patient."

"Dr. Weinberg is a GI specialist, if I remember correctly," Levine said.

"Correct," Jasper said. "You remember him from the hospital picnic last summer?"

Levine had to think about that for a moment. The names and faces of the living didn't tend to stick in her head as well as those of the dead.

"Receding hairline," she recalled. "Gray mustache, eyeglasses. Bifocals. Somewhat overweight."

"That's the guy," Jasper said.

Levine returned her attention to the file. "Patient admitted complaining of severe gastrointestinal pain. Bloody stools, jaundiced appearance, bleeding from all facial orifices, *black vomit*."

"How would you diagnose?" Jasper asked.

It was an almost insultingly easy diagnosis. "Yellow fever, second phase," she said at once. "The term 'black vomit' refers to the presence of blood in the patient's vomit, giving it a distinctive dark coloration. The name 'yellow fever' comes from jaundice caused by damage to the liver."

"Top marks," Jasper said, and for the first time in the conversation he smiled. A little of the tension went out of his shoulders.

"Patient recently returned from Haiti," Levine read. "High likelihood he was infected there."

"He was a volunteer," Jasper said. "Building houses for Habitat for Humanity."

"Rehydration and pain relief drugs were administered," Levine continued. "However, treatment of symptoms was unsuccessful and patient was declared dead. That is unsurprising. Once the patient presents symptoms of jaundice, the probability of fatality is between twenty and fifty percent."

"It's a nasty disease," Jasper agreed. "High mortality rate."

"Why am I here?" Levine asked. "You have a textbook diagnosis, cut and dried. I assume you've followed proper Level Three biosafety protocols with his remains. Is that the containment breach you referred to earlier?"

"That's the problem," Jasper said. "Well, two problems. Mr. Young's daughter is coming to fetch him, but she lives in Denver and was delayed getting here. Bad weather at the airport, I think. She won't arrive until tomorrow. We bagged the body and kept it in the hospital morgue. The bag's been torn open."

Levine nodded. "That isn't serious in itself," she said. "It's possible one or more staff may have been exposed, but it should still be possible to contain any localized outbreak. Have you contacted CDC?"

"Not yet," Jasper said. He was unusually reluctant to come to the point. Levine was starting to find it irritating.

"What's the other problem?" she asked, using a sharper tone than she usually did with him.

"We have another body," he said. "As of an hour ago."

"That's not possible," Levine said. "The incubation period for yellow fever is three to six days. According to his file, Mr. Young was admitted yesterday afternoon. There wouldn't be time for anyone here to show symptoms. Do you mean another traveler from Haiti arrived?"

"No," Jasper said. "The body's one of our hospital staff. Wanda Perkins, a night nurse. And she didn't die of yellow fever."

"Then the events are independent of one another," Levine said.

"No, they're not," Jasper said flatly.

"You have data I don't," Levine said. "My guesses are pointless in the absence of more complete information. What killed her?"

Jasper sighed. "That's why I called you here," he said. "As far as I can tell, Rodney Young did."

Chapter 2

Further conversation would have been a waste of time. It was far more efficient to simply examine the body in question. Levine accordingly borrowed a set of PPE—Personal Protective Equipment—to augment her lab coat. In the case of yellow fever, a Biosafety Level 3 pathogen, that entailed gloves and protection for her mucous membranes and respiratory system in the form of a face shield, goggles, and protective mask.

The situation could have been much worse. Level 4 pathogens necessitated the use of full-body, air-supplied hazmat suits and decontamination showers. If Rodney Young had died of a Level 4 disease, like Ebola, they wouldn't even be talking about examining the body outside a specially-designed laboratory.

"What was the second subject's cause of death?" Levine asked as they rode the elevator down to the basement.

"I'd prefer not to prejudice your judgment," Jasper said.

The elevator settled into place at the bottom floor. There were three reasons to put a morgue as far below ground as possible; two good, one bad. The surrounding earth provided insulation, so more efficient preservation of bodies was possible. It also facilitated quarantine procedures, as it was much easier to prevent airflow and other traffic from accessing the area, which was definitely beneficial in the situation in which they now found themselves. Lastly, and least importantly, it kept the corpses out of sight, and presumably out of mind, of most hospital staff and patients, allowing them to cling to their delusions of immortality.

The morgue entrance was secured by a keycard scanner and two doors, both hermetically sealed with rubber linings. Jasper held up his card to the scanner, which obligingly beeped and showed a green light. The door clicked open.

"Evening, Dr. Ackermann," a man said from a doorway a short distance behind them. He was wearing blue coveralls, upon which was a nametag reading WATERSTON. He held a mop and was engaged in cleaning the floor. A yellow bucket stood next to him. Levine caught the scent of disinfectant.

"Good evening... Leroy, isn't it?" Jasper said. Unlike Levine, he had a good head for names. Levine suspected it was because he cared more than she did about remembering them, so he paid closer attention to introductions.

The man grinned. "That's right, Doc. Who's your good-looking friend?"

"My fiancée," Jasper corrected him. "Dr. Levine."

Waterston's grin widened. "Lucky man, Doc," he said. "Good to meet you, ma'am—Doctor, I mean. I'd shake hands, but you don't want to get any of what I've got on me on you."

"Why not?" Levine asked. "Have you also been exposed? If so, it's not a problem. I'm wearing gloves, and I've been vaccinated."

Waterston's smile faltered. "Right," he said, more uncertainly. Levine often noticed that look on the faces of men that wanted to talk to her. She made them uncomfortable for some reason. She believed most men were intimidated by a well-educated, intelligent woman. Jasper wasn't, which was one reason she liked him.

"Don't worry about it, Leroy," Jasper said, giving a smile of his own. "Just keep up the good work."

"Will do, Doc." Waterston continued swabbing the floor.

Jasper opened the outer door. He ensured it closed behind Levine before opening the inner one. Levine felt a faint but noticeable change in the air pressure as the inner door swung open.

"The morgue is negatively pressurized," she commented. It kept microbes from getting into the air vents and spreading into the rest of the building. Also, less importantly, it kept the smell in.

Levine was aware that most people found the chemical and organic smells of the morgue offensive. She'd never had a problem with them herself. Smell was a useful diagnostic tool for identifying many toxins, and could even help ascertain how long a body had been dead.

"Where's the—?" Levine began to ask, but stopped herself. The mortal remains of Wanda Perkins lay directly in front of her.

Levine's world narrowed and sharpened down into a single point. She knelt beside the corpse and immediately began mentally composing her report.

Female, African-American, aged middle thirties. Heavyset build, height approximately 165 centimeters, weight approximately 95 kilograms. Clad in medical scrubs and tennis shoes. Identification tag clipped to breast of scrubs, picture matching face of victim. Name on card WANDA PERKINS. Obvious injury, laceration of throat; apparent bisection of trachea and slashed jugular vein. Good definition of laceration indicates sharp blade, making a single stroke. Significant pooling of blood on front of scrubs and floor. Bloody footprints on floor, leading further into morgue. Footprints lack definition, suggesting feet dragging.

Preliminary hypothesis: victim's throat was cut by sharp object. Death not instantaneous, but inevitable due to combination of asphyxia and exsanguination. Lack of weapon in hand or near body, and location of wound, strongly suggest homicide.

"Why isn't NYPD Homicide here?" Levine asked.

Jasper pointed to the footprints. They were obviously made by bare feet. Despite the smearing, Levine could clearly make out the marks left by toes.

"Jasper, has the morgue been secured?" she asked. "It's possible the killer is still here."

"I agree," Jasper said quietly. "But I've been through this space. Nobody... nobody breathing is here but us. I haven't touched anything. You're right, we need to call the police, but I wanted your opinion so we have some idea what to tell them. And there's the infectious-disease angle. I don't want a bunch of Patrolmen stumbling around a biohazard hot zone. Ruth... that's Ruth Leibowitz, the other night nurse who has access down here, came looking for Wanda. She called me when she found Nurse Perkins."

"Did she attempt to render assistance?" Levine asked.

"She took a pulse," Jasper said. "So did I. Nurse Perkins was obviously beyond help. No pulse, no respiration, flesh already beginning to cool. I pronounced her immediately."

"You said Rodney Young appears to have killed her," Levine said. "Why did you say that?"

"Those are his footprints," Jasper said.

"How did you determine that?"

"Follow me."

Levine followed Jasper around the examining slab to the storage area, with its rows of metal doors. The blood trail continued until it reached the second door in the second row.

The edge of that door was smeared with blood. The door was shut.

Levine had no fear of the dead; only compassion, respect, and professional interest. Having worked a great many crime scenes, she also understood the importance of preservation of evidence. She reached into the pocket of her lab coat for a pen, which she slid behind the handle on the drawer and used as a leverage point to pull it open. That would minimize the chances of obscuring any fingerprints.

She found herself looking at a pair of bare feet wearing a toe tag, identifying them as belonging to Rodney Young. The feet had blood on their soles.

"I swear, that man was already dead," Jasper said.

Levine nodded. Jasper was a qualified and experienced physician. She was quite willing to take his word regarding the status of a corpse. She didn't say anything, but pulled the drawer out, bringing Rodney Young into the light of the fluorescent bulbs.

He was exactly what she would have expected from the medical file: a man at the tail end of middle age, somewhat overweight, bald. A tattoo on his shoulder and some scars, long ago healed, suggested military service in his past; probably in the Vietnam conflict, judging by his age. He lay partially within a black body bag, and the bag had been swathed in an outer plastic bag, but the body bag was unzipped and the plastic ripped open.

Rodney Young's hands were smeared with blood. In his cold, stiff right hand was a bloody box cutter.

"That is highly unusual," Levine said.

"Unique," Jasper said.

"The Crime Scene Unit will need to examine this," Levine said.

"I know," Jasper said. "But what I need to know is what you can tell me about..."

It was very unlike Jasper not to finish his sentences. Levine straightened up from her examination of Young and turned toward him. "Speak clearly, please," she said.

He cleared his throat. "What can you tell me about zombies?"

* * *

Levine didn't watch horror movies. She didn't see the point. Why would she want to induce an artificial negative emotion? And they were a litany of medical absurdities. So when Jasper asked about zombies, she didn't think of George Romero or brain-eating shambling corpses. She took it as a fairly standard clinical question and answered it accordingly.

"A zombie is a mythical creature from Haitian folklore," Levine said. For the second time that evening, she reminded herself to bone up on her anthropology. It was one of her weaker areas.

"Go on," Jasper said.

"Supposedly, they are the bodies of the dead, enslaved by a voodoo sorcerer," Levine said. "However, since that is impossible given our current understanding of mortality, so-called zombies are more likely living people given a pharmaceutical cocktail which induces a death-like state in which the subject becomes highly suggestible."

"Do you know what drugs might cause it?" Jasper asked.

"Possibly," Levine said. She remembered something she had read years ago, while studying for the tropical disease seminar. It had been a side topic, but due to its connection with mortality had stuck in her head. "There is an article of the Haitian Criminal Code, Article 246, which outlaws 'substances which, without giving death, will cause a more-or-less prolonged state of lethargy.'"

"That sounds promising," Jasper said.

"Wade Davis claimed a combination of tetrodotoxin and datura could be introduced into a victim's bloodstream to induce the proper trance-like state," Levine said. "Though many professionals have discredited him."

"Datura," Jasper repeated. "Deadly nightshade?"

"And related plants," Levine said. She was on much firmer ground with toxicology than with folklore. "Tetrodotoxin is found in pufferfish. It is highly toxic."

"But pufferfish and nightshade poisoning wouldn't present as yellow fever," Jasper said.

"No," Levine agreed. "Tetrodotoxin is a neurotoxin. It causes paralysis and respiratory failure. Datura is an hallucinogen. The only overlapping symptom with yellow fever would be delirium if the patient's fever spiked sufficiently high."

Jasper sighed. "But Weinberg wouldn't have bothered testing for either of those," he said. "Not with Mr. Young exhibiting such obvious yellow fever symptoms. There'd be no reason to screen his blood for exotic toxins. It's not like we look for pufferfish venom in every patient we see."

Levine smiled. Jasper was one of the few men she knew whose sense of humor she appreciated.

"What is your hypothesis?" she asked.

"The Haitian connection is intriguing," he said. "It's just possible Mr. Young might have fallen afoul of someone when he was in Haiti and been the recipient of the drug cocktail you mentioned. He could have contracted yellow fever at the same time. Then, the tetrodotoxin could have paralyzed and apparently killed him. The respiratory failure could have been masked by the yellow fever symptoms, resulting in a premature declaration of death."

"Is he dead now?" Levine asked with interest. She leaned over Young and peered closely at his stiff, cold features.

"Don't touch him!" Jasper hissed, grabbing her shoulder and pulling her back.

"I'm familiar with proper police procedure," she said, annoyed. "I won't compromise evidence."

"That's not what I meant!" Jasper said. "He might be alive. I mean, undead. Ahem. Not dead."

Levine took out her pen again and poked Young's bicep. "Note the rigor," she said. "This man is definitely dead."

"That's what I thought before," Jasper said.

Levine examined the hand that clutched the box cutter. It did not seem to be held tightly. "Neither pufferfish toxin nor datura mimic the effects of rigor mortis," she said. "Not only is this man dead, he has been dead for several hours at the very least. Body temperature is unreliable, due to the refrigeration in this cabinet, but lividity supports the time of death in his file."

"You're saying he's not a zombie," Jasper said.

"I've never examined a zombie," Levine replied. "I don't know how one would present. Neither does anyone I've read about in the literature. It strikes me as an unlikely hypothesis. Who else has access to the morgue?"

"Besides Ruth and Wanda, the night nurses? Dr. Weinberg, myself, and a couple of interns—Lucy Greenberg and Abe Malter."

"The police will want to interview them," Levine said. "Can you ascertain their locations?"

"They're all still on call," Jasper said. "They should be somewhere in the building. I'll double-check."

Levine was still looking at Young's body. "Why would a box cutter be here?" she wondered. "The body is nude. It wouldn't have been in a pocket."

"I don't know," Jasper said. "Maybe someone got careless and left it lying around. Is it the murder weapon?"

"Probably," she said. "It appears sharp, and the blood on the blade is likely to be a match for the victim. This body has no obvious lacerations, so any blood almost certainly came from the other body. However, the cutter was probably not with the body prior to its removal from the bag."

"Why not?"

"The plastic is torn," Levine said, pointing with the tip of her pen. "It is logical that a man attempting to free himself from a bag, and armed with a blade, would cut the plastic instead of tearing it."

"Are zombies logical?" Jasper wondered aloud.

"We have no evidence that Rodney Young is, or ever was, a zombie," Levine said.

"Besides the bloody footprints, the bloody knife in his hand, his trip to Haiti…" Jasper replied.

"None of that is conclusive," she said. "Extraordinary claims require extraordinary proofs."

"We can check his blood for toxins," Jasper suggested.

"That's a good first step," she agreed. "I'd like to continue examining both bodies."

"I'll take a sample of Young's blood and start running it," he said. "I'll start with pufferfish and nightshade, but I'll do a full workup. That'll take some time. The lab's up on the third floor. I'll be there if you need me."

"We should also notify the NYPD," she said.

"Of course," he said. "I'll call them once I'm upstairs. Cell service is pretty spotty down here. Are you going to be okay on your own?"

Levine gave him a look. "I frequently work alone in the morgue," she said. "As long as I follow basic biosafety protocols, I should be in no danger."

"Right," Jasper said. "Thanks for coming here after work."

"You asked me to."

"And I appreciate it." He took her hand and squeezed it lightly. "I hope you find something useful."

"All knowledge is useful," she said.

Jasper nodded. "Just remember you can't get back in through these doors without an ID badge," he said. "You can exit, but you can't re-enter."

"I understand," Levine said.

Jasper walked out of the morgue. The door swung shut behind him, and Levine was left alone with the dead.

Just the way she liked it.

Chapter 3

Rodney Young's body was not eager to give up its secrets. Levine couldn't perform a detailed postmortem until CSU had the chance to photograph the corpse. In the absence of internal information, she had to make do with what she could tell from Young's exterior.

The blood on his soles had not been painted on as he lay in the drawer. The spatter pattern would have been completely different. Either he had walked through Wanda Perkins's blood, or his feet had been dragged through it. The dragging would better fit the footprints she had seen, as well as conforming to Levine's understanding of biology, but the alternative hypothesis could not be conclusively ruled out.

Young's fingertips were bloodstained and had left bloody fingerprints on the box cutter. That could indicate he had shifted his grip after slashing his victim's throat. Levine saw no other fingerprints on the tool. It appeared otherwise pristine, as clean as if it had just been unpackaged. There was a faint, unusual odor in the air.

She bent closer, disregarding Jasper's concerns, and sniffed. Under the expected smell of slow decay and the coppery reek of blood, she identified a cleaning solvent. It was a familiar scent; not simply one she had smelled before, but one she had smelled earlier that evening. The custodian, whose name escaped her, had been using it to wash the floor outside the morgue.

That was a simple explanation. He must have been in the morgue earlier, mopping with a water-and-chemical solution. Levine knew how messy an autopsy could get. There was a reason the morgue had a drain built into the waterproof floor tiles.

She slid Rodney Young's drawer back into its slot in the wall and carefully closed the door. It was important to keep the body as preserved as possible, and the refrigeration was more efficient with the door shut. Levine walked back into the main part of the morgue, taking care to avoid stepping on the blood trail.

There lay Wanda Perkins, exactly the way Levine and Jasper had left her. Levine knelt just outside the pool of blood and stared at the body.

She had examined quite a few victims who had been stabbed or slashed to death, and had studied many more in textbooks and medical journals. Almost endless information could be gleaned from a victim. A skilled medical examiner could determine from which direction the blow had come, what type of blade had delivered the stroke, the handedness of the killer, and dozens of other bits of data. What was missing from a scene could be as important as what was present. Levine took her time, letting her eyes rove to and fro. She knew subconscious intuition often came to conclusions the conscious mind overlooked.

"Bisected trachea," she murmured aloud. "When the windpipe is severed, the victim still attempts to breathe. Blood is aspirated and expelled, both from the mouth and from the site of the wound. It forms an aerosol which spreads in a fan pattern."

She looked at the floor. "No aerosol spatter is visible," she continued. "That leaves three possibilities. Either the victim was not breathing when her throat was cut, or the spatter has been cleaned, or the throat was cut elsewhere and the body was moved."

The first option was definitely plausible, particularly considering that paralytic toxins had already been discussed. If Wanda had been exposed to pufferfish venom, she might have been rendered immobile. Her diaphragm could have been paralyzed and she would have stopped breathing. However, cutting the throat of a woman in respiratory failure was both redundant and counterintuitive.

"If the victim is not breathing, cutting the windpipe is unproductive," Levine observed. "Possibly a ritualistic slaying, but the victim does not appear to have been posed, and there is an absence of visible ceremony."

The blood spatter might have been scrubbed away, which would explain the faint odor of cleaning solution. Under normal circumstances it was nearly impossible to remove all the blood from a scene; a good forensic team would find traces of it. However, this was a morgue. Numerous bodies had been cut open here, and fluids had been spilled and rinsed repeatedly. To isolate a particular blood sample from this floor was effectively impossible.

In any case, Levine failed to see the point of such a cleansing. The victim had bled copiously. Why clean the tiny droplets spewed from her airway and leave the large pool? It made no sense, and Levine preferred her theories to make sense.

"Option three is the most likely," Levine decided. "The victim was, in all probability, cut elsewhere and moved immediately postmortem."

She had no idea why someone would do that. But her theory suggested there was another crime scene, probably nearby, where she would find the fine droplets of blood spray she had expected.

Then she remembered the custodian, whatever his name was, that she and Jasper had met in the outside hallway. He had been scrubbing the floor, probably trying to remove some sort of stain; exactly the sort of stain she might be looking for.

Levine was through both morgue doors in a matter of seconds. It occurred to her only as the second door swung shut behind her that she had just locked herself out of the morgue and away from the bodies she was supposed to be examining.

The basement corridor was empty. The janitor was gone. He had taken his mop and bucket with him, apparently leaving only a damp patch of tile behind.

Levine didn't believe that. The principle of transference was the foundation of forensic science. Whatever he'd been cleaning up, however thoroughly, something would be left behind. She didn't have any of the fancy CSU equipment, but she did possess a keen eye for detail. She removed her protective face mask, lay down flat on her stomach, her face inches from the floor, and started looking.

The custodian had done a good job. If not for two tiny rust-red spots at the base of the wall, where the tile met the plaster, there would have been nothing for the naked eye. Levine noted the wall was also slightly damp.

What had the janitor been doing? Didn't he know he was compromising a crime scene and destroying evidence? The amateurishness of civilians, and even of some police officers, was a constant source of annoyance to Levine. She could only work with what was available. Fortunately, she was still able to determine this hallway was where the victim had died.

Levine wasn't used to thinking like a detective. Her job was to examine bodies and determine cause of death. She gave the detectives their tools and let them figure out the killer's identity. Motives were outside her normal frame of reference. She had no idea why Wanda Perkins had been killed, nor who had killed her.

She did know, however, that Wanda's throat had been slit, almost certainly by a box cutter, and that it had happened in the basement hallway. The killer had then moved the body into the morgue, leaving bloodstains behind which the janitor had then cleaned.

Why had the body been moved?

This was the sort of question Levine hated, because it touched on psychology. This was a "soft" science, given to fuzzy suppositions and assumptions. She much preferred the harder science of forensic medicine. The detectives would be here soon. Jasper had probably already telephoned them. They would ask the psychological questions, interview the suspects, and apprehend the murderer. She would do better to continue examining the bodies.

Unfortunately, she had shortsightedly cut herself off from those bodies, and found herself in a distressingly corpse-free hallway. However, it was also part of the crime scene, and in the absence of both a body to scrutinize and a CSU team to go over the ground, Levine decided to see what she could discover.

Very little evidence was in evidence. She snickered inwardly at the wordplay, though her mouth did not so much as twitch. The corridor was bare of furniture, brightly lit by fluorescent bulbs. She noted the absence of security cameras; yet more proof of humans' unhealthy repression of all death-related matters. Surveillance footage of the morgue and its approaches would necessarily pick up the bodies of the dead, which might offend the sensibilities of the viewers. It would also identify the killer.

Levine considered this. The killer, she decided, was not the late Rodney Young. A zombie, however motivated, was unlikely to have ripped its way out of its bag, shambled out of the morgue, accosted a nurse, slit her throat, and dragged her partway back into the morgue, only to abandon the corpse, wait for the blood to pool on the floor, and take several dragging steps through it back to the drawer from which it had emerged.

Now that Levine considered it, she thought it highly improbable the killer would have been able to move Wanda Perkins without leaving a considerable trail of blood behind. There should have been blood on the door handles, blood in the entryway, blood everywhere.

"Item one," Levine said to herself. "Insufficient bodily fluids at the scene. Conclusion: the scene has been scrubbed. Who scrubbed it? The janitor. Why? He's a janitor. Cleaning stains and scrubbing floors is his job. Nonetheless, he should have reported it. Why didn't he? This is a hospital morgue. Blood is often found here. Perhaps he assumed it was residue from a body which had been transported from upstairs, a victim of a traumatic accident or homicide.

"Item two," she continued. "Murder weapon. Probably the box cutter in the hand of the second corpse. Why place it there instead of leaving it with the body, or removing it from the scene? Conclusion: the weapon was planted on the other corpse in an attempt to misdirect. Secondary conclusion: the murderer is attempting to frame Rodney Young for the killing, in spite of the known fact of Rodney Young's death preceding victim's death."

Levine had to consider the forensic and legal ramifications of that theory. Was it even possible to frame someone who was already dead? Yes, obviously. It was really no different from planting a gun in the home of another man, one who had already died. But to suggest an animated corpse had actually committed a murder was unique in Levine's experience. Would it be enough to foster reasonable doubt in a jury?

"Where did the box cutter come from?" she asked. "Three possibilities: Wanda Perkins had it on her person; Rodney Young had it on his person; the murderer brought it. Young probably did not possess it. Evidence suggests he was not a party to the killing until after the fact. Probability suggests the killer was carrying it, either for the purpose of killing Nurse Perkins or for its intended purpose of slitting packing tape and other packaging materials."

A box cutter struck Levine as a very odd murder weapon for a hospital. Scalpels, bone saws, and all other manner of cutting implements were abundant. Box cutters were something she would expect to find in a warehouse or a supply closet.

She realized she was staring at a door with a label reading PHARMACEUTICAL SUPPLIES. It stood directly across from the section of floor where she had found the traces of blood.

Hospitals were very careful about their drugs. Thieves and addicts were an ever-present concern. All drugs, particularly narcotics, were carefully accounted for and kept locked up at all times. There was a reason they were called "controlled substances," Levine thought with an inner smile.

This door would be locked and only authorized personnel would have the key. Levine knew this, but some oddly irrational part of her made her reach out and push on the door.

It swung open with no resistance whatsoever.

Levine stepped inside, flicking on the light switch. The supply cabinet was lined with bottles of all sorts of drugs, carefully labeled. It was a chemist's dream—or a junkie's. Levine peered more closely at the neat rows of morphine bottles.

Everything appeared to be in order, but there was nothing to prevent her taking a handful of the valuable bottles.

She turned her attention to the door. The lock had been defeated by the simple expedient of a strip of packing tape across the bolt, preventing it from sliding shut when the door tried to automatically lock. A careful observer would notice the door did not latch, but nurses were often in a hurry and would likely simply let the door swing shut while they continued on their way.

Here, then, was a motive for murder. The killer had somehow obtained access to the door, had fixed the lock, and had been pilfering medical supplies. Nurse Perkins had happened along and caught the perpetrator in the act. She had paid for her discovery with her life.

Levine knew almost everything now. She needed to find Jasper and tell him, and then inform the police who should be arriving momentarily. She felt a glow of unaccustomed pride. She had a reputation as a skilled medical examiner, but this was different. She had solved practically the entire crime by herself.

Sarah Levine was actually smiling as she turned to leave the closet. She pulled the door open and found herself face to face with the janitor. *Leroy*, she thought suddenly, glancing at his nametag. *Leroy Waterston. That was his name*.

Waterston was as surprised as she was. He stared at her open-mouthed, a rag in one hand, a bottle of cleaning fluid in the other. Several seconds passed without a sound.

Levine recovered first. "You're in my way," she said. "Move, please. Left or right."

Waterston didn't budge. "What're you doing in there?" he demanded. "That's a restricted area."

"Investigating a homicide," she replied. "The door was improperly secured. I hypothesize a drug dealer has gained improper access to this supply closet and replaced some quantity of morphine with distilled water. When that person was discovered by Nurse Perkins, he or she deployed a box cutter and cut her throat. Then, to deflect suspicion, that person moved the body into the morgue, using Nurse Perkins's keycard to gain entry. The killer then staged the scene to appear as though Nurse Perkins was slain by the reanimated corpse of Rodney Young which was, of course, impossible."

Waterston blinked. "You sound absolutely crazy, Lady," he said. "Reanimated corpses? Like zombies? Who's gonna believe that?"

"Nobody," Levine replied. "There is no conclusive evidence of the existence of zombies, in Haiti or elsewhere. This was a simple homicide, coupled with a clumsy attempt at camouflage. I will report my findings to the hospital authorities and the New York Police Department, who I am confident will promptly resolve the issue. But you are preventing me from doing so by standing in my way."

Waterston nodded. "Gotcha," he said. "So you haven't reported it yet? Does anybody else know about this?"

"No," Levine said. "Just me."

She had to step back at that moment as Waterston moved into the room. He grabbed her shoulder and shoved. Taken off guard, Levine stumbled back against the shelves and nearly fell. Waterston swept a hand behind them and slammed the door, leaving them alone in the supply closet.

Chapter 4

Levine wasn't frightened. She was angry; a cold, professional anger. She glared at Waterston as he forced an arm across her throat, pinning her against the shelf.

"You're the one who killed Wanda Perkins!" she snapped. "You stole from people in pain! You made them suffer needlessly!"

"Oh boo hoo," Waterston growled. "Next you're gonna tell me I should feel sorry for the dead guy."

"You misused human remains to disguise a crime," Levine went on. "You aren't worthy to wear a custodian's uniform. 'Custodian' comes from the Latin *custos*, which means 'guardian.' It is the same word used in the well-known phrase, '*Quis custodiet ipsos custodes?*' There it is translated as, 'Who watches the watchmen?'"

"Lady, what the hell are you talking about?" Waterston said. He didn't know Levine and hadn't had the chance to get accustomed to her unusual thought processes.

"I'm reminding you of your sacred duty," she said.

"I got your sacred duty right here," he sneered. "Damn it, lady, you really screwed the pooch. What am I supposed to do with you?"

"You're supposed to let me go and get out of my way," Levine replied.

"How'd you figure it out?" he demanded.

"It wasn't difficult," Levine said. "It was just a question of following the evidence."

"Bullshit," he said. "This is all that bitch nurse's fault. If she hadn't come down right then, everything would've been fine. And then she started asking all these questions, like what was I doing in the medical supplies, and how did I even have access. What else could I do? It's not like I *wanted* to cut her. But she just wouldn't shut up. She would've got me fired!"

"And incarcerated," Levine added.

"Yeah, that too," he said sourly. "So what about you? Are you smarter than she was?"

"That's difficult to say," Levine said. "I was not acquainted with Nurse Perkins. There are various tests to determine intelligence, and opinions vary as to which is most accurate."

"What I mean is, can you play ball?"

She blinked. "What kind of ball?" She'd played right field on her high school softball team, but she didn't see the relevance of that to the current situation.

"Can you keep your goddamn mouth shut?"

That was a trick question. If she answered it in the affirmative, it would disprove her statement. Levine decided not to say anything.

Waterston was thinking. "I gotta take care of this before the cops show up," he said. "We're going back into the morgue."

"I can't," Levine said. "I don't have an access card."

"Dammit," he said. "Neither do I."

"How did you get in the first time?" she asked.

"I used the nurse's card, of course," he said. "Take off your coat."

"Why?"

"Just do it, dammit!" He forced his arm against her, his forearm digging painfully into her throat.

The possibility of sexual assault crossed Levine's mind, but it seemed unlikely. They might be interrupted at any time, and she didn't think Waterston had any intention of attacking her in that way. "I can't until you remove your arm," she said in a tight, breathless voice.

"Oh." He drew back and picked up a box of disposable syringes from a nearby shelf. He opened the lid and took out a syringe, pointing its tip at her.

It wasn't much of a weapon, but a long, thin point could cause considerable damage if inserted into the correct part of the body. She obeyed, folding her lab coat and placing it on an empty bit of shelving.

Waterston reached out and took one of the morphine vials off the shelf. He removed the cap and drew most of its contents up into the syringe.

"Don't worry," he said. "This won't hurt a bit. It's just like going to sleep."

Levine didn't listen to him. She had already figured out what he planned to do. Postmortem bloodwork would discover the morphine overdose, but that would be too late to do her any good. It was possible he had mistakenly filled the syringe from one of the replacement placebo bottles, but he probably knew which was which.

"Hold out your arm," he said. "This'll only take a second."

"Fatality from morphine overdose is not instantaneous," Levine said. "It normally takes between one and three hours, depending on dosage."

He paused, syringe poised. "Bullshit," he said.

"Assuming your reference to bovine fecal matter is colloquial, you are incorrect," she said. "Prompt administering of naloxone during that time is likely to be able to reverse it."

Waterston hesitated a moment longer. "Shit," he muttered. "This was supposed to be simple! You stupid bitches just keep wandering into it. Why couldn't you have stayed upstairs?"

"The bodies were in the basement," Levine said.

"Whatever," he said. "I'll take my chances."

He grabbed her wrist and pulled her arm toward him. As he did so, he thrust the needle into the angle of her elbow, stabbing at the vein. It was a very small target. Even a trained nurse did not always hit the mark, and Levine was moving. She struggled even as she felt the sharp prick of the needle in her arm. He shoved the plunger home, and suddenly she felt a burning, stinging sensation in her flesh.

"You better sit down," he said.

Levine didn't think that was a good idea, but was no longer sure why. She felt dizzy and lightheaded. Her skin was turning cold and clammy.

"Lots of doctors are junkies," Waterston said, guiding her down to the floor. "Your buddies will figure you found this door open and decided to shoot up. I'll just wipe my prints off this and set it here beside you, like so. Maybe you're right and they'll save you, but I figure it'll take them a couple hours to look in here. So long, Doc. Sorry it worked out like this. You should've never got involved."

Levine could think of three or four reasons why his plan was unlikely to work. She opened her mouth to tell him so, but her tongue felt thick and clumsy. Her vision was blurring. Waterston opened the closet door and switched off the light. He stepped into the hallway and began to close the door again.

"Hey," someone said from the hallway. "Who're you?"

"Leroy," Waterston said. "I'm the janitor. Well, one of them, anyway. It's a big hospital." He laughed.

"Who else is down here?" the other man asked. His voice sounded familiar to Levine, but her thoughts were becoming very sluggish now as the morphine took effect. She felt disconnected and dreamy.

"Just me, I think," Waterston said. "And the dead folks, of course." He laughed again.

"Of course," the other man said. "You haven't seen a woman? Dr. Levine, the Medical Examiner."

"Nope," Waterston said. "Who're you, anyway?"

"Lieutenant Webb, NYPD Major Crimes. I'm here about a couple of bodies."

"Then you've come to the right place," Waterston said with another of his laughs. "But they're in the morgue and I don't have access. You need to go upstairs and get a card from one of the docs or nurses. I can show you where to go."

"I just talked to Dr. Ackermann," Webb said. "He told me Levine was down here and she'd be able to let me in."

"Well, obviously she's not," Waterston said. "Bathroom break, maybe? You know how women are."

Levine, in the pitch darkness of the supply closet, tried to focus. Even thinking was difficult. Moving was even more so. Her extremities seemed to weigh a tremendous amount. She tried to say something, anything. Her mouth felt like it was packed with cotton balls.

"You don't know Dr. Levine," Webb said doubtfully. "She doesn't like to step out in the middle of an examination. That woman's got single-mindedness down to an art form."

"If you say so," Waterston said. He laughed once more, his voice now seeming to come from the end of a very long and dark tunnel.

Levine put all her willpower into a single movement. Lacking all finesse or fine-motor control, she flailed her numbed arm up and back. She caught an armful of glass bottles and swept them to the floor. Glass crashed and shattered all around her. Liquid pooled beneath her and began soaking into the seat of her scrubs.

"What was that?" Webb asked.

"Huh? I didn't hear anything," Waterston said.

"Open that door!" Webb ordered.

"I don't have a key," Waterston protested.

"Baloney! I just saw you come out that door a minute ago!"

"Whoa. Put that away," Waterston said. "You don't need to—"

"If you don't open that door in the next three seconds, you're going to wish you had," Webb said. "Keep your hands where I can see them."

The door swung open. Levine saw the blurry shape of Lieutenant Webb fill the doorway, his silhouette topped by his customary fedora.

"Doctor?" he said. "What's the matter?"

"Mor... mor... morphine."

Levine forced the word through numb, unresponsive lips. She started to say something more, about a forcible overdose, but the room was growing darker. By far the easiest thing was to slip into a deep, soft sleep, and that was what she did.

Chapter 5

The first sense to return to Levine was hearing. Jasper was saying her name. It was a nice sound to wake up to, comfortable and familiar. It was remarkable how a particular person's voice could be so distinct from all others. It was a trick of modulation and pitch, combined with the positive associations of a given voice, but knowing the truth of it didn't make it any less pleasant.

Then she gradually became aware of physical sensations. She was lying on something reasonably soft; a mattress, most likely. Someone was holding her right hand. She inferred, based on the evidence of her ears, that it must be Jasper. She concentrated on the hand and soon recognized the specific contours of his fingers. His palm was slightly sweaty; that denoted either overheating or emotional stress.

Levine tried opening her eyes. The lids felt gummy and heavy, but they functioned properly. She saw a bright blur. She blinked repeatedly and the ceiling came into focus. Then Jasper leaned over her, a look in his eyes she had seen only once or twice before. Jasper was a calm, careful man, not given to overly emotional expression. His eyes were bright and reflective now due to an excess emission from his tear ducts. That meant pain or intense emotion. Levine inferred, on the combined evidence of his hand and eyes, that he was somehow distraught.

"Welcome back," Jasper said. His voice was hoarse. He cleared his throat. "You gave us a bit of a scare there."

"I assume I've been placed on naloxone," she said. "If it was done in a timely manner and the dosage is properly monitored, there should be no cause for concern."

"That's my Sarah," he said, smiling. "How are you feeling?"

Levine considered the question for a moment. "Moderate fatigue and disorientation," she said. "Slight contusions on my right arm and at the base of my throat. Soreness in my right elbow. How long was I unconscious?"

"About a quarter of an hour," he said. "Lieutenant Webb carried you to the elevator and got you to the ER. Dr. Fischbach treated you. He said you ought to be fine, but we'll need to keep you overnight for observation."

"That's a good idea," she said. "You need to ensure all the morphine is out of my system. You should tell Lieutenant Webb the janitor is the man he's looking for. His name is... I forget. You saw him when we first went down."

"You can tell him yourself," Jasper said. "Here he is."

Lieutenant Webb walked into the room. He took off his hat, revealing a head in an advanced state of male-pattern baldness. "Glad you're still with us, Doctor," he said.

"I wasn't capable of independent motion," Levine said. "I would have required assistance to go anywhere else."

Webb shared a look with Jasper and chuckled. "Nonetheless," he said. "Don't worry about Leroy Waterston. He's in custody. O'Reilly and Neshenko are hauling him over to the One-Three for processing, since we're in their Area of

Service. My detectives are a little annoyed they missed all the fun."

"I don't think anyone was having fun," Levine said. "Jasper was running bloodwork, I was examining evidence, and Leroy Waterston was attempting to murder me. All of us were fully occupied by our tasks."

"And I was arresting Waterston," Webb said. "I could tell the man was up to something shady. The way he kept doing that nervous laugh, for one thing. But I didn't realize he'd drugged you. I'm sorry I didn't move faster. I was expecting a cold crime scene, not a crime in progress."

"The morgue is refrigerated," Levine said. "It's definitely cold."

"So what's this I hear about zombies?" Webb asked.

"I found no evidence of zombies," she said. "Mr. Waterston was stealing morphine, and possibly other controlled substances, from the basement. Nurse..."

"Perkins," Jasper supplied.

"Nurse Perkins discovered him in the act of theft," she continued. "He had a box cutter with him, so he cut her throat to prevent being reported. However, he had to dispose of the body, which I believe presented him with a dilemma."

"Definitely," Jasper said. "We don't have cameras in the morgue, but we do have them in the elevator and stairwells. Whoever looked at the tapes would have seen that he and Wanda were the only ones in the basement when she was killed."

"We would have found that highly suspicious," Webb agreed.

"He attempted to frame the only other party present," Levine said. "Rodney Young. However, Mr. Young was already deceased, which complicated the process. Mr. Waterston wiped down the murder weapon to remove fingerprints and washed it in industrial cleaning solution. I smelled it on the weapon. He used the nurse's keycard to open the morgue, knowing it would allay suspicion since he did not have access. He laid her on the floor and opened Mr. Young's body bag, dragged the corpse to the nurse's body, and left the best footprints he could in the blood."

Webb shook his head. "That's unusual," he said.

"He re-bloodied the weapon and placed it in Mr. Young's hand," she went on. "Then he attempted to clean all other traces of blood from the scene, making it appear to the casual observer that the nurse's throat had been cut in the morgue."

"Clever," Webb said.

"Not particularly," Levine said. "While the scene was accurately constructed in broad strokes, the fine details were incorrect. Once I realized the actual murder had taken place elsewhere, I was able to determine what had actually occurred."

"Just in time for Leroy to try to kill you," Jasper said, shaking his head. "I should have stayed down there with you."

"You needed to run the bloodwork for the toxins we discussed," Levine said. "That was impossible in the basement. Neither of us anticipated the murderer would return to the scene."

"It makes sense, though," Webb said. "He wanted to remove all traces of his presence in the supply closet, and make a final sweep for any evidence he might have missed. Not that it matters now. We'll get a warrant to search his home and vehicle. I suspect we'll find large quantities of morphine. And O'Reilly noticed flecks of blood lodged in his cuticles. We've taken scrapings from his nails and expect to get a DNA match to Nurse Perkins. That's not even taking into account the fact that I caught him in the act of attempting to murder our Medical Examiner. That man is never getting out of prison."

"You saved my life," Levine said suddenly, looking Webb straight in the eye.

He coughed. "It's all part of the Job, ma'am," he muttered. "I'm just glad I got there when I did. My only regret is that my back is killing me. I'm too old to carry a grown woman into an elevator."

"Thank you," she said. Jasper had impressed on her how important gratitude was in interpersonal interaction, though she wasn't entirely sure why. It seemed to be making Webb uncomfortable rather than happy, which was confusing.

"You're welcome," he said. "I ought to thank you, too. I've never had a homicide case wrapped up so nicely for me by the time I arrived on scene. The only thing missing was a ribbon and bow to tie it all together."

Levine blinked. "What would I tie together with a ribbon and bow?" she asked. Then she paused. "That was an idiom, wasn't it?"

"Yes," Webb said with a smile. "Congratulations, Dr. Levine. You've closed your first case. You're an honorary detective now."

"I'm not qualified for that," she said quickly. "My medical degree does not transfer to law enforcement."

"That's all right," Webb said. "The rest of the squad won't mind. And speaking of them, I'd better get over to the One-Three before Neshenko picks a fight with their Homicide boys. You just rest, Doctor. We'll have more work for you soon, I'm sure of it."

He shook Jasper's hand, put on his hat, touched the brim, and left. Jasper watched him go. He took hold of Levine's hand again.

"I really thought I'd lost you for a second," he said quietly.

"You had a diagnosis and a clear course of treatment," Levine said. "I had a very high probability of complete recovery."

Something very odd happened. Jasper started to laugh and cry simultaneously. Levine was completely at a loss for what to do. She wasn't good at handling either mirth or sadness on its own, and while the combination of the two emotions ought to mathematically cancel each other out, she didn't think that was happening in this case.

She lay there awkwardly for a few seconds, but that was clearly not the correct course of action. She made her best guess and opened her arms. Jasper leaned in and embraced her, rather more tightly than usual. He kissed her cheek, which was pleasant. She enjoyed his closeness.

"I love you, Sarah," he murmured with his face pressed against the side of her neck.

And for once, Sarah Levine was not at a loss for what to say to her fiancé in an emotional moment.

"I love you, Jasper," she said. "I'm right here."

It was amazing how much comfort a person could take from an obvious, inarguable truth.

About the Author

Steven Henry learned how to read almost before he learned how to walk. Ever since he began reading stories, he wanted to put his own on the page. He lives a very quiet and ordinary life in Minnesota with his wife and dog.

Also by Steven Henry

Ember of Dreams
The Clarion Chronicles, Book One

When magic awakens a long-forgotten folk, a noble lady, a young apprentice, and a solitary blacksmith band together to prevent war and seek understanding between humans and elves.

Lady Kristyn Tremayne – An otherwise unremarkable young lady's open heart and inquisitive mind reveal a hidden world of magic.

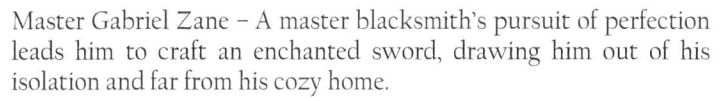

Robert Blackford – A humble harp maker's apprentice dreams of being a hero.

Master Gabriel Zane – A master blacksmith's pursuit of perfection leads him to craft an enchanted sword, drawing him out of his isolation and far from his cozy home.

Lord Luthor Carnarvon – A lonely nobleman with a dark past has won the heart of Kristyn's mother, but at what cost?

Readers love *Ember of Dreams*

"The more I got to know the characters, the more I liked them. The female lead in particular is a treat to accompany on her journey from ordinary to extraordinary."

"The author's deep understanding of his protagonists' motivations and keen eye for psychological detail make Robert and his companions a likable and memorable cast."

Learn more at tinyurl.com/emberofdreams.

More great titles from Clickworks Press

www.clickworkspress.com

The Altered Wake
Megan Morgan

Amid growing unrest, a family secret and an ancient laboratory unleash long-hidden superhuman abilities. Now newly-promoted Sentinel Cameron Kardell must chase down a rogue superhuman who holds the key to the powers' origin: the greatest threat Cotarion has seen in centuries – and Cam's best friend.

"Incredible. Starts out gripping and keeps getting better."

Learn more at clickworkspress.com/sentinel1.

Hubris Towers: The Complete First Season
Ben Y. Faroe & Bill Hoard

Comedy of manners meets comedy of errors in a new series for fans of Fawlty Towers and P. G. Wodehouse.

"So funny and endearing"

"Had me laughing so hard that I had to put it down to catch my breath"

"Astoundingly, outrageously funny!"

Learn more at clickworkspress.com/hts01.

Death's Dream Kingdom
Gabriel Blanchard

A young woman of Victorian London has been transformed into a vampire. Can she survive the world of the immortal dead—or perhaps, escape it?

"The wit and humor are as Victorian as the setting… a winsomely vulnerable and tremendously crafted work of art."

"A dramatic, engaging novel which explores themes of death, love, damnation, and redemption."

Learn more at clickworkspress.com/ddk.

Share the love!

Join our microlending team at
kiva.org/team/clickworkspress.

Keep in touch!

Join the Clickworks Press email list
and get freebies, production updates, special deals,
behind-the-scenes sneak peeks, and more.

Sign up today at clickworkspress.com/join.

Milton Keynes UK
Ingram Content Group UK Ltd.
UKHW040357111224
452348UK00004B/241